SWIMMING WITH THE FISHES

Mia and Jamie exited the car and walked toward the catering hall. "What's that?" Jamie asked. He pointed to a large red bundle floating in the water next to the dock closest to Belle View.

"No idea. Maybe it fell off someone's boat. It could be important. We should see what it is and if we can fish it out."

The two headed toward the bundle, which bobbed up and down in the water. As they drew closer, Mia's heart began to race. *Oh, no. No, no, no, no.*

Jamie grabbed her hand and clutched it. "Is that what I think it is?" he asked, his tone full of dread.

"If you're thinking . . ."

A wave from an incoming motorboat rocked the bundle and an arm floated to the surface.

". . . that it's a body . . ."

Mia saw that the arm was draped in rainbow bracelets. A beautiful, sparkling array of them.

". . . then, yes. It is what you think it is."

Books by Maria DiRico

HERE COMES THE BODY

LONG ISLAND ICED TINA

Published by Kensington Publishing Corp.

Long Island
Iced Tina

Maria DiRico

KENSINGTON
PUBLISHING CORP.

www.kensingtonbooks.com

KENSINGTON BOOKS are published by

Kensington Publishing Corp.
119 West 40th Street
New York, NY 10018

All Kensington titles, imprints, and distributed lines are available at special quantity discounts for bulk purchases for sales promotion, premiums, fund-raising, educational, or institutional use.

Special book excerpts or customized printings can also be created to fit specific needs. For details, write or phone the office of the Kensington Sales Manager: Attn.: Sales Department. Kensington Publishing Corp., 119 West 40th Street, New York, NY 10018. Phone: 1-800-221-2647.

The Kensington logo is a trademark of Kensington Publishing Corp.

First Printing: March 2021
ISBN-13: 978-1-4967-2535-6
ISBN-10: 1-4967-2535-2

ISBN-13: 978-1-4967-2538-7 (ebook)
ISBN-10: 1-4967-2538-7 (ebook)

10 9 8 7 6 5 4 3 2 1

Printed in the United States of America

CHAPTER 1

"*My grandbaby's having a baby!!!*"

Mia Carina winced as Minniguccia Evangelista screeched this into her ear. Becoming a great-grandmother was a huge mark of distinction among the Astoria senior citizen crew. Mia thought of her own poor nonna, Elisabetta, who might never achieve this honor thanks to Mia's train wreck of a failed marriage and the chronic incarcerations of Mia's handsome, charismatic, and felonious older brother, Posi. "Yes, I heard all about it," Mia said to Minniguccia. Which indeed she had, since the mother-to-be was the lovely Nicole Karras-Whitman, one of Mia's closest friends. "I'm so happy for Nicole and Ian."

"I'll be honest. I figured when you're as old as she is, if it ain't happening, it ain't gonna happen." Mia made a face. Nicole was a year younger than her own thirty-one years. "But," Minniguccia continued, "I prayed, and I prayed, and I prayed. I even talked all my neighbors into a weekly block rosary. Well, not all. The Feinbergs passed with regrets, but they said they'd put a word in at their temple, however that works. Anyway, the man upstairs came through for me. *My grandbaby's having a baby!!!"* Minniguccia screeched this even louder the second time. Mia held the phone an arm's length away from her ear. "And we're gonna have one of the showers at your new place, that Belle View Banquet whatever."

Mia pulled in her arm to bring the phone back to normal hearing distance. "Belle View Banquet Manor. *One* of the showers? How many is Nicole having?"

"As many as it takes to celebrate this *miracle*!"

Mia resisted the urge to point out that pregnancy at thirty was less a miracle than a fact of life for her friends, who often waited to start families until they established careers that could support a child or two in the pricey New York tristate area. "Minnie, I'm honored you thought of Belle View for the baby shower."

"I know you'll do it up right."

Mia had only been running Belle View with her father for a few months, but she'd been in the business long enough to know that "I know you'll do it up right" was code for *because we're friends, you need to pile on the free extras.* She was happy to do this for a BFF like Nicole. "We'll do it up *so* right," she promised the great-grandmother-to-be.

"Linda and I are footing the bill," Minniguccia said, referencing her own daughter, who was Nicole's mother. "You get together with Nicole, see if there's anything special she wants, and say yes to it all."

"I'll call her as soon as you and I hang up. Do you

want her input on everything? Decorations? Guest list? Food?"

"Her mother and I will take care of the decorations. As to the guest list . . ." There was a loaded pause. "Linda is insisting we invite the stepmonster."

Mia sympathized with the venomous spin Minniguccia put on the word *stepmonster.* The older woman despised Tina, Ron Karras' second wife, and with good reason, in Mia's opinion. In the five or so years since Tina joined the Karras family post-Ron and Linda's divorce, Mia had never heard a good word about her. This wasn't completely true. Linda, one of the sweetest women ever to walk the earth, tried her best to find something positive to say about the woman who'd replaced her in Ron's affections, while her daughter Nicole instantly changed the subject whenever her stepmother's name came up. It fell to Minnie to articulate animosity toward the former flight attendant, which the octogenarian did with gusto at every opportunity. She'd picked up the word "stepmonster" when it appeared in the zeitgeist and refused to use any other moniker when referring to the second Mrs. Karras. Except for one . . .

"As to the food, it's whatever Nicole asks for except for one dish I insist we include on the menu since the stepmonster will be there," Minniguccia said, her tone dark. "Pasta puttanesca. For the *puttana.*"

That was the other name Minniguccia called Tina: *puttana.* The Italian word for "whore."

Mia heard Minniguccia spit to punctuate the insult. "Pasta puttanesca is a delicious dish," she said diplomatically. "I'll tell our chef, Guadalupe, to dig up the best recipe she can find."

"With an extra helping of *puttana*." Minniguccia spit again.

"I'll get in touch with you after I talk to Nicole," Mia said, aiming for the high road by not responding to Minnie's vitriol. "Dad and I will make sure the shower is a beautiful, memorable event." *But*, Mia thought to herself, *given the fractured family dynamics, not* too *memorable.*

After a hearty string of epithets unleashed against the despised Tina in both English and Italian, Minniguccia signed off. Mia texted mom-to-be Nicole an invitation to meet, flavored with a string of baby-themed emojis. She got an instant reply of **How's tonight?** followed by hearts and exclamation marks. Mia confirmed, then peeled her thighs off the plastic covers that still encased the gaudy furniture she'd been gifted with by a neighbor who had decamped Astoria's 46th Place for a senior living facility on Long Island.

"Ouch. I really gotta get rid of this stuff. It's the worst." She said this to Doorstop, the ginger Abyssinian cat currently splayed out over the gaudy rug Mia had also inherited from her former neighbor. Doorstop, who treated all the plastic-covered furniture with disdain, ignored her. But Pizzazz, the beloved parakeet Mia let flutter around her apartment, chirped what she took as agreement, then pooped on the couch. "My sentiments exactly," Mia said to the bird. She grabbed a paper towel and cleaned up the tiny mess. The one benefit of the slick, uncomfortable cushion covers was that it made this task easy.

Mia had a good reason for the delay in de-plastic-ing her furniture. Business at Belle View Banquet Manor, the catering hall she ran with her father, was brisk. The May and June calendar had boasted weddings every weekend, as well as smaller events, July was going well, and August looked to be a repeat of the previous successful months. Two murders at the manor in early spring hadn't hurt business and may have helped. *It's like they say*, Mia thought to herself while showering, *the only bad publicity is no publicity.* She toweled off, then headed to her bedroom, stepping over the prostrate Doorstop. Mia pulled on a pair of black linen capri pants and a snug purple tank top. She sniffed the air, suddenly redolent with the scent of butter and Italian sausage. "*Mia, vieni,*" her grandmother yelled from the apartment below in the two-family home the women shared. "Come. I made breakfast."

"*Sto arrivando,*" Mia yelled back. "I'll be there in a minute." There was no animus in either woman's voice. Yelling to each other was simply the way the Carina family had always communicated.

Mia scurried down the stairs and made her way through a small foyer into her grandmother's modest first floor digs. Elisabetta Carina, dressed in her uniform of tracksuit and sneakers, stuck a fork into a sausage sizzling on top of her forty-plus-year-old oven and deposited it on a bed of fried onions and peppers already gracing a plate next to a pile of buttery scrambled eggs. Mia took a seat at the room's decades-old dinette set. Elisabetta tore a hunk off a loaf of fresh Italian bread and added it to the plate, which she placed in front of Mia. "*Mangia.* Eat."

"*Si. Grazie,* Nonna." Mia dug into the heavy breakfast, vowing to follow it up with a lunch of carrot and celery sticks. At least one meal in her day needed to be low-cal and less artery clogging.

Elisabetta fixed herself a plate and took a seat across from Mia. "Did Minnie call you?"

"Yes. She and Linda are gonna host a baby shower for Nicole at Belle View." Mia sawed off a chunk of sausage and speared it, along with some peppers and eggs. "I'll finally get to meet the infamous Tina."

"Tina. Puh." Elisabetta made a stink face, then spit, as Minniguccia had done earlier. "*Puttana.* She stole Ron from right under poor Linda's *nebbia.* Linda's an angel. Never says a bad word about her. But we know what she is, a—"

"*Puttana,*" Mia chorused with her grandmother. "I've heard that word more in the last hour than in my entire life. I almost feel sorry for this Tina."

A look of horror crossed Elisabetta's face. She threw her hands in the air. "*Marone,* no! Never even think that. We are, what, how do you kids say it? We're Team Linda."

"Linda's insisting Tina be invited to the shower, so I think she's made her peace with the situation. So, it's more like we're Team Minniguccia."

"This is why I don't like sports," Elisabetta grumbled. "Too many teams."

Mia used the chunk of bread to wipe up stray splotches of butter and olive oil. "*Grazie per calazione,* Nonna. Breakfast was delicious. I've gotta get to work."

Elisabetta curled her upper lip. "It's Sunday. The day of rest. The only place you should be getting to"—she pointed one finger at Mia and one in the direction of Perpetual Anguish, the Catholic church catty-cornered to the house—"is church."

"I'll go next weekend."

"You say that every weekend."

"We're super busy, which is a good thing. It keeps Dad out of trouble." Mia's father, a lieutenant in the Boldano crime family, had received Belle View as payment for a gambling debt, and was under orders to run it as one of the Family's legitimate businesses. Mia was determined to help him succeed.

"*Si*," Elizabeth acknowledged reluctantly. "Fine. Go to work. But next week . . ." She pointed to the church again, then to the heavens. "*Dio sta guardando*. God is watching."

With this ominous warning lingering over her, Mia headed outside. She opened the front door to an assault of hot, humid summer air, which put the kibosh on her plan to bike to Belle View. She debated calling Evans, the catering hall's sous and dessert chef, for a ride. He'd moved into an elderly neighbor's upstairs apartment, the term "elderly neighbor" applicable to pretty much everyone on the block except for recent buyers who were part of Astoria's gentrification boom. Mia balanced her full stomach against the scariest-ride-at-the-amusement-park that was a trip on Evans's motorcycle, and opted for other means of transportation.

She checked the Pick-U-Up rideshare app knowing that she wouldn't hear from Jamie Boldano, the non-mobbed-up son of the Family who was driving to put himself through a graduate psychology program. Despite their mutual attraction, Mia and Jamie seemed to have settled into the friend zone. He was at the beach with his girlfriend Madison, a junior editor at a Manhattan fashion website. Madison had a 1/64th Hamptons share, which seemed to translate into spending a single night at a tiny house miles from the beach with a dozen other people. Still, imagining Jamie and Madison together anywhere made Mia sad. She cursed the relationship PTSD she'd been saddled with, courtesy of her adulterous late husband, which left her wary of embarking on another romance—even one with someone as close to her as Jamie.

Mia shook off the blues and checked her phone again. The app showed no other Pick-U-Up drivers nearby, so she called a cab, which appeared a few minutes later. The route to work passed street after street of the sturdy, red-brick post-war homes that made up Mia's neighborhood. The driver stopped at a red light and Mia gazed out the window while they waited for the signal to change. When she was a child, her father had told her that the Italian bricklayers who built the homes occasionally threw in a whimsical touch like arranging a few bricks to spell their initials or a shape of some kind. Mia still enjoyed seeking out the cheeky masonry messages. By the time the light turned green, she'd found the initials A.R. and the image of a winking eye, all created by cleverly arranged red bricks.

The driver deposited Mia in front of Belle View, a facility whose nondescript mid-century exterior belied its lovely location on a tiny peninsula overlooking Flushing Bay Marina. Mia listened to the rhythmic thumping of water against the boats docked at the marina. The roar of a jet taking off from the LaGuardia Airport runway, which also happened to be in Belle View's eyeline, drowned out the peaceful sound and brought Mia back to earth. She pulled open one of the catering manor's double glass doors and stepped inside. Mia did a visual sweep of the lobby, taking a moment to enjoy the upgrades that a series of weddings, Sweet Sixteens, galas, and assorted parties had funded. The white walls gleamed from a recent paint job and the ornate crystal chandelier glistened from a detailed cleaning. Giant urns standing sentry by the entry to the Marina Ballroom were now bolted to the wall to prevent them from skittering across the tiled floor whenever a plane departed from or landed at LaGuardia.

Mia threw away a few leaves that had fallen to the ground from a floral display filling one of the urns, then headed down a hallway that led to the catering hall offices, which had yet to reap the benefits of Belle View's modest success. She dropped into the battered office chair in front of her ancient computer and began sorting through the hundred or so emails requiring her attention.

By the time she finished confirming and placing orders, e-talking nervous brides off the ledge, and locking in an event for *Le Donne Di Orsogna,* a social club for women descended from the immigrants of Orsogna—which happened to be the picturesque Italian town her family hailed from—hours had passed. Mia checked the time and uttered an exclamation. She was already late to meet Nicole. She texted an apology, then called a cab. *Messina Carina, you* must *learn to drive,* she scolded herself as the cab, under orders to make time, careened down Grand Central Parkway. It pulled up in front of a slightly shabby bar whose exterior hadn't been altered since its opening sometime in the nineteen-fifties. Mia jumped out of the cab and hurried inside. Her friend Nicole waved from a worn red Naugahyde booth. She stood up and the two women hugged, Nicole's burgeoning belly between them.

"Look at you," Mia marveled, gesturing to her friend's stomach.

"Six weeks away," Nicole said, holding up six fingers. Blessed with the best of Italian and Greek genes, she was a Mediterranean beauty, with olive skin, curly brunette hair, and a dimpled smile. She was carrying high and wore an elegant black maternity dress.

Mia made eye contact with Piero, the bartender and restaurant proprietor. He mimed "got it" and poured a glass of Chardonnay. "This place isn't fancy, but the food is fantastic."

"I know." Nicole motioned to a half-empty breadbasket. "Piero introduced himself and brought this. He said he makes everything himself, including the bread, and that dinner is on him. A 'Family' man. With a capital F?"

Mia nodded. "Yes. And dinner's not on him, no matter what he says, but that's for me, not you."

Piero delivered the glass of wine to the women's table and disappeared into the kitchen. The two friends spent a few minutes catching up, then Mia steered the conversation toward Nicole's shower. "I told your grandmother that I wanted to run as much as I could by you first."

"Thank you for that. The thought of Minnie not being reined in is terrifying. She wanted to have one of those proclamations made up when the baby is born, you know like the royal family does, where they put a big sign in front of the palace announcing the birth. I was like, 'Where are you gonna put that, Nonna, in front of the Steinway Street subway station?'"

"Your mother can help me keep her under control." Mia sipped her wine. "So, Minnie said you're having more than one shower."

Nicole slumped in her booth. "Yup. Minnie and Mom's, my friends, Ian's family, my coworkers . . . and Tina."

Mia's eyes widened. "Tina's throwing you a shower? The evil stepmother?"

Nicole pursed her lips. "Oh, don't think she's doing it for me. Tina's convinced that my dad still has feelings for my mom. She's throwing the shower to show off and compete with her. It's infuriating but I can't say no because my parents just want peace in the family."

"Where's she having it?"

"Versailles on the Park."

Mia's mouth dropped open. "*Versailles?* That place is crazy pricey."

Nicole gave a vigorous nod. "I know. Like I said, showing off. *Bella figura.*"

Mia nodded, all too familiar with *bella figura,* the Italian concept of presenting a positive, even superior, social image to the world. She picked up one of Piero's home-made breadsticks and snapped it in half. "Wow. Okay, so you can't get out of *that* shower. But I'm worried the rest of the lineup is gonna wear you out. I think you should combine everything else except the work event into one shower. If you're on board with this, I'll sell it to your mother and grandmother. It'll up their guest list, but I'm sure they won't care."

Nicole straightened up. "I would *love* that. Thank you."

"It's done." Mia looked around the restaurant. A couple of older men she recognized as Donny Boldano's "associates" waved to her and she waved back. "Piero never brought us menus."

"He told me we didn't need them. He had a special order for us.'

"Whatevs. He's an amazing cook." Mia chomped down on half of her breadstick. She followed this up by eating the other half.

Nicole leaned forward. "So, what's going on with you? Deets about your love life, please. You and Jamie . . ."

Nicole wiggled her eyebrows and flashed a knowing

smile. Mia shook her head and held up a hand. "Not happening. Just friends. He's got a girlfriend. And I'm not
dating. No time. Belle View is taking off, which is great,
but we're understaffed. Everyone's working really hard,
even our one slacker employee, Cammie Dianopolis. But
slacking was basically written into her deal, so she's
doing us a favor just by showing up. We have to hire
more people, but I'm not sure where to look." She
frowned and drained her wine glass. "To be honest, I did
an online search for 'how to run a catering hall.' I dug up
some good stuff, but not enough. I wish I could crash a
party at another venue to see how they run things."

"You don't have to crash anything," Nicole said.
"Consider yourself invited to Tina's big fat Greek baby
shower."

Mia brightened. "Really? That would be wonderful. I
can learn a lot from a Versailles event."

Piero emerged from the kitchen holding two large
plates emitting clouds of steam. He deposited one in front
of each woman. "*Ecco,*" he said. "Here you go."

Mia sniffed the steam. "Capers. Tomatoes. Olives.
This is—"

"Pasta puttanesca," Piero said with pride. "By special
request." He mimed tipping a hat and returned to the bar.

"Special request," Mia repeated. She wrinkled her
brow. "Nicole, did you tell your grandmother where we
were eating?"

"Yes." Nicole stared her plate. "She must have heard
about Tina's shower."

"Oh, yeah." Mia looped pasta around her fork, then
deposited it in her mouth. "I have to say, this is the most
delicious stepmother-shaming pasta you will ever eat."

"Amen to that," Nicole said, mouth full.

While the women ate in companionable silence, Mia thought about the baby shower Tina planned to throw for her stepdaughter. Attending would allow Mia to snoop around Versailles on the Park and see how Queens' toniest catering hall operated. Better yet, she'd get to see how Tina Iles-Karras, notorious *puttana* and "stepmonster," operated.

CHAPTER 2

The next few weeks were a blur of long workdays stretching into evening events, fueled by copious amounts of Elisabetta's espresso, a brew so strong that family members joked it should only be available by prescription. Fortunately, planning Nicole's baby shower proved to be a breeze. Nicole dictated an all-women party, eschewing the trend toward co-ed baby showers. This would bring down the liquor bill significantly. In Mia's experience, men generally found baby showers a bore, choosing to congregate at the bar and wait for something to go horribly but hopefully hilariously wrong with the gender reveal.

Since the expectant couple chose to find out their baby's gender when he or she popped out of Nicole, Mia didn't have to worry about cannons shooting out a mess of blue or pink confetti and creating a vacuum-clogging nightmare for the Belle View cleaning crew—which at this point was Mia, her father Ravello, and any waitstaff willing to earn time and a half to stick around and help clean up. Mia had put out general job feelers on a few hiring websites, but while Belle View's notoriety hadn't chased away clientele, it seemed to have shrunk the hiring pool to squat.

Mia's cell rang. She checked to see who the caller was, groaned, and answered the call. "Hi, Minniguccia," she said, faking a chipper tone. "What's up?" Mia knew exactly what was up. She'd already received several emails from the older woman, with the subject line all in caps: NO TEDDY BEAR FOR TINA!

"I wanna make sure you got my email about the favors." For shower favors, Minniguccia had chosen teddy bears clad in little yellow T-shirts that read, WELCOME, BABY WHITMAN.

"Yes, I got your emails. Here's the thing . . ." Mia hesitated, knowing she was about to break bad news. "Both Linda and Nicole told me they don't want to single Tina out. They want her to get a teddy bear."

"What?!" Minniguccia squawked this, following it with a string of Italian invectives. "Why are they being nice? That *strega*, that witch—" *There's one I haven't heard before from Minnie*, Mia thought to herself. "She put a spell on Ron and snatched him away from my *bambina,* my Linda. He had no reason to go anywhere, believe me. My daughter was making him happy, *very* happy, if you know what I mean."

'Oh, I do," Mia said, eager to end the conversation before it became any more uncomfortable.

"No teddy bear for her. Do you hear me? No. Teddy. Bear. For. Her!"

"You talk to Linda and Nicole about this. I'm sure the three of you will figure it out. I'll let you know when the bears come in. Bye-yee." Mia ended the call and dropped her head in her hands. The angry octogenarian was wearing her out.

"Mia, help. Help!"

The cry came from event planner Cammie Dianopolis' office. Ravello had hired Cammie, a neighborhood friend, to help him run Belle View when Mia's move home to Queens from Florida hit a bump. Palm Beach police had tagged her as a suspect in the mysterious disappearance of her husband Adam Grosso and his cocktail waitress mistress. Fortunately for Mia but not so much for the waitress, a boat washed ashore containing the adulteress's body. Adam was assumed lost at sea and Mia was free to move about the country. Cammie had agreed to stay on at Belle View with the proviso that she work as little as possible. The crush of activity at the catering hall was seriously cutting into Cammie's personal schedule of beauty treatments and gym visits.

Mia raced into Cammie's office. She found her coworker crawling around the shabby carpeting under her desk. "Cammie, what's wrong? Are you okay?"

No, I am not okay." The fortysomething woman held up a hand. Each finger but one featured a long nail colored in a shade of mauve popular in the nineteen eighties, the decade where Cammie's style stood frozen in time. "I lost a nail. I've been so busy here I haven't had time to get them re-glued. Help me find it."

Mia dropped to her knees and felt around the carpet.

"Maybe you should put on your readers. It'll help with looking close up."

"Never. I hate those things. They're the eyewear version of saying, *I give up*."

"Aha!" Mia sat back on her haunches and triumphantly held up the errant fingernail. "Found it."

"Thank God." Cammie grabbed the nail and stood up. She pulled a small tube of nail glue out of a drawer and stuck the nail back onto her index finger. "This is a temporary fix. I gotta get back to the salon. And for my hair, too. Look." Cammie bent at the neck and pointed the re-nailed finger at the scalp of her frosted hair. "Roots. On *me*. I'm devolving."

"I'm sorry. I'm working on getting more help, I swear. It's harder than I thought it would be to staff this place. Dad and I are so grateful to you for helping out."

"Hey, this is the best job in the world except for when I actually have to work. Speaking of which, I'm taking off the entire month of January."

"It's a slow month. You got it."

Cammie held out a hand to Mia, who grabbed it and let Cammie pull her to her feet. Cammie eyed her. "I gotta wonder . . ."

She hesitated. "Wonder what?" Mia prompted.

Cammie studied her friend. She tapped a finger against her pink frosted lips, then spoke. "If you're booking all these parties so you have an excuse not to date."

Mia gaped at her. "*What?* Are you serious? Cammie, you know exactly why I'm working this hard. If this place folds, Dad goes back to the Life. Secrets. Danger. Jail time. I cannot—I will not—let that happen."

"I appreciate that, *bella*," a male voice said. Mia and

Cammie turned around to see Ravello Carina standing in the doorway. "But I don't want you ever using me as an excuse not to move on with your own life."

"Dad." Mia went to her father and kissed him on both cheeks.

The tall, broad man enveloped his daughter in a bear hug, then released her. "Your brother sends his love."

"You went to see Posi?" Positano Carina, Mia's sole sibling, was finishing up a jail stint for car theft at the nearby Triborough Correctional Facility. "How is he?"

"Good. He's trying to talk the prison staff into putting out a calendar featuring him doing different prison tasks. Bare-chested."

"Of course he is." When Posi Carina wasn't working some illicit angle, he was trying to jumpstart a career as a male model. So far, he'd had more luck jumpstarting the expensive cars he was stealing and selling to China until the Feds nabbed him. "I owe him a visit. I haven't had time." Mia turned back to Cammie and said in a triumphant tone, "See? It's not about dating. I don't even have time to visit my own brother."

"I can't talk. My nail fell off again. I am living a *nightmare*."

Ravello excused himself and, after locating Cammie's errant nail a second time, Mia returned to her office. She checked her phone and saw a text from Nicole: **Ignore my nonna. Tina gets a teddy bear. See you tonight at her shower. Remember, it's formal attire. Which is insane.**

Mia texted back, **Yes, it is. See you there.** She checked the time on her phone and decided to put in a few more hours at Belle View before getting ready for the baby shower blowout, if for no other reason than to prove

Cammie wrong. *I'm not avoiding dating. I* do *have to work this hard.* Mia ignored a niggling feeling of skepticism as she scrolled through her emails.

Rather than be fashionably late to the baby shower, Mia chose to arrive on time so that she could take in every aspect of the Versailles on the Park experience. The ornate building, which had only recently been kitted out as a party venue, sat in the middle of Flushing's largest park. The building was a holdover from France's contribution to a long-ago World's Fair. Built as an homage to one of the world's most iconic sites, the stately replica was currently bathed in a sea of pink and blue lights, an obvious nod to the night's festivities. Mia exited the cab onto a cobbled drive that made walking in four-inch spike heels a challenge. She hiked up her full-length black jersey halter dress so she could see the ground beneath her feet and made her way onto a red carpet that extended from the drive to Versailles' grand entrance. On either side, massive fountains featuring statues of half-clothed women shot up choreographed sprays of water. Each statue extended a marble hand to the walkway as if to welcome guests. Men in tuxedos and women clad in the black gowns dictated by the invitation stopped to pose in front of the kind of step-and-repeat usually found at a movie premiere.

Mia climbed the banquet hall's stone steps, following the red carpet into a clone of the Hall of Mirrors where a string quartet played. She sunk into a depression. The banquet hall business in Queens was fiercely competitive. In a *bella figura* battle between Versailles and Belle View, her humble workplace didn't stand a chance. She

looked around, unsure where to go, and was relieved to
see Nicole waving to her. She went to her friend, and they
hugged. "So?" Nicole said with a grin. "What do you
think?"

"A red carpet? A step-and-repeat? A string quartet? For
a baby shower? No words."

"This is only the beginning."

Nicole took Mia's hand and led her into an enormous
room decorated with the most ornate selection of carved
molding Mia had ever seen, all colored with gold gilt.
The walls were upholstered in rose damask and a line of
chandeliers, each twice as big as Belle View's solitary
chandelier, cast a warm light on the room, which featured
an array of buffet stations. A combo played jazz standards
as waiters wandered through the crowded room offering
hors d'oeuvres. Mia opened her mouth and closed it.
She'd partied in some fancy venues during her lifetime—
the Family was not known for subtle shindigs—but she'd
never seen anything like this. "It's supposed to be the
Throne Room at Versailles," Nicole explained.

Mia found her voice. "Wow. Okay. Well, at least Tina
made this only a cocktail party."

"Wrong," Nicole said. "This is the cocktail *hour*."

Mia followed her friend to a door sporting florid carving. Nicole pushed it open a crack and Mia peered inside.
Like the room she was in, this one was slathered in gilded
Baroque trim, but with white upholstered walls instead of
red. The barreled ceiling showcased frescos of babies
floating in clouds. The theme carried over to the table settings, where each of the many, many tables featured a
centerpiece comprised of white flowers shaped to form a
cloud that a ceramic statue of a baby floated above. "I-

I—" Mia searched for a response. "Where's Ian? What does he think of all this?"

Nicole let the door close. She motioned to a nice-looking man in his thirties standing by one of the many buffet stations. Next to him, a WASP-y middle-aged couple clung to each other. All three looked lost. "He's over there with his parents. They just got in from St. Louis. I'll introduce you. I think you're the only person Ian will know here. You're practically the only person *I* know."

The two women were about to start toward Ian and his parents when there was a drumroll. The combo's bassist called for everyone's attention. "Ladies and gentlemen, please join me in welcoming your host and hostess, the guests of honor for this evening . . . *Ron and Tina Karras*!"

Mia did a double take. "Excuse me. Aren't you and Ian the guests of honor? You know . . . the parents-to-be?"

"It's Tina," Nicole muttered. "She *had* to make an entrance."

Mia glanced at her pregnant friend, who was clearly trying to suppress her anger. Worried for Nicole, Mia took her hand and squeezed it. "Think of this whole thing as a joke," she whispered. "It's gonna make for some great stories."

Nicole relaxed and smiled. "You're right."

The combo played a flourish. Waiters pulled open the room's grand doors, and Nicole's father, Ron Karras, walked in with a stunning woman on his arm. Mia stared at her fascinated. There was no denying Tina Iles-Karras was beautiful. Nicole had mentioned her stepmother was somewhere in her mid-fifties, but perfect bone structure aided by subtle facial procedures took ten to fifteen years off Tina's real age. Still, there was a tightness to her that went beyond shots of wrinkle-erasing toxins. She gave off the vibe of a sleeping cobra, dangerous whether awake or at rest.

While the guests had all hewed to the invitations and dressed in black—including Nicole, who Mia had naively assumed was the actual guest of honor—Tina wore a silky, fire-engine red gown. Her arms sparkled with what must have been a dozen rainbow bracelets—bracelets comprised of either sapphire or topaz stones arranged in the color order of a rainbow. Mia, who'd always wanted a mere single rainbow bracelet, was consumed with jealousy. Ron, an average-looking man in every way including height, led his model-thin spouse to the combo, where she took the mic from the bassist. "Welcome, everyone," she said in a throaty voice with the tiniest hint of an accent. "Ronald and I cannot thank you all enough for coming tonight and helping us celebrate this wonderful occasion. We are so thrilled and grateful that we have the honor of sharing it with you." Tina beamed at her guests and threw her hands up in the air. "Now, *kalí diaskédasi!* Have a good time!"

The guests applauded and the combo struck up a jazzy tune. It occurred to Mia that Tina never mentioned her stepdaughter in her welcoming remarks. The party might as well be a celebration of Tina. Which, Mia surmised, is exactly what the stepmonster wanted.

Cocktail hour turned into two. Bored with making small talk with strangers, Mia decided to explore Versailles. She began her self-guided tour by checking out the other banquet rooms, most of which opened onto the sumptuous main gallery, much like the rooms at the original Versailles. They were all lovely, but none were as ornate as the two housing the current festivities. It was obvious that Tina Karras had sprung for Versailles' top-of-the-line package. The only thing Belle View had to offer that Versailles didn't was its view of Flushing Marina. And LaGuardia Airport. *If only we could get LaGuardia to freeze landings and takeoffs during our events,* Mia thought with a sigh.

Having finished checking out the rooms and adjacent gardens, which were perfectly manicured and equally lovely, it was time to take a gander at the kitchen facilities. She watched a waiter, carrying an empty plate of hors d'oeuvres, push open a door hidden in one of the hall's ornately paneled walls. Mia waited a moment, then followed him inside. She did her best to be unobtrusive as she examined the scene in front of her, which offered a blinding array of brand-new, state-of-the-art stainless-steel equipment. A chef shouted orders at kitchen staffers who were plating lobster, steak, ravioli, and chicken on hundreds of dinner plates. Mia noted Tina's commitment to Best in Show extended to this extravagant main course.

"May I help you?"

Mia jumped. She turned to face a man who appeared to be in his late forties. He was elegantly attired in a black suit tailored to his taut frame. A shock of white stood out in the middle of his slicked-back black hair. The sneer on his face undercut his handsome features. He folded his arms in front of his chest and stared her down. Mia stuffed down her guilt at being caught sneaking around and said in her most officious tone, "Yes, hello. I'm Mia Carina, the assistant general manager of Belle View Banquet Manor. A fellow hospitality executive."

She threw in both qualifiers in the hopes they would help legitimize her snooping, then extended her hand.

The man responded with the kind of quick shake of someone who feared a virus might be transmitted. "Castor. General Manager."

Mia wondered if he went by one name or didn't think she ranked learning his full name. "I've been admiring your facilities," she said, then piled on the flattery. "Stunning. Everything from the kitchen to the rooms to the service is the ne plus ultra of our business." She gave herself props for throwing in one of the few phrases she remembered from high school Latin.

"*Merci,*" Garvalos responded. Mia bristled at his condescending tone. "I'd give you a personal tour but as you can see, we're a skosh busy."

"Thanks," Mia responded, adding in a light tone, "It's nice of you to offer, considering I'm the competition."

Castor burst out laughing, then stopped himself. "I'm so sorry. That was incredibly rude. This is no excuse, but I've seen Belle View, and . . ."

Mia glared at him. "And what?"

A fanfare blared from a trumpet in the Throne Room. "Dinner's being served," Castor said. "The salad is a mélange of locally sourced lettuce varieties, artisan buffalo mozzarella, and a drizzle of twenty-five-year-old, barrel-aged balsamic vinegar. You won't want to miss it."

"Balsamic," Mia said with a sniff as she headed for the door. "That's so nineteen-nineties." She pretended not to hear the general manager's response that the nineteen-nineties was when the rare and expensive balsamic dated from.

Later, having polished off the to-die-for salad, amuse-bouche, appetizer, and main course, Mia loaded a plate with delicate desserts during the party's Viennese Hour. She forced herself to pass on the ice cream sundae station and cotton candy machine. Ian, Nicole's husband, sidled up to her. "All this food. Crazy, huh?"

Mia chomped down on a custard-filled profiterole and moaned. "Crazy good, much as I hate to admit it. It's almost midnight. How's Nicole holding up?"

"I sent her home two hours ago. Tina didn't even notice."

"No surprise there. At least you don't have to worry about transporting all the gifts home." The invitation from Tina warned guests to send baby gifts directly to the parents and not bring anything to the shower.

"We have a two-bedroom apartment. I had to rent a storage facility for everything from this party alone. I'm grateful but . . ."

"A little overwhelmed?" Ian gave a vigorous nod.

Mia patted his hand. "Welcome to the world of Italian and Greek celebrations. You will never go unfed or ungifted, even if a lot of it is just an excuse for someone to make someone else look bad by comparison."

The trumpeter sounded another fanfare, startling Mia and Ian. He put down the trumpet and held up a microphone. "Ladies and gentlemen," he intoned, "All hail—"

"Did he just say, *All hail*?" Ian whispered.

"He did indeed," Mia whispered back.

"Tina and Ron's gift—"

"Hey, she let Ron take some credit," Mia whispered to Ian.

"For a change," he murmured back.

"For the Karras-Whitman baby!"

"I didn't know you were going to use both your names," Mia whispered.

"We weren't."

Ian ran his hand through his hair so hard he pulled out

a small chunk of it as Versailles staffers wheeled out a portable stage set with a lavish display of nursery furniture. The crowd vigorously clapped while Tina preened and gestured to the furniture like a game show spokesmodel. Mia noticed her husband Ron had the decency to look embarrassed.

Ian gulped, then pulled out his cell phone. "I have to check the storage facility's website. We're gonna need a bigger space."

Tina held up a hand to quiet the crowd. "We're not done."

"We're not?" Ian whispered this to Mia with a terrified look on his face.

"Please join me outside for"—Tina motioned to the trumpeter, who responded with yet another fanfare—"the gender reveal!"

"I thought you weren't going to do a gender reveal," Mia said as guests trooped by them.

"We weren't." Ian paled. "We don't even know the baby's sex. How does she? I'm scared."

The two of them joined the throng exiting the banquet hall. Everyone reconvened on a flagstone patio overlooking a pond surrounded by perfectly manicured greenery. The *Star Wars* theme blasted from speakers disguised as boulders. Ian's mother whimpered. His father enveloped her in his arms protectively. A yellow display of fireworks suddenly erupted. Confused shower guests muttered to each other. Tina sauntered to the front of the crowd, a mic in her hand. "When Nicole's doctor said he wouldn't reveal the sex of a patient's baby for any amount of money, he wasn't kidding," she said in a jocular tone. "So, I give you . . . yellow!" The guests hooted and cheered. Tina threw her arms up in the air and rattled her bracelets. "And now, I give you . . . a rainbow!" Behind her, a multicolored array of fireworks exploded.

Mia watched the extravagant display in silence. The fireworks, the furniture gift, the high-end party, that array of rainbow bracelets . . . Ron owned a diner in Astoria. Mia knew it did well, but not *that* well. "Ian," she asked as a fireworks rainbow burst in the sky and then dribbled down into the pond, signifying the end of the show, "where does Tina get all her money? Because I know it's not all coming from Ron. If any of it."

Ian, who seemed close to tears, gave a helpless shrug. "No idea. She was a flight attendant, and Nicole and I always assumed she retired with a great pension. Now she works from home doing investments. Says she's a day trader."

Mia pursed her lips. "Day trader, huh?" In Mia's world—or rather, her father's—"day trader" was the younger goombah generation's code for *No way am I gonna tell you where I'm getting all this money.* There was something hinky about Tina's seemingly endless stream of cash.

"Don't leave without your party favor," Tina called out to her guests, who were starting to disperse. "They're custom Swiss chocolate baby rattles. Solid chocolate, not hollow."

"Solid, not hollow," one partygoer said to another as they hurried back inside to line up for their favor. "Price-*ee.*"

Very price-ee, Mia thought to herself. Even for a successful "day trader."

CHAPTER 3

Off-putting as Tina's over-the-top baby shower had been, the evening proved useful. Mia may have been annoyed by Castor Garvalos's attitude—she'd found the snooty G.M.'s full name on the Versailles' website—but by poking around the venue, she'd learned what Belle View was missing. She and her father needed to hire a retail manager, someone whose sole job was to order food and beverage supplies, as well as rental equipment. Currently, those tasks were divided between her, her father Ravello, the ever-elusive Cammie, and even chefs Guadalupe and Evans. A dedicated retail manager would lift the load off everyone.

When Mia showed up at work the next morning, she couldn't help comparing Belle View to the grandiosity of Versailles. The upgrades she'd been so proud of only days before now recalled the expression, *lipstick on a pig*. She tried replacing the thought with a judge-y internal labeling of Versailles as garish and nouveau riche. The tiled floor beneath her feet rumbled and she heard the roar of a jet departing from LaGuardia. Mia watched a tiny crack appear in the brand-new paint job of the wall to her left. The sight made her heart heavy. It confirmed that there was only so much she and her father could do in terms of cosmetic fixes. The facility needed structural work, sound-proofing, better plumbing, and a new roof. The bathrooms, currently museums of mid-century Formica finishes, would require gutting. New carpets, drapes, paint . . . the list of repairs and upgrades necessary to turn Belle View into Astoria's premiere event destination felt longer than a drugstore receipt.

For a moment, Mia felt overwhelmed by the fear that she wasn't up to the challenge. Then she flashed on an image from her childhood—her father wearing a prison jumpsuit singing "Happy Birthday" to her in a penitentiary visiting room. She couldn't recall which prison or which birthday—there had been several "celebrated" this way. Mia fought back fear and summoned up her reserve of inner strength. *I can do this*, she told herself. *Baby steps*. And step one was finding a retail manager.

She was typing the job description into a hiring website form when Ravello appeared in her doorway, having returned from lunch with Donny Boldano, the Boldano Family godfather and her literal godfather. "Hi, Dad. How was Roberto's?"

"*Eccellente,* as always." Ravello lunched at the popular eatery every weekday. The restaurant rewarded him with a gold nameplate above his booth, in addition to many freebies. "Minniguccia Evangelista was there. She had a special meal made for Donny and me and picked up the tab."

"Let me guess. Pasta puttanesca."

"How did you know?"

"She's sending me a message." Mia closed her eyes and leaned back in her chair, which rolled backward. "Nicole's shower is this weekend. I love her like a sister, but I can't wait until it's over and I get a break from hearing about stepmonsters and *puttana*."

"*Capisco.* I understand." Ravello threaded the meaty fingers on his large hands together and cracked his knuckles. "I told Donny about our staffing need and he has someone he wants us to meet."

Mia cast a wary eye at her father. "Oh-kay. Does this person have hospitality experience?"

"Not that I know of."

"What's his background?"

Ravello shrugged. "Got me."

She stared down her father. "He's in the Family, isn't he? Dad, we gotta keep this place clean—"

"He's not in the Family."

"That's a relief."

"He's in the Tutera Family."

Mia rolled back to her desk and slammed down her fists. "*What?*"

Ravello held up his hands. "Calm down, *bella.* He's a good kid and wants to do his own thing. He's Vito Tutera's grandson."

"I thought Donny and Vito hated each other."

"Donny had kidney stones last week and Vito sent him a get-well basket from the Abruzzo Deli."

Mia crooked her mouth. "And in exchange we hire

Vito's grandson who we've never met and has no experience to do an important job here? That must've been some nice basket."

"We want to keep Donny happy. And it wouldn't hurt to make Vito happy, too."

Mia couldn't argue this point, but she wasn't happy about it. "Fine. You get to hire him and explain the job. But he doesn't start until after Nicole's shower. I don't need to babysit a newbie on top of everything else that day."

Ravello saluted his daughter. "Yes, ma'am." He started to go, then turned back and asked sheepishly, "How does the new job work again?"

Mia let out an exasperated sigh. "I explained it to you. A couple of times. But I'll forward the description I wrote up for the job websites."

"*Va bene, grazie*. I'm sorry, *bella*. I know I'm off my game."

"Is it Lin?" Mia softened. Finally, some years after having his disastrous marriage to her self-centered mother annulled, her father had started dating again. More than dating–he had a steady girlfriend, Lin Yeung. Formerly a prosecutor, Lin now ran a high-end florist shop in Manhattan's East Village. Not only was she a lovely woman who'd taught Ravello the art of floral design, her proviso for dating him was that he eschew all criminal activity. Mia appreciated that the relationship motivated her father to stay straight.

"Yeah." Ravello beamed. "I forgot what it feels like to care so much about someone in a romantic way. You know, get like, heart flutters when you think about them. It's a good feeling."

Mia smiled at her father. "It is." Her own heart

clutched a touch. She wondered; *will I ever feel that way again in a relationship?* She shook it off. "Go take care of Vito Tutera's grandson. The teddy bears for Nicole's shower showed up without their T-shirts on, so I got fifty bears to dress."

As opposed to Tina's extravaganza, which didn't end until the wee hours of the morn, Nicole's shower at Belle View was scheduled for a respectable early afternoon slot. Deliverymen traipsed through in the morning, depositing rentals, decorations, and supplies. Mia helped her staff set up for the event, then changed into a summery dress patterned in shades of purple. Since she was doing double duty as guest and host, she opted for comfortable black sandals with a small heel that would make being on her feet less onerous. She joined Guadalupe in the kitchen to give the food a once-over. Nicole had asked for a tea party theme, so Mia rented enough three-tiered serving stands to provide guests with a generous selection of finger sandwiches. Along with . . .

"If you ask me," Guadalupe, Belle View's chef, said as she surveyed the spread on the long kitchen prep table, "those big bowls of pasta puttanesca next to the girly sandwiches look nuts." The tall, robust woman, formerly an Army cook in Iraq, wasn't one to mince words.

"That pasta tastes good, though. Nice blend of flavors." This came from Evans, who was focused on decorating the cake he'd designed for the party. It was in the shape of a baby carriage, but rather than place a baby inside, Evans had created a question mark out of vanilla cake, a clever nod to the unknown gender of the Whitmans' incoming progeny.

"The guests are all family and friends," Mia said.

"They'll assume the puttanesca is a nod to Nicole's heritage on her Italian mother's side. Love the cake, Evans."

Evans responded with his usual monosyllabic grunt,
but Mia thought she caught a glimmer of a smile.

Cammie, who was also a guest-slash-hostess—with the
emphasis on "guest"—pushed open the swinging door
and stuck her head in. "The first guests clocked in. Speaking of which, a reminder that I'm clocking out before
cleanup." She held up her hands, showing off fingernails
that glistened with frosty pink polish. "Fresh manicure.
No thanks to the hours at this hellhole." She winked at
Mia. "And by *hellhole,* I mean the best job I will ever,
ever have."

"Hoo-ah!" Guadalupe clapped her hands together and
barked at everyone like the Army cook she'd once been,
"Let's do this, people!"

The first hour of the shower ran more smoothly than
Mia could have dreamed possible. It was a beautiful summer day, which made for a perfect view through the floor-
to-ceiling glass windows of boats gently bobbing in
Flushing Marina. Even the airport seemed to cooperate.
Being that it was the weekend, there were fewer flights to
rumble Belle View's walls. With distance from the forced
grandeur of Versailles, Mia could enjoy the merits of her
homey banquet hall.

The room filled with warm, happy chatter. Cardboard
ducks dangled from yellow crepe paper strung across the
room. The gift table wobbled under the weight of presents from Nicole and Ian's loved ones, to the point
where Mia texted Ian that he better ratchet up the size of
his storage facility yet again. Elisabetta, clad in a simple
navy dress instead of her requisite tracksuit, gossiped

with the senior friend group surrounding great-grandma-to-be Minniguccia, who had jazzed up her walker by wrapping crepe paper around the legs and dangling a row of plastic rattles from the handles. Mia hung with Nicole's crew. Much to her chagrin and embarrassment, she discovered that even women she was meeting for the first time knew the story of her philandering hubby, Adam. Everyone had someone they wanted to set her up with, including a lesbian friend of Nicole's cousin Sophie. "If that's what you're into," Sophie hastened to add.

"It's what I'm into," said Justine Cadeau, a stylish thirty-something art gallery owner.

Touched by the concern for her moribund social life but tired of deflecting the invitations, Mia encouraged Sophie and Justine to exchange contact information, and grabbed the chance to move on. She gravitated toward Nicole's mother, Linda, who kissed her on both cheeks and then hugged her. "It's a beautiful party, sweetheart," Linda said. She was a petite woman who shared the olive coloring of her Italian heritage with her daughter. Linda had curly hair she wore in a short cut that accentuated delicate gamine features. It wasn't unusual for people to mistake her and Nicole for sisters.

"I'm just the hired hand," Mia said. "You and Minnie get all the credit for the party."

"I'm glad it's going well. For Nicole's sake."

Linda smiled, but with a hint of sadness Mia couldn't ignore. "We're already an hour into the shower," Mia said. "Maybe Tina won't come."

"She'll come," Linda said. "I want her to. With a baby almost here, there has to be peace in the family."

Cammie tottered over, wearing a pair of pink heels

she'd proudly tell anyone who asked that she bought in nineteen-eighty-six. "Food's out."

Mia gave her a thumbs-up. "Thanks."

They began herding the guests toward the tables. The double doors of the Marina Ballroom suddenly flew open and Tina Iles-Karras strode in. She wore a rayon jumpsuit in fire-engine red, which Mia now pegged as her signature, attention-getting color, and once again her arms were loaded with the coveted rainbow bracelets. "Am I late?" she asked, all innocence. Mia knew this was a rhetorical question. The event's time frame was crystal clear on the invitation. Tina was a woman who had to make an entrance.

"Your timing is perfect," Linda said, her tone gracious. "We're just sitting down to tea."

"Thank you, Linda." Tina motioned for Nicole's mother to precede her. "Oops. I almost said, 'age before beauty.'" She said this to Mia and Cammie under her breath with a half-grin.

"You did say it," Cammie pointed out. She motioned for Tina to walk ahead of her and flipped off the woman behind her back. Mia bit the knuckle of her index finger to keep from laughing.

The energy in the room shifted with Tina's entrance. Tension permeated the air. Minniguccia fixed Tina with a glare so white hot that for a second Mia wondered if the octogenarian Italian possessed some *strega*-like power to reduce her to ashes. Nicole stood up and came to her stepmother. "Tina, thank you so much for coming." She kissed her on both cheeks.

"We saved you a spot at the table with the best view," Linda said to her replacement in Ron's affections. She led

Tina to the table closest to the ballroom's expansive glass window and farthest away from Minnie's location. The tension dissipated and happy chatter returned as everyone turned their attention to tea. Guests devoured the finger sandwiches, and no one questioned the pasta puttanesca side dish, to Mia's relief. Photos of Evans's adorable cake garnered so many social media postings that Mia thought it had a shot at trending. There was one dicey moment when Mia feared the party might take a dark turn. The waitstaff delivered a three-tiered dish of pastries and cookies to each table. In a break with traditional treats like pecan squares and lemon tarts, all the sweets were Italian-themed, including a top tier of *trecolore*—three-color cookies—which also went by another name.

"Rainbow cookies!" Delighted, Tina held up a cookie. Then she held up a bracelet-loaded arm. "A tribute to her step-mama—who is me—from the beautiful mother-to-be. Tina—or Tino—would be a good name for a baby, huh?" She held up a hand to a nonplussed tablemate, who gave her a tentative high-five.

"Ucciderò quella puttana di vita bassa," Minniguic-cia muttered, which Mia translated in her head as a threat to murder the despised Tina.

Minnie made a move to get up, but Linda pulled her back. "Mama, *basta*. That's enough. We need to make nice." Linda waved and forced a smile at her rival, and her mother dialed back her rage to a simmer.

The meal over, Nicole hied herself to the giant stack of presents. Tina waved a large, thin package in the air. "Before you start with those, open this." She made her way across the room, the skinny heels of her designer sandals making a rhythmic clicking sound as she walked.

"Tina," Nicole said, embarrassed, "you already gave me a wonderful present."

"That was from your father and me. This one's just from me."

Trapped, Nicole unwrapped the package. Her mouth dropped open. "I-I-I don't know what to say."

"What is it?" Justine Cadeau, who was sitting at Mia's table, called out.

Nicole held up a replica of a check resembling the graphic from a Publishers Clearinghouse giveaway in the amount of ten thousand dollars. The room gasped.

"That amount has been deposited in a savings account for Baby Whitman." Tina shared this with an attempt at a wide smile. Her upper lip didn't move.

Botox, Mia thought to herself.

Tina clicked her way back to her table, graciously acknowledging a round of applause for her gift. As she passed Linda, who was sitting next to Mia, she muttered out of the side of her mouth, "Top that."

Linda waited until Tina was out of earshot, then whispered to Mia, "I'm providing free childcare so Nicole can go back to work after her maternity leave ends."

Mia choked back a chuckle. "Linda for the win," she said in a quiet voice. She and Nicole's mother discreetly low-fived.

Nicole continued to open presents and a pile of wrappings accumulated as time passed. Mia left the ballroom to retrieve a new trash bag. She was distracted by the sound of women yelling in the ladies' room. Her concerned ratcheted up when she recognized Minnie's voice.

Cammie came running out of the bathroom, a panicked look on her face. "Mia, thank God. Tina and Minnie are going at it. I'm afraid it's gonna get physical."

Mia dropped the trash bag and ran into the bathroom. Nicole's grandmother and stepmother were in a face-off, screaming at each other. "Call me a *puttana* one more time and I will sue your shriveled-up old Italian butt!" Tina yelled at Minnie.

"Fine, I'll call you other names!"

Minnie hurled a stream of Italian profanity at her nemesis, who gasped.

"How *dare* you," Tina said, outraged. "I know exactly what you're saying. You don't live in Astoria without learning street Italian."

"And you don't live here without learning street Greek."

Minnie shot this back at Tina, then switched to cursing in Greek. Tina responded with a stream of Italian invectives.

"Did they just switch languages?" Cammie asked. "I'm so confused."

Mia thrust herself between Tina and Minnie's walker. She held up her hands. "Ladies, please—"

The women ignored her. Justine Cadeau stepped into the room as Minnie and Tina continued their fight. "Bad time to use the bathroom?"

"Ya might wanna use the one upstairs," Cammie advised.

"I can hold it in," Justine said, unable to tear herself away from the drama.

Tina poked a finger in Minnie's chest. "Yell at me all you want. It'll just put you in the grave faster. Remember that, Minniguccia. I'll be around long after you're gone, you old bat."

"Hey." Linda burst into the room. She grabbed Tina's collar, yanked her away from Minnie, and held her at eye level. Everyone froze—including Tina. Linda blazed with fury. Mia, who'd never seen Nicole's mother lose her temper in any way, found it a frightening sight. "If you *ever* talk to anyone in my family that way again," Linda said to her rival through clenched teeth, "I will yank the engine out of that fancy sports car you drive, tie it to your ankles, and drop you in Flushing Bay." She let go of Tina's collar and the woman stumbled backward. "This is my daughter's baby shower. I don't want her to know about this insanity. The party is gonna end on a high note. You got that? Get out there and pretend to be a human being. Then I never want to see your sorry, skinny face again unless it's looking up at me from a casket."

Mia, Cammie, and Justine all sucked in a breath. Tina regained her balance. She glanced in the restroom mirror and patted her black hair in place. "What insanity?" she said, then strode out.

Linda enveloped a weeping Minniguccia in her arms. The room was silent for a moment. "We need to get back to the shower," Mia finally said. "If we're gone too long, Nicole will figure out there's a problem."

"*Si,*" Minnie said. "You're right."

Linda released her mother. "You sure you're okay?"

Minnie nodded. She pulled a tissue from box on the vanity and wiped her eyes. "*Andiamo.* Let's go."

Linda took Minnie's hand and led her from the restroom. Mia lingered behind. Disturbed by the altercation, she needed to regain control of her own emotions. She inhaled a shaky breath, released it, and then headed back to the baby shower.

Elisabetta spotted her granddaughter as soon as Mia

entered the ballroom and pulled her aside. "Something's wrong. I can see it on your face."

"Can't talk now," Mia said. "I'll tell you later."

"You don't look good."

"I'm fine. Just a little shaken."

Elisabetta patted Mia's stomach. "Eat something. You'll feel better." She said this despite the fact everyone at the party had just enjoyed a hearty meal. In the Carinas' Italian household food was a cure-all for everything from a hangnail to a heart attack.

Nicole continued opening gifts. Mia tried to focus. She oohed and ahhed with the rest of the women, but without commitment. She was concerned that the animosity between the Karras family members had become toxic. *It's not my family,* she reminded herself. Still, she couldn't shake the ugly scene she'd witnessed.

The mom-to-be finally reached the last gift in the pile, a flat, rectangular package wrapped in a black-and-white polka dot patterned wrapping paper and a gauzy, sparkling silver ribbon studded with rhinestones. "Tina, no. Another gift? You have to stop."

The smug look that generally colored the expression on Tina's face disappeared. She looked stunned. "I did. That's not from me."

Nicole wrinkled her brow. "There's a card with your name on it." She unwrapped the present, revealing a painting. A buxom woman sat atop a cow, depicted in a style that Mia, who'd taken an art history class in high school because it was rumored to be an easy *A*, recognized as cubism. Nicole held up the painting and Tina paled. "It's lovely," Nicole said politely. "Although it might be a better fit for our living room than the nursery."

Justine Cadeau jumped up from her chair. "Let me see that." She took the painting from Nicole and examined it carefully. "This painting is called *Cow and Woman*. It's by the late Spanish artist Ferdinand Vela, and was stolen from the Malcolm Miller Art Collection about twenty years ago in one of the most famous art heists of all time."

Nicole looked mystified. "Why would someone give me a copy of that painting? And say it was from Tina?"

Justine turned the painting around and checked out the back of it. "This isn't a copy. It's the original painting."

Tina Karras let out a shrill scream. Then she collapsed to the floor.

CHAPTER 4

Mia dropped to the floor to help Tina as the party erupted into a cacophony of confusion. "Nobody leave!" she yelled to the guests while slapping the prostrate woman to revive her. She considered this the best part of her day.

"We're not going anywhere," one of the guests responded. "This is like some awesome reality show."

"I got smelling salts," Elisabetta said, pulling them out of her ancient handbag. "Because you never know."

Mia grabbed the smelling salts and waved them under Tina's nose. Nicole's stepmother coughed and choked her way back to consciousness. "The painting," she murmured as Mia helped her to a chair. "Where . . ."

"Justine has it."

Cammie ran up to Mia. "The police are on their way. Pete said they also asked Manhattan to send over the

NYPD art cop." Detective Pete Dianopolis was Cammie's ex-husband who lived in the hopes of correcting the mistake he'd made by divorcing her. Cammie figured they'd eventually get back to together but for now she was having too much fun making him work for it.

Mia handed Tina, who was weeping, a napkin. She followed Cammie into the Belle View foyer. "NYPD has an art cop?"

"Yeah. Apparently stealing pricey artwork is a big thing. Even ugly stuff like that." Cammie used her thumb to gesture toward the painting Justine Cadeau clutched in her arms. "I'm not into modern. I like my cows to look like cows."

"Why?" Tina moaned. "*Whhhyyyy?*"

"The police are coming," Mia said. "Hopefully we'll find out why soon enough."

To Mia's relief, Pete and his young partner, Ryan Hinkle, arrived minutes later, along with several law enforcement officials she didn't recognize. A man she assumed was the art detective immediately commandeered the painting. He briefly conferred with Pete, then headed out of the building, stopping to hold the door open for a young woman. Mia groaned when she saw who it was.

Teri Fuoco, ace reporter for the *Triborough Tribune*— at least in her own mind—marched into the building. A headband corralled her mess of dirty blond hair and her lumpy body was clad in its usual uniform of khaki chinos and pastel polo shirt. She looked more like someone who'd hand out towels in a golf course clubhouse than a crack investigative journalist. "What I wouldn't give to do a makeover on that girl," Cammie muttered to Mia.

"If by makeover you mean make her disappear, I'm all for it," Mia responded with asperity. Teri lived to dig up dirt on the Boldano Family. She and Mia had struck a wary truce after Teri helped rescue her from the clutches of thugs, but Mia still didn't trust the reporter.

"Mia, hi," Teri said in a tone that made them sound like old friends.

"What do you want?" Mia snapped.

"Word's out about the Vela painting. Slow news day so when that hit the police scanner, everyone jumped on it."

Teri motioned for Mia to follow her to the catering hall's glass double doors, which she did with reluctance. The reporter pointed to news vans from local stations that were pulling up to the entrance. Mia muttered a few choice words, then texted Ravello. He'd left the all-women shower in her hands, but she'd need backup to fend off the media. "Cody," she said to a part-time staffer dragging off a full trash bin. "Wait on tossing the trash. I need you to man the doors and keep out anyone who isn't law enforcement."

Cody, a former Marine, instantly let go of the bin. "Yes, ma'am," he said, managing to restrain himself from saluting.

"Good thing I'm already inside," Teri said cheerfully. "I get first dibs on the story."

Mia unleashed a few more choice words. "I am so not talking to you."

She headed back to the ballroom, Teri on her heels. "You do know that the Miller Collection art heist was assumed to be the work of the Boldano Family."

"Yes," Mia lied. If the heist happened twenty years prior, she would have been eleven at the time, and more worried about an impending set of braces than the crime syndicate's activities.

"Donny Boldano swore on a bible—literally, he had it videotaped and sent to the media, he was very ahead of the curve on that one—he swore his people had nothing to do with the theft," Teri said.

"Then I'm sure it's true. If Donny swears the Family had nothing to do with it, then that's usually the case."

Teri looked skeptical. "Considering how many activities the Boldano Family denies doing, I don't know how it stays in business."

Mia scanned the ballroom. Pete and Ryan were divvying up the guests for interviews. "As you can see, I'm busy. Feel free to leave."

"You're kidding, right? I'm not going anywhere." Teri noticed an uneaten row of sandwiches. "Ooh. Yummy."

Teri sat down at the table and fixed herself a plate of leftovers. Pete crooked a finger at Mia. "I'll take a group to the ballroom upstairs. Hinkle's gonna do interviews down here. You stay and keep an eye on him. His baby's got colic so he's not getting much sleep. Cammie can come with me." He smoothed down his thick thatch of salt-and-pepper hair. "I look okay?"

Mia, who knew Pete considered every male, including her father, a rival in his affections for Cammie, was determined to stay on the detective's good side. "You look great."

"Thanks." He stroked his chin. "Interesting case for Steve Stianopolis." Pete, a mystery buff, wrote a self-published series under this pseudonym. It had yet to find the mass audience he assumed it would, instead selling in the ones of copies.

Pete marshaled his group of guests to interview and

headed upstairs to the Bay Ballroom. Mia's head pounded. The party had gone south in a big, unforeseen way. *But, she comforted herself, at least it doesn't involve dead bodies, like what happened in the spring.*

She approached Ryan Hinkle who was deep in conversation with Nicole. Mia could see that her pregnant friend was fighting to keep it together. "You want the combination bouncer-walker," Hinkle advised. "Don't let anyone talk you into buying them separately. Oh, hey, Mia."

Mia placed her hands on her friend's shoulders. "It's been a long day for Nicole. I'm thinking maybe you could finish up with her and talk to her stepmother Tina. She had a big reaction to the painting. Like"—Mia bent her arm at the elbow and bent it forward to mime falling over—"dead faint big."

"I'm all done with Nicole." Hinkle took out a card and handed it to her. "You got any questions about baby stuff, gimme a call. Believe me, by now I'm an expert."

Nicole took the card. "I will. I appreciate that." She hugged Mia and mouthed, "and thank *you*."

Mia led the junior detective to where Tina had stretched herself out on four chairs shoved together. "Tina, if you're feeling better, Detective Hinkle has some questions for you."

Tina bolted up. "It's *them*." She dramatically pointed a finger at Minniguccia and Linda, who were huddled together at a table across the room. "They both hate me. They must've found that painting somewhere and used it to get me in trouble."

"How so?" Hinkle asked.

"By making it look like I stole it. Wrapping it up, putting a card with my name on it. It's a setup."

"So, you've never seen the painting before?"

Tina shook her head back and forth with vigor. "Never in my entire life."

Having grown up around an organization where lying was in the job description, Mia had developed a radar for people's tells when they lied, and Tina Karras was currently a tsunami of tells. She broke eye contact and looked everywhere but at the detective as she continued to deny any knowledge of the painting with a vociferousness that rang false. She bit nervously on a beautifully manicured nail. Even Hinkle look skeptical between yawning the yawns of a father with a colicky infant.

Mia heard the thud of familiar footsteps. She was relieved to see Ravello stride in. "Dad, you got my text."

"Yours, Cami's, Guadalupe's, Evans's. That's why I didn't get here quicker. I was too busy reading texts."

He kissed his daughter on both cheeks, then gently pulled her to her feet. Ravello replaced Mia in the seat next to Hinkle. The detective thrust his phone in Ravello's face. "Hey Carina, recognize this?"

Maria looked over her father's shoulder, to see an image of the *Woman and Cow* painting. Ravello made a face. "No. Stupid painting. Why would anyone ride a cow? How would you even get on top of one? It doesn't make sense."

Hinkle put his phone away. "I thought maybe if I surprised you, I'd get a reaction. Not an art critique, a guilty look or something."

"That was a good plan. Sorry to disappoint you." Ravello said this with a wry smile. He addressed his daughter. "Go take care of Nicole. I'll handle everything here." He extended a hand to Tina, who was staring at the Mob lieutenant with an expression Mia couldn't identify. "I'm Ravello Carina. And you are?"

Tina opened her mouth and paused. Then she found her voice. "Tina. Tina Iles-Karras."

"Ah. Nicole's infamous stepmother."

Fury colored the woman's face. Tina inhaled and exhaled through her nose, like an angry bull. "And the victim of a very, very cruel joke."

Ravello's smile thinned. "That painting's gotta be worth a fortune. I wouldn't exactly call it showing up here with your name on it a joke. What do you think, Detective?"

Hinkle gave a vigorous nod. "Agreed."

Mia left her father and the detective to their unlikely partnership and went to find Nicole. She saw Teri Fuoco had cornered Justine Cadeau in the foyer and was in the middle of an interview. Much as the reporter annoyed her, Mia was curious to hear the art dealer's take on the situation. She sidled over to the women.

"It's extremely difficult, if not impossible, to sell famous paintings, even on the black market," Justine said into the tiny mic Teri held up to her. She pushed her Manhattan-trendy black eyeglasses back to the top of the bridge of her nose. With her flawless blonde bob and black pants/white shirttail, the kind of deceptively simple outfit that cost a fortune, the dealer gave off the vibe of coming from money.

Probably went to one of those fancy sister schools where they drink champagne and talk about their trust funds. Mia hated that women like Justine made her feel insecure. She shook off the side trip and turned her attention back to the conversation.

"But these weren't great works of art," Teri said. "I looked up all the paintings stolen from the Miller Collection. They were the lesser-known works of great artists."

Mia reluctantly acknowledged that Teri had done her homework.

"That was the brilliance of this heist," Justine said. "Each painting had enough cachet to command a high price from wealthy financiers or oligarchs, yet wasn't so iconic that it could instantly be identified by whoever viewed it. Stupid art thieves steal famous paintings. They're impossible to move. But what's weird about the Miller Collection robbery is *Cow and Woman* is the only stolen painting that was ever seen again." Ryan Hinkle appeared at the door and motioned to Justine. "Sorry, that officer wants to talk to me."

"No worries," Teri said. "I've got your contact info."

The art dealer disappeared into the Marina Ballroom. Teri did a happy dance. "Oh, man, I love this story. You know what it is? Sexy, that's what. It's a sexy, sexy story. A beautiful stepmother, a stolen painting suddenly showing up again. It's got so many good elements I barely have to mention the Boldano Family."

"Or not at all," Mia said, hopeful.

"I said barely. That's very different from *not at all*."

Mia checked her wrist. "Oh, look, it's Teri-was-just-leaving time."

"You're looking at freckles, not a watch, but I've got my story. Which none of them do." Teri, with a cocky grin, gestured to the news vans outside. "Call me if anything interesting breaks."

"Will do that . . . *never*."

Teri blew Mia a kiss and left. Mia shot a middle finger at her back and resumed her hunt for Nicole. She found her lying down in the upstairs bridal lounge and hurried to the pregnant woman's side. "Are you okay?" she asked.

Panicked, she added, "That baby isn't coming now, is she? Or he?"

"No, although it would be the perfect end to today," Nicole said, her tone sardonic. "Ian just got here with the van he rented. Mom and Nonna are done being interviewed by the detective and some of your very nice employees are helping to load the van. The detective said it would be okay to take everything as soon as the crime scene unit finished taking pictures and dusting for prints. They don't need to hold on to anything for evidence except the painting. It's not like I unwrapped a dead body."

"Thank God for that." Mia flashed on visions of a body lying in the bottom of a bachelor party jump-out cake and a body found in a dumpster, both victims of murders that nearly doomed Ravello, as well as Belle View, in the spring. She banished the images.

It took a few more hours, but eventually the police finished their investigation and interviews. Mia and the staff cleaned up the baby shower detritus, and then Mia released the employees who were still there—Cammie had departed with ex-husband Pete, who promised a stop at her favorite jewelry shop if she joined him for dinner. "Do you mind taking Nonna home?" Mia asked her father as they double-checked the rooms for any missed trash. "I wanna put a call into Posi." Given his dicey connections, there was a good chance her inmate brother had some insider knowledge about the Miller Collection theft.

"Sure. I can drop her off." Ravello gave a shout to his mother. "Hey, Mama! *Vieni qui.*"

Elisabetta emerged from Mia's office. "What's up? I was on the phone. Annette Cornetta was at my table and *marone*, did she have a story. You know how her husband

Gugliemo died a couple of months ago? They buried him without his shoes. Terrible mistake on the part of the funeral parlor. I told her she should sue."

"Not sure that that's a sue-able offense, Nonna," Mia said. "In fact, I pretty much doubt it."

Elisabetta brushed off her granddaughter's comment with a wave of the hand. "That's for the lawyers to decide. But poor Annette's been having the same dream over and over again. Gugliemo shows up, begging and crying for shoes. His feet are so cold, he says. Annette can barely sleep. But I called her with the perfect solution. We're gonna send up a pair of shoes for Gugliemo in someone else's casket." Elisabetta looked pleased with herself while Mia and Ravello managed to hide their reactions to Elisabetta's bizarre idea. "*Andiamo*," she said to her son. "I gotta get home and find a funeral to go to. Queens is a big borough. Somebody's dying somewhere."

Ravello escorted his mother out of the catering hall, tossing an eye roll back at Mia on his way out. She retreated to her office. Putting a call through to a prison inmate wasn't easy, even at a minimum-security facility like Triborough, where the goal was to transition offenders to life on the outside. But Posi was a regular at the facility, and Ravello had done a stint or two back in the day as well, so Mia was put through to her brother relatively quickly. She detailed the day's events to him. "Do you know anything about the Miller Collection heist?" she asked.

"Not much. I was only a few years older than you when it happened."

"Have you ever heard anyone in the Family talk about it?" Posi was more connected to Boldano activities than Mia, even if the connection was peripheral.

"Only in the way anyone who read about it or saw it on TV would."

"It sounds like an inside job to me," Mia said.

"Agreed. From what I remember, the cops thought so, too, but they could never connect anyone from the Collection to the heist."

"Tina Karras passed out the minute she heard the painting was real. I swear she was lying when she told Detective Hinkle she didn't know anything about it."

"And if anyone has a nose for a lie, it's my baby sister."

"It must be a gene that runs in the family," Mia said. Posi had a history of covering up his illegal activities like car thefts with lies.

"I'll ignore that. You want my advice, sis? Forget about the whole thing. This is one for the cops. The last thing Belle View needs is another crime drama on the property. And what does it have to do with you anyway?"

"Nothing," Mia had to admit. "Except that it happened here."

"Could've happened wherever the party was. So, move on. Dad said you want to learn how to drive. Since I can't teach you on account of my current incarcerated state, I set you up for the next best thing. Tomorrow's Sunday, you got no parties going on. Jamie Boldano's gonna pick you up in the morning and give you a driving lesson in the Belle View parking lot."

"*What*?" Mia protested. "Posi, you can't just—"

"Time's up. Bye."

Her brother ended the call. "Stop acting like some kind of a dating app," Mia said to the dial tone. She hung up the landline and began tapping Jamie's telephone number into her cell to cancel the lesson. Then she stopped. Posi had a point when he recommended leaving the art investigation to actual investigators and focusing on her own life. Jamie was a terrific driver and had more patience than the average Italian man, especially the ones in her family. He'd make a good driving instructor. "This has nothing to do with wanting to spend time with him," she told the phone. "And I just lied to myself." She did one last sweep of the Marina Ballroom, then hied herself and her lies home.

In the morning, Mia fed Doorstop and Pizzazz, then changed three times before settling on a learning-to-drive outfit of skinny jeans and a lacy turquoise tank top. The color brought out the bright blue in her eyes, and the cool tone complimented her winter coloring of pale skin and dark hair. She ringed her eyes with navy blue liner, then added two coats of black mascara. She finished the look by outlining her full lips and filling them in with a soft pink lipstick. *In case I run into someone I know*, she told herself. *This has nothing to do with Jamie. And I just lied to myself again.*

A text alerted her that Jamie was five minutes away. Mia used the brief wait to check her computer. She saw several media outlets picked up Teri Fuoco's story about the discovery of *Cow and Woman*. "Not my problem, right guys?" she said to her pets. Then she headed downstairs and outside.

A beat-up old brown sedan pulled up in front of Mia's front stoop. She ignored it, scanning the street for Jamie's pristine silver Prius. The sedan driver honked. Annoyed,

Mia waved it away. Jamie Boldano got out of the car. "Mia, it's me." He grinned, creating a perfect dimple in each cheek.

"Oh. Sorry." Mia ran down the steps to him. "Is your car in the shop?"

"No. I'm teaching you to drive on this one. I got it from someone Little Donny recommended."

"Meaning it has a sketchy history." Mia considered Jamie's older brother a big-time *cafone*, a.k.a., a jerk. She surveyed the vehicle. The back fender was missing. Sun had fried the paint on the car's roof. Both back doors sported dents. "Wow. You don't have a lotta faith in my driving skills, do you?"

"I figured this way you don't have to worry about dinging my car."

"Right," Mia scoffed. "You know, I've had some experience driving. Remember that Barbie Jeep I had when I was a kid?"

"All too well. Which is why I'm teaching you to drive real cars in this junker. Hop in. I'll get us to Belle View."

There were only a few cars in the banquet hall parking lot when they got there, belonging to people who had taken out the boats they docked at the marina. Jamie parked and turned off the engine. He handed her the key. "Your turn."

The two got out of the car and switched places. "This is so nice of you," Mia said. "You're sure Madison doesn't mind?"

"Oh, she's totally supportive. Doesn't care at all."

Mia found the fact that Jamie's girlfriend wasn't threatened by her somewhat insulting but pushed this aside to concentrate on driving. She placed a foot on the brake, released the hand brake, put the key in the ignition, and started the car.

"When you accelerate," Jamie cautioned, "make sure you do it—" Mia pressed down on the accelerator and the car shot forward. "Aaahhhh!" She slammed on the brake and the car jolted to a stop, throwing them forward and backward against the car seats. "—slowly. We'll work on that."

For the next hour, Mia practiced braking and accelerating. "I'm doing pretty good, huh?" She lifted a hand off the wheel to pat herself on the back and the car swerved right. She grabbed the wheel with both hands and hit the brakes.

"I think that's enough for today," Jamie said. He flinched and rubbed his neck.

"If you need a neck brace, there's probably one in the lost and found," Mia said. "You wouldn't believe the stuff people leave here."

"I'll live," Jamie said. "But I wouldn't mind getting something to eat."

"Let's see what's in the fridge. I think there might be some of Evans's cake left over from the shower. It's so good."

Mia and Jamie exited the car and walked toward the catering hall. "What's that?" Jamie asked. He pointed to a large red bundle floating in the water next to the dock closest to Belle View.

"No idea. Maybe it fell off someone's boat. It could be important. We should see what it is and if we can fish it out."

The two headed toward the bundle, which bobbed up and down in the water. As they drew closer, Mia's heart began to race. *Oh, no. No, no, no, no.*

Jamie grabbed her hand and clutched it. "Is that what I think it is?" he asked, his tone full of dread.

Mia fought back the bile rising in her throat, hating what she was about to say. "If you're thinking . . ."

A wave from an incoming motorboat rocked the bundle and an arm floated to the surface.

". . . that it's a body . . ."

Mia saw that the arm was draped in rainbow bracelets. A beautiful, sparkling array of them.

". . . then, yes. It is what you think it is."

CHAPTER 5

Mia and Jamie watched in silence as the police retrieved the body of Tina Iles-Karras from its watery grave. The parking lot and marina docks, both designated as crime scenes, were cordoned off. Crime scene technicians worked the entire area. An unmarked car parked in the spot closest to the marina. Pete Dianopolis and Ryan Hinkle exited the vehicle. They conferred with several police officers, then walked by Mia and Jamie on their way to the crime scene technicians. "Don't go anywhere," Pete said to Mia as he passed.

"I wasn't planning to," she said.

The heat index put the feel of the warm, humid air somewhere in the nineties, but Mia shivered. Jamie put a comforting arm around her. It said something about Mia's state of mind that she barely noticed. The air stank from rotting garbage in the nearby dumpster and whatever lurked

in the murky marina waters. Mia prayed the rank scent
had nothing to do Tina's corpse. The thought that it might
made her choke down the urge to throw up.

Pete had a brief conversation with the lead technician
and returned to Mia. "We'll need a family member to officially ID the vic, but I figure you already know who it is."

Mia nodded. "Tina Iles-Karras. From the shower yesterday. Was she . . ."

Mia couldn't finish the sentence, so Jamie took over.
"Was her death unnatural?"

"You mean, was she murdered? I can't tell you that."

"I'll let Cammie know how helpful you were," Mia
said.

"Too early to say for sure and the coroner will determine the exact cause of death, but it's definitely suspicious," Pete instantly replied. He called to his partner.
"Hinkle, look alive. Track down phone numbers for the
two women I told you about who got into a fight with the
vic at the baby shower." He pulled out a notepad and
checked it. Mia's heart sank as he said read out the names.
"Minniguccia Evangelista and Linda Karras." He looked
up at Mia. "The art gallery owner who was at the shower
told Cammie about the ladies going at it in the bathroom.
And that you were there, too."

Mia tensed. She pulled away from Jamie. "They ar-
gued, but not in an *I'm gonna kill you* way."

"So you say." Pete checked his notes. "But this Justine
Cadeau also said Linda Karras threatened to dump Tina
Karras in Flushing Bay. Which, as we can all see, is ex-
actly where she ended up."

Mia thought of Nicole, and what might happen if her
mother was accused of murder. The stress could endanger
her pregnant friend's life, as well as the baby's. The

stolen painting might be none of Mia's business, but Nicole's health was. "The painting," she blurted. "The stolen one that suddenly showed up at the shower, with Tina's name on it. She knew something about it, I know she did. Ask Detective Hinkle. He thought so too, I could tell. The painting appeared yesterday, Tina's dead today. There has to be a connection."

"There doesn't have to be a *has to be*," Pete said. Mia bristled at the mocking tone, but kept her mouth shut as he continued, "If the death wasn't accidental or natural, I lean more toward a crime of passion, given the catfight at the party." The detective scribbled in his notebook. "A lotta good stuff here for my next Steve Stianopolis mystery."

"Catfight is a sexist term," Mia said.

"Sorry. How's 'an exchange of blows rendered by those that are of the female persuasion?'" Pete put away the pad. "Or, here's another way to look at the situation. The Boldano Family was suspected in that art heist. The body of Tina Karras is found in the water behind Belle View Banquet Manor, run by a Family lieutenant—"

Mia and Jamie exchanged a nervous glance. "Go with your first instinct," Jamie said. "The passion thing."

"We can guarantee NYPD a bazillion percent that nobody we know had anything to do with the heist," Mia declared. "*And* I've known the Karras family almost my whole life. Nicole and I were in preschool together. If this is murder, you're gonna have to cast a way wider net, Pete." She glanced over to where representatives from the coroner's office were transferring the late Tina from the large net that divers had used to retrieve her, into a body bag. "Not the best choice of words on my part."

Jamie gave Mia a gentle poke in the ribs with his

elbow. He motioned with his head toward the parking lot entrance. Several news vans had pulled up to the crime scene tape blocking entry to the lot. A slim woman, immaculately dressed in a sleek maroon dress and black heels, hopped out of a van. Mia recognized her as the investigative reporter from the local station's six p.m. newscast. The reporter stuck a mic in the face of the officer guarding the entrance.

"Incoming," Jamie said.

"Great," Mia muttered. "Time to make ourselves outgoing. Are you done with us, Pete?"

"For now." The detective glanced at the news vans. "Ugh. Don't talk to them."

"No worries on that score," Mia said.

She and Jamie ran to the beater car and made their escape with Jamie behind the wheel. As they peeled out of the parking lot, Mia saw Teri Fuoco drive up in her tiny Smart car. Mia garnered pleasure from seeing that for once the *Triborough Trib* journalist was late to a Boldano Family story.

Mia texted her father the bad news on the drive home and warned him not to go by Belle View. **Do NOT put yourself in Pete's crosshairs.**

Ravello responded with a long row of thumbs-up. Jamie dropped her off with a promise to touch base later, and Mia went inside. She found Elisabetta, readers perched on her nose, scouring the obituaries in the print edition of the *Triborough Trib*. Mia kicked off her sneakers and plopped down on the couch next to her grandmother. "Looking for funerals?"

"Yeah. People are living so much longer, there's way less of them than there used to be."

"I can tell you one that'll probably be taking place

soon, but I wouldn't use it as a chance to send Gugliemo some shoes."

Elisabetta arched her eyebrows and closed the paper. *"Parlami."*

Mia did as ordered and shared the story of Tina's strange demise. Elisabetta gasped and crossed herself. "*Madonna mia.* What kind of world is this where people go around murdering each other? That Pete doesn't suspect your father again, does he?"

"It's not officially a murder until the cause of death is determined," Mia cautioned. "But I don't think he suspects Dad. I mean, that's Pete's go-to take on any crime near Belle View. But Dad wasn't even at the shower and he never even met Tina. As far as I know." Given how closed-mouthed her father was about his past ventures, Mia felt compelled to add the last sentence.

Elisabetta fell back against the couch and released a sigh of relief. "*Grazie a dio.* But poor Nicole. Do you think she's okay? This is the last thing she needs in her condition. I'll make a lasagna and send it over." As usual, if there was a question in the Carina household, food was the answer.

"I don't want to bother Nicole right now. I'm sure she's with her dad. But I'll call her later." Mia planted a kiss on top of her tiny grandmother's head. "I'm gonna take a nap. Between the heat and Tina, this morning really took it out of me."

Mia went upstairs to her apartment. "Hi, babies," she said to Doorstop and Pizzazz. "Who wants to take a lie-down with Mommy?"

Doorstop, who was already prone on the bed, stretched and purred. Mia opened the door to Pizzazz's birdcage. The parakeet flew out and made herself comfortable on top of the gold-gilded, ostentatious headboard that crowned Mia's hand-me-down bed. Mia substituted cotton draw-string shorts for her jeans and collapsed onto the bed. She closed her eyes and instantly flashed on the image of Tina's body being fished out of Flushing Bay. Her eyes popped open. She tried again. This time she flashed on the image of Tina's body being zipped into a body bag. She gave an annoyed exclamation and sat up in bed. "It ain't workin', Doorstop," she said to the cat, who was emitting peaceful little kitty snores. "If I'm not gonna sleep, I might as well do something useful."

Mia got off the bed, took the laptop from her desk and returned to bed, propping herself up against the head-board. Despite her cautionary tone to Elisabetta, Mia didn't believe some untimely accident landed the hated woman in the drink. She created a document titled SUSPECTS IN TINA'S MURDER. Mia paused and pondered. After a min-ute, she typed "Linda Karras" only because Justine the art dealer had blabbed about the bathroom imbroglio. Then she highlighted the name and deleted it. "I don't care how much Linda hated Tina. I know in my bones she wouldn't kill anyone." Doorstop didn't respond to Mia's declara-tion, but Pizzazz cheeped what she chose to see as agree-ment. Next, she typed Minnie's name. But she deleted it as well, unable to imagine the frail, diminutive old woman doing whatever it took to bump off Tina, then deposit her in the bay. Instead, Mia typed "Other People." "That's not too vague," she muttered.

She thought for a moment, then typed *Cow and Woman* into the search bar. A long list of articles pertaining to the painting's heist popped up on her screen. Mia read the first five, which were all different variations of the same story, the one she overheard Justine share with Teri Fuoco. She closed that search and typed in "Tina Iles-Karras." The announcement of her wedding to Ron appeared, plus a few social media tags, but nothing of interest and since her identity hadn't been revealed, there was no reference to her death. Mia yawned. Her eyelids fluttered shut.

"DINNER!"

"Agh!" Mia screamed and bolted up from bed, almost knocking her laptop onto the floor. She picked up her cell phone and checked the time. It was six P.M. Exhaustion had overcome her buzzing nerves, and she'd slept for five hours. She changed back into her jeans, then hurried downstairs to Elisabetta's kitchen, passing through the living room, where voices chattered from the television her grandmother liked to have on in the background while she cooked. Ravello, clad in slacks and a button-down shirt, which he considered casual wear, was sitting at Elisabetta's ancient dinette table fussing with an exquisite floral arrangement of lilies, roses, hydrangea, and snapdragons. "Look at what I made in Lin's class today," Ravello said proudly. "I figured you could use something cheerful around here after the last couple of days."

"It's gorgeous." Mia bent down and breathed in the pungent scent of lilies and roses. "You got a real gift, Dad."

"Meh." Ravello gave a modest shrug. "I just do what Lin tells me."

Elisabetta opened the oven door and Ravello's flowers duked it out with the rich, tomato-y scent of lasagna. She plated three portions and placed them on the table, along with a hunk of parmesan cheese and a cheese grater. Then she sat down and said a quick prayer in Italian. "*Adesso.* Now we eat."

Ravello shoveled a forkful of lasagna in his mouth. "I went by Belle View."

Mia stopped eating. "Dad," she said, frustrated," I told you not to do that."

"It's okay. The cops were very respectful. I think I'm off the hook on this one. I had to show Benjy Tutera around the place. He starts tomorrow."

"Right." Mia resumed eating. "I forgot about him. Is he excited?"

"Yeah. Sure."

Ravello focused on his plate. Mia gave her father the side eye. "Wow, could you sound any less convincing?"

Ravello waved off her concern. "He'll be fine. Worry about other things."

"Like who offed Tina." Elisabetta worked the cheese grater with ferocity as she said this.

"Nonna, you sound like a nineteen-forties P.I."

Mia's cell rang. Elisabetta wagged a finger at her. "No phones at the dinner table."

"It might be business." Mia checked. "Argh, it's Teri Fuoco, the reporter from the *Triborough Tribune*. Not answering, turning off ringer." She did both. A text popped up. Mia cursed, then read it aloud. "'Turn on channel 5.'"

"The TV's already on 5," Elisabetta said. "They got a real weatherperson, not some model girl dressed like she's going to the prom."

Mia got up and hurried into the living room. Her father and grandmother followed. The reporter Mia had seen jawing with the police officer was reporting live from the marina parking lot. Mia rewound the story to the beginning. "A body was recovered from Flushing Bay this afternoon," the reporter intoned. The Carinas hovered around the television as she continued with the story.

"At least she didn't mention Belle View," Ravello said.

". . . In the marina located behind Belle View Banquet Manor."

"And there it is," Mia said.

"At least she didn't bring up the Family," Ravello said, hunting for a bright side.

". . . Belle View Banquet Manor recently came under new ownership and the business is now reported to be operated by members of the Boldano crime family."

Mia crossed her arms in front of her chest and shot her father a baleful look. "At least she didn't mention the murders from the spring?" he said hopefully.

"The upscale catering facility was the scene of two murders only a few months ago," said the reporter.

"Hey, she called us upscale," Ravello said, genuinely excited.

"Yeah, we can take that to the bank. And see if we can trade it for bail money." Mia leaned against the back of an old armchair covered with one of the multicolored crocheted afghans Elisabetta birthed like rabbits.

"Belle View, which shares a name with a New York hospital renowned for its psychiatric care, was also the site of the mysterious reappearance of *Cow and Woman,* a long-lost painting stolen in the infamous Miller Art Collection heist."

"Sounds like Belle View Banquet Manor could use a little therapy itself," the newscast's male anchor joshed.

Elisabetta chuckled. "He made a funny. I like when they do that. It's a nice break from all the bad news. I swear, somedays I don't know who's gonna go first, me or the world."

Mia used the remote to mute the TV. "I keep going back to that *Cow and Woman* painting. Dad, are you a hundred percent sure that the Boldanos had nothing to do with the art heist?"

"A hundred *thousand* percent sure," Ravello said with total conviction.

Mia couldn't help smiling at her father. "You put a lot more behind that than when you talked about Benjy."

"You know how I know the Family had nothing to do with the heist? Donny was jealous. He couldn't believe how well someone pulled off the operation. To be honest . . ." Ravello lowered his voice by habit. No one had bugged a Carina home in years, but he didn't believe in taking chances. "Donny looked into doing his own version of the heist. There's a lot of new-money people out there, all over the world, who think the way to flaunt it is by hanging fancy art on their walls, and they don't care how they get it. But museums and galleries stepped up security in a big way after the Miller Collection paintings got stolen. Once that happened, Donny didn't think the payoff was worth the risk, especially since none of those paintings except the cow one ever showed up again. What's the point of stealing stuff if you can't sell it?"

"What indeed."

Mia's sarcasm didn't go unnoticed by her father. "Which is why I don't do it," he said in a defensive tone, adding under his breath. "At least anymore."

"Okay." Her father's assurances rang true and Mia relaxed a little. "I pray they find Tina's killer fast. In the meantime, I'll welcome Benjy to the Belle View family tomorrow, and that's family with a small *f*."

"There." Elisabetta pointed to the TV. "You see?"

A severe-looking woman in a long-sleeved, conservatively styled dress pointed to a graphic of the week's expected temperatures. "That's how a weather lady should dress. Not like she's going to one of those singles bars looking for dates."

Ravello and Mia exchanged an amused glance. "*Buona notte, Mama.*" Ravello bent down and kissed his mother on both cheeks. He did the same to his daughter. "I'll see you tomorrow. And remember"—he pointed a finger at her—"be nice to Benjy."

Mia held up her hands. "*Ma, certo.* Of course."

Unfortunately, being nice to Benjy proved harder than Mia imagined. She'd arranged for the new hire to share Cammie's office. "Does that mean I have to come in less?" Cammie had said. "Totally on board with that plan."

Twenty-four-year-old Benjy had the blond good looks of his mother's Teutonic heritage, which softened the sharp Sicilian lines of the Tuteras. He also had the slightly glazed look of a generation that spent too much time staring at screens. The fact Mia thought of Benjy, seven years younger than her, of another generation, made her feel old. The small company of Belle View full- and part-timers cheerfully welcomed him to their ranks. Ravello greeted him with a manly plant—a thorny cactus—from Lin's shop. But Benjy took to the job with the enthusiasm of a Guantanamo Bay prisoner. Working at Belle View—or possibly anywhere—was obviously ordered by a grandfather aggravated by his grandson's slacker attitude toward life.

Mia stuck her head into Cammie's office. She found

Benjy consumed by typing something which she hoped was work-related but given his lackluster response to assignments Mia had given him, she doubted. "Did you submit the liquor order for the DeNunzio wedding?"

"Not yet," Benjy said, still focused on his typing. "I'm about to."

He'd only been working at Belle View for three days and Mia had already enough *about to*s for a lifetime. "Let's change that *about to* to *right now,* 'kay?"

" 'Kay."

Mia's phone buzzed with a text from Chef Guadalupe. **Get in here NOW**.

Mia rubbed her forehead. A headache was beginning to take root. "I need to talk to Guadalupe."

"Huh?"

"Guadalupe," Mia repeated. "The head chef. Tall. Very tall. A little scary." This was of no interest to Benjy. He returned to typing. "Remember to put in that liquor order."

"About to."

Mia clenched her fists. She headed to the kitchen. Guadalupe, whose chef's toque added a foot to her given height of six-plus feet, tapped a knife against her hand with the look of a tropical storm brewing in the Atlantic. She used the knife to gesture to sacks on the kitchen workstation. "You know what these are? Beets. That idiot new hire ordered beets instead of beef. I got the Rotary Club luncheon today. I'm doing barbecue. I double-checked the order I gave the kid. Beef, tri-tip. What do I do with these? 'Yippee, barbecued beets!' said no Rotary Club member ever. Oh, but I got parsley. Lots and *lots* of parsley." Guadalupe thrust a giant bag of the garnish under Mia's nose. "I know, I'll make beet and parsley surprise. The surprise is, it will suck. Wait, that won't be a surprise."

Mia groaned in exasperation. "Great. Let me think, let me think." Her face cleared. "Got it. We use the beets and parsley in a side dish. Do you have potatoes? Can you add them and make up some recipe we can sell to the Rotary Club crowd as trendy?"

"Rotary Club and trendy aren't words you generally see in the same sentence. I can try but we still need beef. This is a meat-eating crowd if I ever saw one."

"Okay. I'll send Benjy to the grocery store to buy out all their tri-tip."

"No! Don't send that kid anywhere but home."

"Oh, how I wish. But I can't. I'll put in the order myself. All he has to do is pick it up. He can do that much." *I hope, I hope.*

Guadalupe glowered at Mia. "He better."

Mia retreated to her office. She placed the meat order, then paid Benjy a visit. She found him still typing away on Cammie's computer. "Benjy, stop typing and look at me." He reluctantly did so. "You messed up a supply order. Your first one. That doesn't bode well."

Benjy stared at her. "What'd I do?"

"You ordered beets instead of beef and a boatload of parsley."

"Oh, man. Sorry. I'm doing a run on parsley. I got it on the brain."

"A run?" Mia said, confused.

"Yeah, a comedy run. You know . . . what's the deal with parsley? Nobody needs it. It's like that Facebook friend you never met, but you accepted their request, so they won't feel bad and now they won't shut up with their comments." Mia responded with silence. "That's funny for my generation. I guess you're too old to get it."

Mia suppressed the urge to throttle Benjy. But she was getting a clearer picture of him. "You want to be a comedian? I'm guessing that didn't go over well with your parents or your grandpa Vito."

Benjy snorted. "You'd think I wanted to be a serial killer. And what's the deal with serial killers? Why are they always quiet, scary loners? There should be some app that sends out a Scary Loner Alert. You know, like . . ." Benjy mimicked an alarm going off. "Scary Loner Alert, Scary Loner Alert, beware the serial killer white van in your weird neighbor's driveway."

Wow, Mia thought. *My sympathies are with you, Vito.* "You know," she said, mustering up a supportive tone, "Cammie's ex-husband Pete is a detective and he writes mysteries on the side. He doesn't let them interfere with his day job." Which wasn't completely true. Fictional detective Steve Stianopolis had cracked a lot of cases that stumped real-life detective Pete Dianopolis.

"Are they funny mysteries? Because that's a thing."

"I don't know," Mia admitted. "I tried to read one once but couldn't get past the first chapter. Too many typos. He publishes them himself. A lot of people do that well, but Pete, not so much. My point is, it's great to pursue your dream. But when you're starting out, you have to balance it with a functional work life."

"I guess." Benjy didn't look too happy about this.

Mia handed him a sheet of paper. "I need you pick up an order of tri-tip. It's waiting for you. All you have to do is get it from the grocery store and bring it here. Do. Not. Mess. This. Up. Got it?"

" 'Kay."

To Mia's relief, Benjy got the simple task right, returning within the hour with pounds of tri-tip. The Rotary Club luncheon was a hit. Mia was thrilled to see a website review that gave a special shout-out to the beet-and-potato salad side dish Guadalupe came up with. Mia, who snacked on a bowl of it mid-afternoon, could attest to its deliciousness. She was washing her bowl in the capacious Belle View kitchen sink when her cell rang. She checked and saw the caller was Minniguccia. "Minnie, hi? Everything okay with Nicole?"

"She's fine, but her mother isn't. Tina *was* killed. The police are questioning Linda." Minnie let out a loud, operatic moan. "They like her for the murder."

CHAPTER 6

Minnie's moan transitioned to histrionic sobs. Mia tried to calm the senior down. "First of all, 'like her for the murder?' Stop watching cop shows, they always juice things up for TV and they'll make you crazy. And I'm sure Linda is only the first in a long list of suspects. I only met Tina twice and I hated her. I imagine a lotta people felt the same way."

"Messina, *bella mia*, you have to help us," Minnie pleaded. "Your grandmother told us how you're the one who solved the case of the stripper and waiter who got killed at Belle View last spring, and how the police wanted to give you a key to the city and begged you to join the force."

Mia managed not to burst out laughing at how Elisabetta had embellished her granddaughter's role in helping bring a killer to justice. "Nonna's kicked that whole thing up a notch. I'm not exactly a detecting genius. I almost got offed myself by the psycho."

"I'm so worried about Nicole. The stress. It could bring the baby early."

Despite Mia's disavowal of her sleuthing skills, she was worried about her friend, too, and would do anything to help her have a safe, on-schedule delivery. "Like I said, I'm not Nancy Drew, but I'll do what I can, Minnie."

"*Mille grazie, bella.*"

The call over, Mia headed back to her office. Having successfully completed his one simple task, Benjy was released by Mia for the day. When she passed Cammie's office, she saw someone sitting in the desk chair holding up a giant needlepoint canvas. "I got a new hobby," Cammie said, lowering the canvas to reveal herself. She turned the canvas around to show Mia the front of the canvas, which boasted a detailed portrait of a villa overlooking the sea. "It cost Pete a fortune."

"I assume you plan to do your stitching on company time."

"I don't have a choice. My free time's pretty much eaten up with nail, spa, and gym visits."

Mia parked herself on the folding chair in the corner of the room. "I need to talk to you."

Cammie pulled a threaded needle through the canvas. "You mind if I stitch while we talk?"

"Go for it." Mia leaned back in the chair until it met the wall. "I just got off the phone with Minniguccia. Tina was officially murdered. The cops brought Linda in for questioning." Cammie raised her eyebrows but continued stitching. "Minniguccia thinks Linda's the number one suspect and even though I'd never say this to her, my instincts are telling me she's right."

"Better her than anyone here."

"Cammie, that's callous," Mia scolded, then added, "but not wrong. Still, I'm worried about Nicole. Having her mother questioned about the murder of her step-mother is N.G. Not good. Can you do whatever it is you do with Pete to see if you can get any updates?"

"You mean, talk to him? Cuz truthfully, it doesn't take much more than that for me to get his attention these days. He's all, *I never should've left, I made a mistake.* And I'm all, *yeah, ya got that right and you're not done paying for it.*" She showed Mia the canvas. "Those are French knots. Made with a very expensive fiber."

"Pretty. Back to Linda. See if you can find out if the cops have any other suspects. Why did they bring in Linda first? I know she and Tina got into it in the bath-room here, but as far as I know, Linda made her peace with Ron and Tina's relationship."

"As far as you know." Cammie threaded her fiber under other stitches to anchor it. "Who knows how much you don't know?"

Mia thought about this. She'd been living in Florida during the entire span of Ron and Tina's marriage. All her insight into Linda's feelings about the dissolution of her marriage and the woman who replaced her were based on Minniguccia's and Nicole's reports. Minnie painted her daughter as a saint. Nicole was more circumspect but never indicated that her mother endured more than the usual stages of grief over the breakup. "Good point, Cam. Which is why anything you dig up from Pete might an-swer some questions."

"Give me a minute." Cammie put down the canvas and picked up her cell phone. She tapped on it, then pressed Send. "I asked Pete for deets and added a photo of me in a suggestive yoga pose. Five, four, three, two . . ." A *swishing* sound indicated an incoming message. "Tina was gone before she hit the water. Strangled with a piece of ribbon the police believe came from one of the shower gifts. That's why the police are all over Linda."

"Good to know. Thanks."

"My phone's acting wonky. Can I borrow yours?"

"Sure."

Mia handed Cammie her phone. Cammie futzed with it, then returned it to Mia, who glanced at it and groaned. "Oh, come on. Did you load another dating app?"

Cammie picked up her canvas and resumed stitching. "Yes, ma'am. You need to get back on the horse, Mia. Or the cow, depending on the artist."

Mia glared at her friend. "What is with everyone getting all up in my personal life? I'll swipe right or left when I'm ready to, which is not now." She pressed a button and the apps on her phone jiggled. Then she pressed the X in the corner of the app Cammie had loaded. She held up her phone. "See? Deleted."

"You say that like it's a good thing."

Mia stood up and went to Cammie. She peered at the canvas. "You missed a stitch. A bunch, actually."

Cammie's face fell. "I did?" She followed Mia's finger to the missing stitches and cursed in Greek. "Now I gotta rip out this row and start all over again. The fiber will be ruined." She brightened. "Which means more overpriced fiber on Pete's dime."

Mia left Cammie for her own office. She emailed Benjy step-by-step instructions on how to place an order and then pick up orange juice jugs. In addition to being a rare combination of sous and pastry chef, Evans had developed an interest in mixology that Mia wanted to encourage. A unique drink selection at Belle View would help distinguish them from other local venues. Benjy had managed to return with the correct meat order; hopefully a juice jug run was also in his bandwidth. Mia checked the time and began to pack up her things. The Belle View landline rang. "Belle View Banquet Manor," Mia answered. "Be the belle of the ball at Belle View."

"Cute." The caller was a man. "Is this Mia?"

"Yes, here to meet all your event needs."

"I like how you stay on message. This is Castor Garvalos. From Versailles on the Park."

Mia reacted with surprise. "Castor. Hi. Nice to hear from you." Considering how rude he'd been to her at Tina's big fat Greek shower, this was a lie.

"I feel like I owe an apology for the other night," the Versailles manager replied as if he read her mind. "That party was what we call here a mega event. Even I was overwhelmed." *He got in that Versailles hosted a "mega event" and that he's usually Mister In-Control,* Mia thought. *The rare double humble brag.* "Please let me make it up to you."

"Okay," Mia said, intrigued. "If you insist."

"I do. If you're free tomorrow night, how about coming over to Versailles?"

"Let me check my schedule." Mia stared into the air and counted to ten. "I can move some things around. How's seven?"

"Perfect. I'll see you then."

Mia hung up and sashayed over to Cammie's office. "Here's a little news for you. I may not have to swipe on any of those freaky dating apps. All I have to do is pick up the phone. That call was from the general manager of

Versailles. I met him at Tina's—the late Tina's—gonzo shower for Nicole. He invited me to Versailles tomorrow night for dinner."

"So he's too cheap to take you out," Cammie said, eyes focused on the canvas.

"He's showing professional courtesy," Mia said, knowing this was a lame defense. Cammie's comment triggered the wary, well-honed instincts of a mobster's daughter. If pressed, she had to admit she didn't feel an iota of attraction to Garvalos. He was a good fifteen years older than her, and on the smarmy side. Oddly enough, she didn't pick up any sexual tension on his part, either. Granted, it was only a phone call but still, she wondered if the manager's invitation to make up for his rude behavior disguised an ulterior motive.

The next night, Mia thumbed through her wardrobe and landed on her blandest black dress, one that sent absolutely no message whatsoever. She called a cab. As they drove toward Versailles, Mia decided to make the ride useful. She mimed steering, braking, and accelerating along with the cab driver. He looked at her askance through the rearview mirror. "Everything okay back there?"

"A friend's teaching me how to drive," she said. "I'm practicing."

The cabbie's face cleared. "Ah. My grandkid does the same thing. I'll do what I do with him. I'll talk you through it. Now I'm putting my foot on the go pedal." He accelerated. "Uh oh. Red light. Now I'm putting my foot on the stop pedal. When the light turns green, I'll wait a couple of seconds in case anyone in cross traffic runs the light and then put my foot on the accelerator. Hey look, the light changed. Ten Mississippi, nine Mississippi, eight Mississippi . . ." The driver's well-intentioned narrative made the fifteen-minute drive feel endless, but Mia gave the kind man a generous tip.

Castor awaited her at Versailles' palatial entrance. He was dressed in a perfectly fitted charcoal gray suit with a blue-and-maroon-striped tie. He gave her hand a quick, weak shake. Mia noticed that the stripes on his tie were comprised of tiny maroon wine bottles. She wondered if this indicated a sense of humor or that he'd bought so much wine from a vendor that they'd rewarded him with a bespoke gift. Judging by the man's stiff posture, she had a feeling it was the latter. "Welcome back to Versailles," the general manager said. "Everything is set up in the Throne Room. Come."

Mia followed Garvalos to the elegant room she remembered from Tina's bash. Tonight, its half-dozen chandeliers were set to dim. As a banquet hall proprietor, Mia understood the move. No need to have the lights blazing and incur a high electrical bill when there wasn't an event taking place. She saw four tall cocktail tables in the middle of the room, each set with the kind of display she used to give potential customers a sense of the packages Belle View offered. The settings featured elaborately patterned china resting on gold or silver chaser plates. The silverware also ran gold or silver, depending which color best complimented the china on display. All of the settings included cut glass wine and water goblets. "I know you're interested in how we operate," the manager said, "so I thought I'd walk you through a few of our packages. We'll start high and work our way down." He led her to the nearest table. "I'm sure you recognize this Platinum Package from the event you attended. It features lobster, filet mignon, a mélange of the freshest vegetables . . ."

Mia's stomach rumbled as Garvalos continued the food tour without offering a bite of anything. They finished at an unadorned table. There was no place setting, only a bag of chips and what looked like a cheese sandwich. "Is this for a kid's party?"

"Oh, no, we do way better for our children's events. That's an example of what we feed the staff. If you're not careful, they'll eat you blind."

Mia thought of Belle View's staff and couldn't imagine one of them taking advantage of her. She scanned the tables and it occurred to her that there were no chairs set up. Her empty stomach rumbled again. *Time to drop a hint that I'm ready for dinner.* "You really set the bar high here, Castor. The settings, the food. I've worked up an appetite just looking at it."

Garvalos patted his trim stomach. "I never eat after six. But if you're hungry, we've got some leftover wedding cake from an event we hosted this weekend. I'm pretty sure it's still good." As the manager led a glum, hungry Mia toward the facility's massive kitchen, two things occurred to her. One, he'd never specifically said dinner when he called. And two, Cammie was right. The man was cheap.

The minute they stepped into the kitchen, Mia was overwhelmed by a delicious scent. A man of Indian descent who looked to be in his late thirties stood in front of a stove burner stirring ingredients in a cast-iron skillet. He was clad in a chef's jacket. Mia recognized him as the chef running the kitchen at Tina's party. She sniffed the air, trying to identify the mix of herbs and spices. "Whatever you're making smells incredible," she said to him.

He turned off the gas under the skillet. A lock of thick black hair fell onto his forehead, covering one of his brown eyes, which were the color of melted milk chocolate. He brushed the hair off his face and favored Mia with a warm smile. "Thank you. We have an Indian wedding on the agenda and I'm experimenting with my personal take on *murgh makhana*. Butter Chicken." He extended a hand to her. "I'm Sandeep Singh. Executive Chef here at Versailles."

Mia took the handsome man's hand, then reluctantly released it. "Mia Carina. Senior event planner at Belle View Banquet Manor. And if I knew what was in that recipe, I'd steal it for our guests."

Sandeep responded with a deep, genuine laugh, which seemed to annoy Garvalos, who muttered something Mia couldn't make out, then pulled open a gleaming stainless-steel refrigerator door and removed the remnants of a sad-looking cake. As Sandeep transferred his dish into a storage container, Garvalos cut and plated a piece of cake on a leftover paper plate he scrounged from a drawer. He placed it before Mia with a fork. "Here."

Mia gave Sandeep's creation a longing stare, hoping the chef would take the hint. When he didn't, she went with a bold approach. "I'd love to sample that merga . . . mega . . . butter chicken."

"Of course," Sandeep said. "I'm sorry, I should have offered."

He scooped a spoonful of rice from a rice cooker next to the stove, added a dollop of butter chicken and gave Mia exactly what she'd asked for—a sample. Her disappointment increased after tasting the delicious dish. She could have inhaled a bowl of it. "It tastes as good as it smells."

Sandeep acknowledged the compliment with a slight head bow. "I'm glad you approve." He removed his chef's jacket and placed it over his arm. "I need to go," he said to Castor. He motioned to the container of chicken. "When this cools off, put it in the refrigerator. The Kumars will be here for a tasting at noon." Garvalos grunted acknowledgment. Sandeep rewarded Mia with a smoldering glance. "It was nice meeting you. *Very* nice."

Mia, now hungry *and* cranky, grunted an acknowledgment of her own, and the chef departed. She ate the slice of stale, almost inedible cake Castor had deposited in front of her quickly, the better to make a quick escape from the dud of an evening. Done, she handed the empty paper plate to Garvalos, who tossed it into a large trash receptacle. "Thanks for the tour," Mia said, determined to be polite. "I appreciate the professional courtesy."

"I had an ulterior motive," the manager confessed.

He leaned in toward Mia. *Please don't hit on me, please don't hit on me.*

"I'm interested in buying Belle View."

Wow. Talk about giving myself way too much credit. And also . . . what? "It's not for sale. And my family doesn't own it. My birth family, that is."

Garvalos made a dismissive gesture with his hand. "I know. Your father Ravello runs the place for the Boldano Family. But I have an investor with deep pockets. And I believe we could make your 'boss' an offer he can't refuse." Mia didn't bother to suppress a groan at the tired joke, but Garvalos either didn't hear it or ignored it. Instead, he waxed poetic. "What I could do with Versailles on the Water. Crown molding everywhere. A new center staircase with a solid brass railing. Sea-green and blue velvet drapes to showcase the marina view." Mia had to admit the man possessed a passion for his job. And she didn't hate his vision of upgrades for Belle View. When the Belle View balance sheet showed a bigger uptick, she might even "borrow" one or two of them. "I know it's not officially on the market," he continued. "But I've heard Donny Boldano is a good businessman. Considering the negative publicity from recent events, I think he'd be open to a conversation with me."

Mia bristled. "I doubt it. Business has been better than ever the last couple of months. None of the deaths have been linked to the Family, including Tina's."

Garvalos looked puzzled. "Tina? I did my research on Belle View and neither of the two murder victims from that incident this past spring was named Tina."

Mia realized that the police had yet to publicly identify Tina as the body in the water, waiting until the family was notified. Judging by Minnie's panicked telephone call, the family now knew, so sharing the name wasn't a violation of privacy. "There's been a third . . . incident. The body of a woman was found floating in the marina. It's the woman who hosted the party here that I came to. Her name is—was—Tina Iles-Karras."

The Versailles general manager went so pale Mia thought he might pass out. He gripped the edge of the worktable. He closed his eyes and muttered something in Greek. He drew in a deep breath, then exhaled and opened his eyes. "It's late and I have an early start in the morning." He hurried Mia out of the kitchen, down Versailles' long hallway, and outside onto the building's front steps. "Good luck with Belle View."

The giant carved double doors closed behind Mia and she heard Garvalos lock them. She was about to summon a ride through the Pick-U-Up app when a linen supply truck drove toward Versailles. As it passed, Mia made out a logo for Quality Control Linen Supply. She ran through a list of local linen supply companies in her head. None sported this name. Mia followed its path with her eyes, watching as it stopped at a side service entrance. The driver hopped out of the truck. He was met at the door by executive chef Sandeep, who pushed a laundry bin toward him. The driver hefted the bin into the back of the truck with ease, indicating it held a light cargo, and pulled down the truck's roll-up door. Sandeep then strode toward the employee parking lot while the truck driver got back behind the wheel. He backed up the truck, turned it around, and drove away from Versailles. Mia's skin prickled, the result of suspicious instincts drummed into her from childhood. *There could be a logical reason I don't recognize the linen service,* she told herself. *But why are they picking up at this weird time? And why just one bin?*

Spooked, Mia tapped in a rideshare request hoping Jamie might respond. He didn't. A message popped up that a driver would reach her in three minutes. Standing alone in the dying daylight of the quiet park, three minutes never felt longer. Finally, much to her relief, a Queens College student driving an older-model sedan whose back fender was covered with Grateful Dead stickers showed up. "You mind if I change my destination?" she asked.

"No probs," her young driver said.

"Great. Drop me at Salambini's Pizza and Pasta."

"Yes." The driver pumped the air like his team had just

scored a winning run. "Best pizza *ever*. Okay, now I want a slice. Ride's on me, my friend!"

Ten minutes later, Mia had inhaled a wedge of mushroom and sausage pizza that she washed down with a beer. She ordered a second slice, which she ate more slowly. As she crunched on the thick end crust, Mia contemplated the night's events. There was the odd bin pickup from a mystery linen service. But that was less intriguing than Castor Garvalos's unexpected reaction to the news of Tina's death. It indicated to Mia that Tina was more than a client who threw a pricey bash at Versailles to Garvalos.

The big question was, how much more?

CHAPTER 7

Mia returned home. Still hungry, she snacked on Elisabetta's lasagna while perusing the Versailles website for any clues that might explain Garvalos's behavior or the mysterious late-night linen service. She found nothing of interest, although she did emit a shocked gasp at the exorbitant cost of the banquet hall's event packages. At midnight, she gave up the fruitless search and crashed for the night.

When she woke up, she decided to prioritize her amateur sleuthing. Step one would be a deep dive into the machinations of the Miller Collection heist. She sat down at her desk and flipped open her laptop. Doorstop draped himself over her feet and Pizzazz perched on her shoulder as she called up her original search for stories on the heist. Mia landed on a long story in a leading art magazine and gave it a thorough read.

Malcolm Miller was a man whose fortune came from "old money." He'd inherited wealth and added to it through the kind of financial wizardry Mia couldn't begin to understand. He used a hefty percentage of his millions to amass a huge art collection. Rather than donate it to a museum, he chose to keep it in tony Millville—a town his family helped found two hundred and fifty years ago and was loosely named after them—and built a building to house it on the family's vast Long Island estate. One night more than twenty years earlier, thieves broke in and made off with a score of paintings, some priceless, some merely worth buckets of money. The security system was conveniently on the fritz that night; a new one was set to be installed the next day.

Mia heard her grandmother huffing her way up the stairs and stopped reading. Elisabetta appeared in her doorway, followed by Hero. "*Marone*, I'm getting too old to come up here," she said, clutching the doorframe for support.

"I told you to call and I'll come downstairs to you. What's up?"

"I made a frittata for breakfast. Eggs, tomatoes, cheese, mushrooms, with some sausage." Hero, who heard the word sausage so much in the Carina household he was trained to respond to it, barked and wagged his tail. "Minniguccia made the sausage herself as a thank-you for helping to get Linda off the hook with the *polizia*."

"I haven't done that yet and don't know if I even can, Nonna. Do me a favor and stop making up stories about how I'm some genius amateur detective."

Elisabetta shrugged. "Meh. Can I help it if I'm proud of my granddaughter?"

"Be proud of me for something else. Like helping to

steer Belle View into the black instead of the red. But as long as you're here and we're talking about Tina Karras, listen to this."

Elisabetta settled down on the foot of Mia's bed. Hero jumped on the bed and parked himself close to her. Doorstop followed. He playfully swatted at the chubby terrier mix, who wasn't entertained. Hero growled until Doorstop grew bored and chose to curl up on one of Mia's pillows instead. "That cat of yours is gonna push my Hero too far one day."

"Lucky for Doorstop, he can out-run Hero because that dog of yours is weighed down by all that pasta you sneak him." Mia turned her attention back to the computer. "I'm reading about the Miller Collection heist. You know, where that painting at the shower came from."

"Crazy painting. Who rides a cow?"

"It's modern art."

Elisabetta made a face and shook her head. "Feh. Gimme a picture of a nice bowl of fruit that looks like fruit."

Mia fought back her annoyance at Elisabetta's digressions. "*Si*. Bowl of fruit. Got it. Back to the heist. Like I thought, the police suspected it was an inside job. One person involved with it was caught, a man named Liam O'Dwyer." Mia read from the article on her computer screen.

"A smalltime crook, O'Dwyer's assignment was to drive the stolen paintings to a beach parking lot where two masked men transferred the stash to another car. The heist made national headlines. O'Dwyer was nabbed by the police after he got

*drunk and bragged to patrons about his role in the
operation when the story appeared on TV at his
local bar. O'Dwyer swore he had no idea who
masterminded the theft, and either couldn't or
refused to identify associates in the plot. He's
currently serving a ten-year jail sentence. The
paintings were purported to have crossed the
Atlantic and made their way into the hands of a
European art dealer who was also rumored to be a
fence for stolen art goods. Law enforcement has
never figured out how the collection of famous and
semi-famous paintings was transported from one
continent to another."*

Mia squinted at the date on the article. "This article is
fifteen years old, which means O'Dwyer must have completed his jail sentence." She typed in the ex-con's name.
A list of Liam O'Dwyers from around the world popu-
lated her screen. "Well, this isn't helpful." Mia checked
the time. "Yikes, it's late. I gotta get to work."

"After frittata," said Elisabetta, who'd assumed a
prone position on the bed, with Doorstep at her head and
Hero at her feet.

"*Si.* After frittata."

Two helpings of Elisabetta's frittata meant a bike ride
to Belle View to burn off some calories. Mia sliced
through the warm summer air on her ten-speed, welcoming the breezes her fast pace engendered. She locked up
the bike and made a pit stop in the ladies' room to fix her
hair and makeup, both of which had taken a beating from
the wind.

As Mia brushed her hair, she re-lived the fight be-tween Tina, Minnie, and Linda. She tried to recall Linda's exact threat. Something about weighing Tina down and dumping her in the bay. Considering how close that was to the nasty woman's actual demise, even Mia had to con-cede the police were justified in suspecting Nicole's mother and Ron Karras's jilted ex. Still, she'd practically grown up with the Karras family. Mia couldn't imagine the woman who once nursed her through a horrible sun-burn and left five-dollar bills under her pillow when she lost a tooth at the Karras house, being driven to murder. *She was more of a mother to me than my own mother,* Mia thought with a pang in her heart. Gia-formerly-Carina-now-Gabinetti was living in Rome with her second hus-band Angelo Gabinetti, deported back to his homeland after serving a jail stint for forgery. Mia rarely heard from her mother, a beautiful clinical narcissist. *Some people have daddy issues*, Mia thought to herself as she re-freshed her blush and lipstick. *I have mommy issues. Maybe that's why I feel so attached to Linda.* Mia rested her hands on the sink and stared at her reflection in the mirror. "Be honest," she said to the reflection. "Are your personal feelings getting in the way of reality here?" She shook her head. "No. Remember the painting."

"Uh . . . hello?"

Mia turned to see Evans standing in the doorway. "Oh, hey."

"I was looking for you. I thought I heard two people in here."

"Just talking to myself," Mia said to allay the chef's concerns, whose expression indicated fear about her mental state.

"Ah. Got it." He relaxed. "Are we hosting one of those Mommy and Me get-togethers this week?" Belle View had endeared itself to locals by allowing non-profit groups to use their facilities for meetings or meetups during off hours.

"No. Why?"

Evans held up a juice box. "Because a few flats of these showed up in the kitchen instead of the industrial-size jugs I asked for. It's gonna be hard to make an updated version of the Harvey Wallbanger for that seventies-themed class reunion with juice boxes."

Mia slapped her hands to her face and cursed. "Benjy. I told him exactly what to get and how to do it, and he effed it up. I'll talk to him. And get you your jugs."

Mia left the bathroom and marched down the hall to Cammie's office. Benjy was at the desk pounding away at the computer keyboard. Mia didn't waste time wondering if he was working on Belle View business. "Benjy, you messed up the juice order."

He glanced up from the computer, a puzzled look on his face. "I got orange juice like you said."

"I told you to get jugs. You got juice boxes."

The puzzled look was replaced by a blank stare. "Does it matter?"

"Yes!" Mia bellowed this. She took a deep breath to calm herself down. "Sorry. I know you're new to this business. I should have explained things more. The price differential between an industrial-size container of orange juice and those little boxes is huge. When we order industrial-sized supplies, we get the wholesale rate. They're meant for business, not individual, use. Evans— you remember who he is, right?"

"Yeah, the black guy."

"Oh, please do *not* describe him like that." *Am I too young to have a stroke?* Mia wondered. Then she continued. "Evans is a man of many talents. The latest is coming up with cool drinks for our parties. He's working on a signature drink for the class reunion this weekend where the theme is the nineteen-seventies. We can't mix that drink for a hundred people using juice boxes." Mia mimed ripping open one juice box after another. "You see what I mean."

"Kinda."

Ohmygod!

"Put a call in to the supplier," Mia said, speaking slowly so as not to blow. "Tell them you need to exchange the juice cartons for jugs. Today."

"Okay." Benjy face lit up. "I just got a great idea for a run. What's the deal with those tiny straws they give with juice boxes? You can never get them into the box. It's like, why wait until you grow up to fail at something, kids? Learn to fail when you're a toddler."

Mia grabbed the keyboard before Benjy could jot down his brainstorm. "That's more depressing than funny. Call the supplier. Then you can type."

The twentysomething pouted but picked up the phone, and Mia put down the keyboard.

Rather than return to her office, she went outside and pounded on the stucco-ed back wall of Belle View in frustration. This proved more painful than satisfying. She leaned against the wall, staring out at the marina as she nursed her bruised fists. She thought of Nicole's late step-mother. "How did you wind up here, Tina Karras?" she murmured. "How? And why? Why here?" A thought suddenly occurred to her. Was it farfetched, or might it offer the answer to these questions? Either way, it was a thought worth running by someone. And she knew exactly who.

A few hours later, Mia sat across from her brother at the beat-up old metal table in the Triborough Correctional Facility's visitor's room. Henry Marcus, a guard who'd grown close to the family due to the multiple incarcerations of the Carina men, leaned against a wall checking his cell phone, casting the occasional perfunctory eye at the duo.

"So, how was your day?" Posi asked.

"Are you asking to be polite or are you genuinely interested?"

"Both, to be honest. It's the polite thing to do but also, once I get out of here, I'm hoping there's a spot for me in the new family enterprise. I believe I could charm a lot of business our way."

Posi smiled his trademark sexy smile, a smile that Elisabetta once said could charm a nun out of her vows. The comment was extreme, but not wrong. In fact, according to Family rumors, it might also be true. "Consider yourself hired," Mia said, adding, "if you stay straight. But speaking of hiring, that's what I wanted to talk to you about. The most recent addition to the Belle View staff." Mia shared the backstory of Benjy's hiring with Posi. "I'm starting to wonder if Benjy is purposely messing things up. Like, is he a plant?"

Posi furrowed his brow, then stopped. "I gotta remember not to do that, I'll get wrinkles. But a plant how so?"

"Maybe Benjy's grandfather has an ulterior motive for parking his grandson with us."

"Such as?"

"Revenge for something we don't know about. Or . . ." Mia sat up straight. Was she about to connect some disparate dots? "I met with the general manager of Versailles on the Park. Obnoxious guy named Castor Garvalos. He got together with me because he wants to buy Belle View. He said he had an investor with 'deep pockets.' Could it be Vito Tutera?"

Posi looked doubtful. "Seems like a longshot."

"Maybe," Mia acknowledged. "There's still a lot of work to be done on the facility, but from a booking angle, Belle View's looking pretty good these days. I think some of the other Families might be seeing how the catering business could work for them, and not in the laundering money way. As a legit business they can be proud of. But if you wanted to buy us out, you'd wanna do it a low price. Vito could have planted Benjy at our place to mess things up. Business goes down, he swoops in with an offer that we'd have to take or go under."

Her brother crossed his arms in front of his chest and leaned back in the rickety visitors' room chair. "Sis, you been reading those Steve Stianopolis books?"

"No," Mia said, annoyed at Posi's patronizing tone. "What I'm saying isn't so farfetched."

"Maybe not. I've been out of commission here for a while, so I don't know what's going on outside. Hey, Henry. You been listening? What do you think?"

"I've had some of the Tuteras in here before," the guard said. "Between us, they're a hinky bunch. But they been quiet lately. Might be like your family right now, you know, trying to play it straight. Or using straight as a cover for something not straight. You never know with these guys."

"Amen to that, my friend," Posi said. "You might wanna wait before running this by Dad, sis. You don't want to go putting ideas in his head. That could go bad in a big way."

Mia sighed. "You're right. Benjy might just be incompetent. He doesn't want to be there, that's for sure. He's got this dream of being a comedian."

Posi snorted. "Seriously? Have you heard any of his material?"

Mia wrinkled her nose. "So far, not so good. I wish I could fire him, but the last thing I wanna do is start a war between the Families. I don't need that."

"You don't, but it keeps us in business," Henry said, with a chuckle that Posi echoed.

"Okay, I'll put that theory on hold. There's also some major weirdness with the Versailles on the Park staff. This Garvalos guy almost passed out when I told him Tina had been killed. Like, he knew her in some way. And I happened to see a linen company pick up a laundry bin."

Posi's expression was skeptical. "Which happens every day at every party place. How is that a thing?"

"It's a thing because it was only one bin at eight o'clock at night, which means overtime, and who wants to pay that? And why a run for one bin? Also doesn't make sense. Unless you were desperate for those linens, you'd wait until you had a full load and schedule a pickup during work hours. Also, I didn't recognize the linen company."

Her brother stroked his chin. "Now, that adds up to a thing."

A cell phone rang. "That's my ring tone," Mia said. She had turned her phone over to Henry upon checking into the visitors' room. "Henry, you mind checking for me to see who it is?"

"Sure." Henry checked. "It's your grandmother."

"I'll call her later. Thanks."

Henry declined the call. The phone pinged a text. "Some guy named Benjy says supplier doesn't have juice jugs, oh, well."

Mia uttered an epithet and pounded her fists on the desk. "Now you do think the Tutera angle is a longshot?"

"A little less so," Posi acknowledged.

"Henry," Mia said, "Can you do me a favor and type, 'Go to a grocery store?' Make it all caps with a lot of exclamation marks."

"Yes, ma'am."

Henry tapped out the message. Mia's phone rang again and he ignored it. A text tone dinged. "If that's that idiot Benjy with some excuse," Mia said, her tone venomous, "I will take him out myself."

Henry peered at the text. "It's not. It's your grandma again. She says it's important. Oh, and here's a response from Benjy. He wrote back, 'Will do.'"

"Good," Mia said. "He just bought himself another day on this planet." She stood up. "I better go talk to Nonna." She blew her brother a kiss. "Later, *fratello mio*."

Posi blew a kiss back to her. "Love you, *mia sorella*."

Mia checked out of Triborough and retrieved her

phone from Henry. She exited the facility into a blast fur-
nace of August air. She speed-dialed her grandmother as
she walked toward the subway. "Sorry I couldn't talk. I
was with Posi, and Henry had my phone. What's up?"

"What's up," Elisabetta said, her tone grim, "is that
I'm with Minnie at her house. She called me, hysterical.
Nicole is in the hospital."

CHAPTER 8

Mia stopped walking. She held her hand to her mouth, then let it go. "What hospital?"

"One in Manhattan. On the East Side. A name like the singer in those TV music videos we watched together when you were little. Annie Lennox or something."

"Lenox Hill. I'm on it."

Mia ended the call and dashed into the street. She waved her hands in the air to flag down a cab. A few already carrying passengers whizzed by. She jumped up and down to attract one from the far lane. An empty cab shot across two lanes of traffic to the sound of horn honking and a lot of cursing from other drivers. Mia pulled open the door and jumped in. "Bless you. Lenox Hill, please. As fast as you can drive without getting pulled over or killing us both."

The turbaned driver said something in a language Mia didn't understand, then pulled a U-turn and screeched toward Manhattan. Mia sent a flurry of texts to Minnie, Linda, and Ian while the driver did a masterful job of negotiating potholes, street constructions, and cars going either too fast or too slow. They flew over the Queensboro Bridge, making it to the hospital in a speedy fifteen minutes. Mia rewarded the driver with a hefty tip and ran inside the building. She followed directions to the Emergency Department, where she found Linda pacing in the waiting room, her lovely face lined with worry. Linda saw Mia and her lower lip quivered. "Mia, *bella*."

Mia went to Linda and embraced her in a tight hug. "What's going on? Is Nicole okay? Is she in labor?"

Linda rung her hands. "We don't know. We're waiting to hear from Ian."

A man sitting across the room lifted his head up from his hands—Nicole's father, Ron. "Hello, Mia. Thank you for coming. It means a lot to us."

"Of course." It occurred to Mia this was the first time she'd seen Ron Karras since his second wife's death. She debated whether to pull him aside and extend her condolences but was spared the awkward moment by Ian's arrival in the room.

Nicole's husband went to Linda. "It's false labor. Braxton-Hicks contractions."

Linda's shoulders sagged with relief. "Oh, thank God."

"Nicole's fine, the baby is fine. Even if they had to deliver, she's at thirty-seven weeks, which is considered full-term. But the doctor thinks our little guy or girl might end up being late, so this is a better scenario."

Linda clutched her son-in-law's hands. "They're not gonna send her home right away, are they?"

"No. They're going to keep her overnight and when she comes home, she'll be on bedrest for at least a few days. Belated hi, Mia."

Mia hugged Ian. She released him. He rubbed his eyes. "You look exhausted," she said. "Can I do anything? Babysit Nicole? Bring over meals?"

Ron stood up and approached them. "I'll be sending over all their meals from the diner. No arguments, Ian."

"Yes, sir."

There was an awkward pause. "I could use a coffee," Ron said. "Anyone else?"

The others chorused yes, and Ron departed to do a coffee run. "I'm going back to Nicole," Ian said. "She's sleeping right now. I'll let you know when she wakes up so you can both make a quick visit."

"*Grazie, figlio mio.*" Linda gave Ian a gentle kiss on the cheek. "Go to your wife."

Ian left. Mia took Linda's arm and led her to one of the room's hard plastic chairs. "You look exhausted, too. Here. Sit. I'll call my nonna and have her tell Minnie what's going on."

The two women sat down next to each other. Mia called Elisabetta, who thanked God several times and instantly relayed the update to a worried Minniguccia. Mia ended the call. "Minnie said not to go home. You should stay with her tonight."

"That's a good idea. I will. I'd rather not be alone." Linda began to quietly weep. "This is all my fault."

"Linda, that's crazy talk. This has nothing to do with you."

The distraught woman shook her head vehemently. "It's all on me, Mia. I had that fight with Tina and then she died, and the police think I may have done it. The stress of that got to Nicole, I know it did."

"Not to speak ill of the dead"—Mia craned her neck to make sure Ron wasn't walking down the hall with the coffees—"But I think Tina had more than a few enemies, which means there are other suspects. Someone put that stolen painting in the stack of shower presents. It was like a warning to Tina. I'm sure the police are looking into that angle."

Linda gave Mia a weak smile. "I appreciate the support, but I don't know. The painting may have been someone's idea of a bad joke."

Mia pulled her cell phone out of her purse. "I'm curious about something." She typed in a search with the words "Ferdinand Vela" and "auction." A list popped up. She scanned it and opened the first document, and then the second. "One of Vela's paintings sold for over nine hundred thousand dollars at a recent auction. Another sold for only a little under that. *Cow and Woman* isn't only a painting by him, it's notorious, so I'd bet you it's worth even more money. Whoever put out that painting wasn't joking. And that person may be the murderer."

Linda's phone pinged a text. She read it and her face lit up with a genuine smile. "Ian said Nicole is awake and feeling much better."

Mia brought her hands together in tiny claps. "Yay!"

"She wants to see us. *Andiamo.* Let's go."

Mia and Linda made their way through a maze of hospital hallways to Nicole. She was the sole occupant of a room designed to house two patients. The mom-to-be was propped up in a bed raised to a forty-five-degree angle. There was a slight pallor to her skin but aside from that, she looked well. Ian, positioned like a sprinter, perched on the side of her bed, ready to bolt and meet whatever need she might have.

Nicole held her arms out to her mother. "Mama."

Linda choked back a sob and went to her daughter. The two embraced and held each other tightly. "I better let you go before I squeeze that baby out of you," Linda said, laughing between teary sniffles. "I'm all nervous now."

She released Nicole, who beckoned to Mia. "Your turn."

Mia blew her friend a kiss instead. "Your mom scared me with that squeezing-the-baby-out-of-you thing." The room had two chairs for visitors. Mia pulled both next to Nicole's bed, offering one to Linda, who sat down. She parked herself in the other one, placed her hands on her thighs, and got down to business. "Your mom here blames herself for your false labor and we know that's a crock. But—and this is a big but—she's not all wrong. Tina's death has created a nightmare and Linda here being a suspect adds to all the stress. What we have to do is come up with another suspect for the police to check out. I know they're looking into this too—Pete Dianopolis isn't a total idiot. He does know how to do his job, but it's NYPD. They got a lot going on. So let's help them."

Nicole held a fist up in the air. "I'm in," she declared. Her husband and mother seconded and third-ed this.

"I can personally vouch for the staff that worked the

party," Mia said. "It was a small crew of people I totally trust. Which means one of your guests planted a painting that made Tina faint and I think led to her being killed."

"Ian, hon, can you get me my phone?" Ian practically leaped off the bed, delivering the phone to Nicole in an instant. "I kept a copy of the guest list in the Notes app. I'll forward it to you and Mom to go over. We all had friends there who one of us might not know."

The room was quiet as the three perused the guest list. "I didn't have that many guests and I've known them all for years," Linda said. "With all the gossiping in my crowd, you'd think I'd know it if someone had been holding on to a stolen painting for twenty years."

"I'm looking at my list and I kind of feel the same way," Ian said. "But I'll tell you someone who's really milking the whole thing, Nic. Your friend Justine, the art dealer."

Ian held up his phone to display a photo of Justine Cadeau accompanying an article about the mysterious reappearance of *Cow and Woman.*

Nicole looked confused. "Justine's not my friend. I thought she was yours."

Ian shook his head. "Not mine. I'd never seen her before the party. I figured she was on your side."

Mia's heart thumped. "None of you know this woman?" The others shook their heads. She jumped out of her chair. "You guys, we have a suspect!" She paced the room, rubbing her hands together as she walked back and forth. "She sat at my table. I'm trying to remember our conversation. Now that I think about it, she kept things very generic and never focused on either one of you. Someone asked her who she was friends with, and she said, 'I love them both.' She never directly answered the question. She's an art dealer, so there's a logical link between her and the painting. I'm sure the cops would be all over that if they weren't distracted by all the family drama, Linda, don't even think about blaming yourself again."

"How did she find out about the shower?" Nicole wondered.

"Tina," Mia said.

"But Tina didn't seem to know her," Ian said.

"Maybe she didn't," Mia said. "But Justine must have known *her*. Or about her. Tina had buckets of money for a retired flight attendant. I checked out the Versailles website for the cost of that shower she threw. The package she went for is so expensive, they don't even give a figure on the site. It just says *price upon request,* like it's one of those bazillion-dollar homes in the real estate section. You have to wonder why she has that kind of money. There's something very sketchy about her."

"I've got the coffees."

Mia froze. She turned to see Ron standing behind her. "Ron, heh, hi," she stammered. She gave up trying to cover. "Did you hear me?"

"Yes." The middle-aged man glanced down at the holder full of coffees still in his hand, emanating an air of defeat. "All I know is that my second marriage was a mistake." His voice broke. "I'm so sorry."

Ian relieved his father-in-law of the coffee. "Thanks for this, Ron." He handed them out.

Ron shook off his emotions. "Thank God you're all right, *koritsi mou omorfo,*" he said to his daughter. "My beautiful girl. I'll check on you tomorrow."

Nicole reached out a hand to her father. "Dad, stay. Please."

Ron, uncertain, glanced at his ex-wife. "Stay," Linda said.

Mia snuck out of the room, leaving the family to their complicated dynamics. She found an empty table in the hospital's second-floor cafeteria and sat down to drink her coffee and do a little research on her phone. Finding Justine Cadeau's gallery was easy. It was called The Justine Cadeau Gallery. The dealer represented contemporary artists. Mia didn't recognize a single name on the gallery list but judging by the prices, she assumed they were well known. *Note to self, schedule a refresher visit to the Museum of Modern Art sometime.* She checked the gallery's hours, and then her watch. It had closed at seven. It was now seven-thirty. She put in a call to Cammie. "Hi. Were you planning to show up at Belle View tomorrow?"

"I have to," Cammie said. "I'm teaching a Zumba class in the Marina Ballroom. I got a training certificate in my free time, which thanks to a very cushy job, is pretty much all my time. I figured you wouldn't mind if I borrowed the room. I made everyone sign a waiver absolving Belle View—and me—of any responsibility or liability should injury or death ensue. One of my students is a lawyer and created a legally binding document in exchange for a month of free classes. We good?"

"We're good but in between salsa and samba numbers, could you cover for me? I have an errand to run in Manhattan."

"Oooh." Mia imagined an intrigued Cammie raising a

bleached eyebrow. "Anything to do with the mystery of the ugly painting?"

"Everything to do with it. I'll fill you in if there's anything to tell you. Oh, and do me another favor: keep an eye on Benjy. He's a questionable employee."

"Ain't that the truth," Cammie said with a snort. "He's making my job harder by making me actually have to work."

The call over, Mia headed back to Queens, choosing to economize by taking the subway. A sweat-soaked hour later, she staggered down the stairs onto Ditmars Boulevard, vowing to do whatever it took to finagle another driving lesson out of Jamie, who'd been suspiciously out of reach since the last one. She walked the mile home, showered off the city summer grime, fed her pets, and collapsed on top of her bed with the room's box air conditioner cranked up to maximum chill.

The next morning, Mia donned the black dress she'd worn to meet Castor Garvalos. She made her way downstairs. Elisabetta, also dressed in black, was in the vestibule. She checked out her granddaughter's outfit. "You going to a funeral, too?"

"No. I have to go to a gallery in Tribeca. The one owned by that art dealer who ID'd the painting at Nicole's shower. Turns out no one at the party knew her. I'm looking for a connection between her and Tina that I can share with Pete Dianopolis to take the heat off Linda."

"That's my girl." Elisabetta opened the door and peeked outside. "*Bene*, there's Philip. He's coming with me today." Mia glanced outside and saw Philip, half of the gay couple that had moved in down the street, walking toward the house. "Finn took the babies to his mother for a week so Philip said he could come to the funeral today and distract everyone while I deliver Gugliemo's shoes." Elisabetta held up a bag. "The man who passed away was a pipe fitter, in his eighties, and president of his union local. Should be quite a crowd."

Mia quirked the corner of her mouth. "A handsome gay man at a blue-collar funeral is gonna be quite a distraction."

Her grandmother dismissed her with a *pfft* sound. "Probably half the mourners' kids are gay. They just don't know it. *Ciao, bambino*."

Philip came up the steps to the top of the stoop. He greeted the women with kisses on both of their cheeks. "Am I dressed correctly?" He ran a hand up and down his dark suit like a spokesmodel. "I've never been to an Italian funeral. I'm a little nervous."

"Don't be," Elisabetta said. "They're just like your WASP-y ones but with more crying and better food."

"The handkerchief's an impressive touch." Mia nodded toward a neatly folded white silk hankie peeping out of Philip's breast pocket. "Don't lend it to someone. You might not get it back."

Elisabetta left for the funeral with her accomplice. Mia, mindful of the sweat storm from the evening before, called a cab. "Can you ball-park the cost to Tribeca?" she asked the driver after climbing in his car. He did so and she sighed. "Ditmars Boulevard, please." Luckily, an entrepreneurial Senegalese immigrant was selling personal fans at the bottom of the subway stairs. Mia bought one, using it as she transferred between subway lines in her quest to reach Tribeca. She got off at Franklin Street and darted up the stairs out of the hellmouth that was a New York subway stop in August, and exited onto the street, which didn't provide much relief from the heat. Mia kept the fan going as she traipsed along to The Justine Cadeau Gallery, earning envious looks from her fellow city dwellers. "I'll give you a hundred bucks for that thing," said a young guy who was dressed like a taco, handing out flyers for a new restaurant.

Mia, taking pity on him, handed over the fan. "Here. You got it way worse than me."

After profuse thanks and an offer of tacos for life, Mia eventually found herself on Leonard Street. She kept walking until she came upon the gallery. It was housed in one of the many century-plus-years-old cast-iron buildings that made the neighborhood, as well as nearby Soho, famous. Mia pushed on the door handle. It didn't move. She jiggled it, but to no avail. The door was locked, the gallery closed. Mia double-checked the gallery hours, which were listed in a small box on the door: 11 A.M. TO 7 P.M. The time was currently 11:45 A.M. Could Justine be late, Mia wondered? Or conversely, taking an early lunch? She looked up the gallery's number on her phone and called it. The call went straight to voicemail, followed by an announcement that the number's mailbox was full.

Frustrated, Mia rested against one of the building's cast-iron columns. A trickle of sweat dripped off her forehead and fell to the ground. *I wish I still had my fan,* she thought glumly. A hipster-looking waitress wiping down a table at the upscale café housed in the building next door, waved the rag in her hand to get Mia's attention. "Hi," she called to her. "If you're trying to visit the

gallery, it hasn't been open in days. The owner lives upstairs, but I haven't seen her lately. She must be on vacation.
Although you'd think she'd put up a sign or something."

"Thanks, I appreciate the intel," Mia called back to the
waitress. It was a nice theory. But Mia's gut was sending
the message that Justine wasn't on vacation. She had disappeared . . . or been disappeared.

CHAPTER 9

Mia evaluated the situation. The outdoor area of the café was empty of customers and its lone waitress looked bored. On the chance that boredom would translate into small talk that evolved into gossip, Mia sauntered over and took a seat. The waitress brightened and handed her a menu. "I'm Santia. Welcome to Sourced, where everything is ethically sourced. Everything, even the napkins. They're Fair Trade, made by survivors of Ebola in the Republic of Congo. And, little tip, the coffee here is *lit*. It's from the owner's private plantation on the Kona side of the big island of Hawaii."

There was a slight clicking sound as Santia spoke. Mia noticed her tongue, as well as her nose, was pierced. Lines of earrings marched up each ear, ending at cartilage piercings. "Hawaii plantation? Lucky owner. I'll go with an iced coffee."

"You got it."

Santia took Mia's menu and went into the café. She emerged a few minutes later with a large glass of iced coffee, topped with a scoop of coffee ice cream and a dollop of whipped cream. An artisanal cookie that looked like a rolled-up pizzelle stood at attention in the middle of the cream. Santia deposited the drink in front of Mia and waited expectantly for her to taste it.

Mia did so. "Wow. Delicious. Thank you." She stirred the melting ice cream into the drink. Mia got the feeling that Santia might have some dirt to share, so she gave her an opening. "This makes up for not being able to get into the gallery. I'm super bummed it's closed. And without a sign or anything on the answering machine about it. It's weird, you know?"

Santia's eyes lit up, and Mia gave her instincts a smug pat on the back. "I know, right? Justine, the girl who owns the gallery, always came down in the morning for coffee and one of our croissants. They're made with butter from our owner's organic farm in Vermont and flour from virgin wheat that he has milled at his ranch in Colorado."

Kuai coffee plantation? Vermont Farm? Colorado ranch? I wonder if the owner is single, Mia thought, then forced her attention back to Santia.

"So, I brought Justine her coffee and croissant, like I always do." Santia shared this in a gossipy whisper. "She was scrolling through her phone and she suddenly freaked out. I asked if she was okay and she said, 'Someone I know died.' Then she ran out of the café without her order."

"Was that the last time you saw her?"

Santia scrunched up her face. "Now that I think about

it, yeah. About a week ago." Her attention wandered to a couple pushing a Boston terrier in a stroller. They parked the stroller next to a table and took a seat. "Customers. Excuse me."

About a week ago, Mia thought while Santia tended to the couple and their dog baby. Which lined up with Tina's murder. If that's what motivated Justine's "freak-out," it might remove her as a murder suspect. But it also indicated a connection to Tina. This was a development she could share with detective Pete. Mia held up a finger to Santia and gestured for her check. The waitress nodded. She finished taking the couple's order and returned to Mia, handing her the trendy restaurant version of an iPad. "We're a cashless restaurant. We take credit cards, Apple Wallet, and bitcoin."

"I have at least one of those." Mia pulled out a credit card. She looked at the charge and her mouth fell open. "Nineteen dollars for an iced coffee? Now I know how your owner has the money for farms and plantations up the hoo-ha."

"Sorry," Santia said. "Tribeca prices."

Mia paid for the drink, then emptied it and ran her finger around the inside of the glass to get every last drop of the expensive beverage. She evaluated what she'd learned from Santia and decided on her next move: tracking down Liam O'Dwyer, the sole heist culprit who was caught and did time. *That nineteen bucks bought me some seat time at this place to do a little research.* Mia took out her cell phone and typed in the name "Liam O'Dwyer art heist." The internet search only yielded old articles about O'Dwyer's trial, conviction, and jail sentence. Nothing came up about his current whereabouts. *The best way to track down an ex-con is through a current con*, she thought. *And I just happen to know one.* She called Tri-borough Correctional and learned Posi was on a work crew at Astoria Park. Mia drained her glass of a little melted ice at the bottom, then pulled ballet flats out of her tote bag, traded her heels for the more comfortable shoes, and took off for Queens.

She found Posi and his fellow workers, along with several guards, picking up trash on a section of trail near the Hell Gate Bridge. "Sis, what a treat." Posi reached out for a hug. Guard Henry Marcus cleared his throat as a warning, and Posi dropped his hands.

"Hey, Po. Henry, is it okay if I ask my brother something?"

"Long as he keeps working."

"Got it." Mia followed Posi as he speared littered wrappers and deposited them in a bag strapped across his chest. "I've got some updates on the Tina murder sitch. Turns out this guest at the shower, Justine Cadeau, was a party crasher. I'm guessing she's the one who put the stolen painting with the gifts. She owns a gallery in Tribeca named after her, so there's an art connection."

"She used her own name?" Posi said, bewildered. "Can't be a career criminal."

"Agreed. Even I know not to do that, which is why the fake ID I got when I was fifteen said *Mariah Clarey.*"

"An homage with a twist. Nice touch."

"Thanks. Anyway, a waitress at the place next door said Justine disappeared after learning someone died. I'm thinking that person who died was Tina, and Justine either panicked and ran or . . ."

"Or another body's gonna pop up soon."

Mia grimaced. "It sounds awful when you put it that way, but yeah."

Posi speared what appeared to be a balloon. He checked it out and recoiled. "Ugh, a used condom. Disgusting. And people think us cons are animals." He deposited it gingerly in his sack. "I'm assuming you didn't come here to give me a rundown."

"No. I need to track down Liam O'Dwyer, the one guy who did time for the crime. I didn't find an obit, so as far as I know, he's still around. I thought maybe you could help me find a contact for him."

"Sure. Let me work my magic. Yo!" Posi yelled this to the crew, following it with an earsplitting whistle. They all stopped and turned to him. "Anyone here know a Liam O'Dwyer?"

"I do," a scrawny con with a full neck tattoo said. "I did time with him at Sing Sing." He leered at Mia. "You looking to get in touch with O'Dwyer? Gimme your number, I'll pass it on."

Posi cast a baleful glance at his fellow inmate. "Yeah right, Belsky. Like that's gonna happen. Get *me* the number and I'll pass it on to my sister. Who happens to be engaged to Donny Boldano's son."

Mia opened her mouth to protest the lie, but it replaced the leer with fear on Belsky's face. "Sorry, miss. Congratulations, and best wishes for a long and happy future."

"Here, here," Guard Henry seconded with a smattering of applause. Mia swallowed her annoyance at Posi and forced a smile.

There was an anguished cry from a child, followed by bawling. Mia glanced toward a line of trees next to the trail and saw a boy around five throwing a tantrum. A young woman was having no success comforting him.

Mia looked up and saw a kite stuck in one of the trees. Posi noticed, too. "Henry?"

The guard nodded and the two approached the tree. Posi grabbed a branch and hoisted himself up. He climbed to the kite and untangled it. It fell into the arms of the little boy, who instantly stopped crying. Posi climbed down a branch and swung off the tree like Tarzan. "Thank you so much," the young woman said. She tossed her bleached blond hair back and flashed a flirty smile. "I love a man in uniform."

Mia shot her a look. "You do know that's a prison jumpsuit."

The woman ignored her. "I'm a single mom," she said to Posi. "Joint custody, so plenty of downtime. I'll give you my number. Call me when you get out."

Mia left Posi to his love connection and hailed a cab for the ride to Belle View. She walked into the building to find Cammie, dressed in circa-1980s Jane Fonda aerobics togs, yelling at Benjy in the middle of the foyer. "Who asked you to do that, who? No one, that's who!"

Mia wasn't happy to see two of her employees going at it. "Everything okay?"

She kept her tone sunny, hoping to dissipate the tension. It didn't work. Cammie, furious, pointed at Benjy. "Mister Saturday Night here pulled aside a bunch of my Zumba students and forced his comedy act on them."

"Forced, nuthin'," Benjy said, defensive. "They liked it. They all laughed at my jokes."

"You're Vito Tutera's grandson!" Cammie yelled. "They were afraid you'd kill them if they *didn't* laugh."

"My comedy kills," Benjy said with dignity. "I don't. Now, I got a job to do. I have to order holly for the bar mitzvah comin' up. Why the Jews want holly, I don't know. It's not even Christmas. But to each his own."

Mia drew in a breath. "It's *challah,* not holly. It's a type of bread. Call Katz's Bakery and tell them it's for the Telsey event. They'll know what to do."

Benjy gave a nod and left to, hopefully, do his job. As soon as he was out of sight, Cammie mimed strangling someone. "The wrong body ended up in the marina," she said darkly.

"I'll see if Dad can talk some sense into him."

Pete Dianopolis emerged from men's room, clad in a tank top and short shorts. Mia found the image of the detective in workout gear disconcerting but managed not to telegraph this. "I heard you yelling," he said to his ex. "I been on the receiving end of that, so my pity's with the other guy, but I wanted to make sure you're all right."

Cammie waved him off. "It's over. Although," she hastened to add, "I'm a little shaken. Some retail therapy will help me a lot. With your credit card."

Pete flinched, but willing to do whatever it took to win her back, said, "Do what you need to feel better, babe."

"Pete, I'm glad you're here," Mia said.

"That's a new one coming from you," he said, surprised.

"Some interesting information has come to light pertaining to the Tina Karras murder," Mia said, hoping she sounded as official as the characters on the procedural TV shows she watched. She detailed what she learned about Justine Cadeau, then waited for Pete's impressed reaction to her sleuthing.

"Good lead," he said.

"Thank you." Mia imbued her response with modesty.

"Except I got a better one. We got the marina surveillance feed. It shows Linda Karras and Tina Karras meeting on the dock and getting into an argument."

Mia, left speechless by the unexpected twist, stared at Pete. Was she wrong about Nicole's mother, misdirected by fond memories of the past? After a minute, she found her voice. "You didn't say it showed Linda strangling Tina."

"It didn't," Cammie chimed in. "Linda stormed out of frame and then so did Tina."

"Babe, you weren't supposed to share that," Pete said, gently reproaching her.

"Oops." Unseen by her ex, Cammie winked at Mia.

Mia struggled to justify this new development. "There has to be another reason Linda was there. Maybe Tina called her to meet and Linda went, hoping to make things right with them." She had a brainstorm. "Or maybe the real murderer got them *both* there."

Pete glowered at Mia. "Have you been talking to Linda Karras? Because that's the excuse she came up with. Not that the murderer called her and Tina, but that someone who wasn't either of them called both of them. She says that's why they were arguing. *You called me. No,* you *called* me. It's a little hard to buy, in my book. And by 'in my book,' I mean the new Steve Stianopolis book I'm writing."

Mia returned Pete's glower. "If you're so sure Linda is guilty, why haven't you arrested her?"

Pete hesitated, so Cammie jumped in. "The D.A. is still ticked off about Ravello's false arrest in the case of the stripper murder this spring, so Pete's in the doghouse. He has to come up with an airtight case to get an arrest warrant issued or his career will be on the skids and his life will be a living hell. Did I get that right, sweetie?"

"You called me sweetie," Pete said, melting.

Cammie gave him the side eye. "I also call my kitty sweetie, so don't get too excited."

"Kitten? When did you get a kitten?"

"Last week. She's what they call a Peterbald. I named her Olga since Peterbalds are a rare Russian breed."

"Rare." Pete paled as he said the word, which Mia knew he had translated to "expensive" in his head.

"If you give me a ride home, I'll let you stop in and meet her—"

Pete perked up. "Great."

"—after you buy me dinner."

"Wait, what?"

Cammie was already out the door. He jogged out after her. "Don't forget to look into that art dealer's disappearing act," Mia called after him.

Her mood thoughtful, Mia went to her office. For the rest of the day, she shoved aside freelance sleuthing and focused on her job. She confirmed with relief that Benjy had ordered "challah," not "holly" from Katz's Bakery, then she booked a photographer for an upcoming wedding, and scheduled tours of Belle View for three potential customers. Her tasks for the day completed, she allowed her mind to wander back to the murder. Tina was dead and Linda was still the prime suspect. Justine Cadeau was MIA; Mia had yet to receive any contact information for Liam O'Dwyer. "What to do next," she murmured to herself. "What to do . . ." It occurred to her that she'd yet to run an online search for the mysterious Quality Control Linens. She entered the name into her computer. Nothing came up. "I knew it," she murmured. She texted Pete her discovery and theory that Versailles was a hotbed of suspicious activity and received a non-committal thumbs-up emoji in return, along with the photo of a tiny hairless kitten, followed by dollar signs and tears emojis. Undaunted, Mia texted, **Any paintings stolen lately? Laundry bin good means of transport.**

Pete responded, **Having dinner with CAMMIE AND OLGA!! Off the clock. Re: stolen art, prob not or would've heard. Gnite!**

Mia, aggravated by a lack of forward motion, debated walking away from the whole complicated situation. Then she flashed on Nicole in her hospital bed, surrounded by her worried family. The image erased all doubt, and she typed in yet another search for images of paintings stolen from the Miller Collection. This time, photos of the location itself came up. Mia saw a website address and clicked on it. She perused the site, starting with the "About" page, which didn't reveal any new information. She studied the website tabs and clicked on "Gallery." A page filled with images from a variety of events appeared on the screen. A line in scripted font at the bottom of the screen read, THE MILLER COLLECTION CAN BE MADE AVAILABLE FOR SUITABLE EVENTS. "La di da, Miller Collection," Mia said to the screen. "Let's see if you're interested in talking to Queens' most exciting catering company about providing staff and cuisine for these 'suitable events.'"

Mia dialed the number at the bottom of the web page.

CHAPTER 10

Larkin Miller-Spaulding, the Miller Art Collection's director, proved receptive to Mia's call, scheduling a mid-afternoon meeting for the following day. Mia, unsure her ruse would fly, suddenly found herself pulling together what she hoped was an impressive presentation of catering options the facility could provide. Guadalupe and Evans stayed late to help. The coworkers set up and photographed several levels of service, ranging from cocktail party to sumptuous five-course meal. Exhausted, Mia finally fell into bed at two A.M. *Why am I awake at six A.M.?* she wondered as she stared at the ceiling when she woke up four hours later. She spent a half hour trying to fall back asleep and gave up.

"I'm nervous about going back to the scene of the original crime," she told Pizzazz after removing the parakeet's cage cover. The bird hopped around tweeting happily, then pecked at her breakfast. Doorstop lounged on the bed, waiting for the sound of his kitty kibble to drop into his bowl. Mia filled the bowl and the cat strolled into his kitchen. She poured herself a cup of coffee, and watched Doorstop go through his usual routine of sniffing his food with disdain, walking away, then deigning to eat it. She'd only told Pizzazz half the story. Yes, she was nervous about visiting the Miller Collection, the genesis of the chain of events she was convinced led to Tina Karras's death. But there was more at play than that. The Millers were a classy lot, reeking of refinement and old money. People like them pushed Mia's less-than buttons. Her accent was too Noo Yawk, her clothes too cheap or too flashy. *Stop it*, she scolded herself. *You're not* pretending *to be a successful businesswoman looking for new venues for Belle View's growing offsite catering business, you* are *one.* If only she wholeheartedly believed this.

Mia spent the next hour going through her wardrobe for the perfect outfit and hating everything in her closet. Her go-to bland black dress was showing signs of being gone-to too often. It begged for a trip to the cleaner. She tried on skinny black pants with a white shirttail top. *I look like a cater-waiter* was her morose thought as she stared at her reflection in the mirror. She traded the top for a gray silk T-shirt and accessorized with silver jewelry. *A solid B, which is as good as it's gonna get today.*

She traipsed downstairs, where she heard her grandmother humming "*Non Domenticar*," a favorite family tune. She found Elisabetta in the bedroom, modeling her own outfit of simple skirt and top, all in black. "Another funeral? What happened to yesterday's?"

"They closed the casket just as we got there. But the

funeral lunch was *eccellente.* That new place, *Tres Amici.* I brought home some leftover gnocchi in a doggy bag. Help yourself."

Mia sat down in a rickety wicker side chair dating back to the late nineteen-sixties that decorated a corner of the room. She gave Elisabetta a dubious glance. "If you crash a funeral, should you be helping yourself to lunch? It seems kind of . . . scammy."

"*Ma, che success?*" Elisabetta said, affronted. "When did my granddaughter get so nervy? It just so happens that I knew a couple of people at the funeral, so it wasn't *scammy.* But I'll tell you one thing. Philip was, how do you say? A man magnet. A couple of guys slipped him their numbers."

Mia chortled. "Ha. Not surprised. Is he coming with you today?"

"Yeah. He did some acting in high school and is great at being sad." She buckled a black belt around her waist. "You look nice. You got some tours lined up at work?"

"No. I'm going out to the Island. I've got a meeting with the people at the Miller Collection." Elisabetta raised an eyebrow. "They rent out the place for events," Mia explained. "I set up a presentation for our offsite catering business but what I really wanna do is poke around and see if I learn anything useful about the heist and Tina's maybe involvement in it."

"You think she was involved?"

"I do." Mia swung her legs back and forth. The old wicker creaked a warning, and she stopped.

"*Va bene,* but be careful. I don't trust rich people. They got enough money to do whatever they want. They kill someone and then pay a lawyer a million bucks to get them off."

"I don't think that's always true."

"It's true enough times for you to watch your back."

Mia's phone signaled an incoming text. She checked it and stood up. "Jamie's here. He's going with me."

"Good."

"We're using it as a driving lesson."

Elisabetta made the sign of the cross. "Nonna, that's not nice," Mia scolded.

"Nice or not, I want *Il Dio* in the car with you. And I bet Jamie does, too."

Mia huffed out of the house and scurried down the front stoop to where Jamie and the brown beater car were parked. He lowered the driver's side window. "You look great."

"Thanks." Mia allowed herself a frisson of pleasure at the compliment. She waited for him to exit the car. He didn't move. "Aren't we gonna trade places? Me driving, you in the passenger seat?"

"Not until we get off the expressway." He patted the seat next to him. "*Andiamo*."

Mia stomped around to the side of the car and pulled open the passenger's side front door. "It would be nice if people had a little faith in me," she grumped.

"I'm willing to give you another lesson after the last one," Jamie said. "I'd call that faith."

Jamie took off, following a labyrinth of local roads until he reached the Long Island Expressway. A half hour later, they exited the Island's main artery. "Now?" Mia asked, impatient with anticipation.

"Not yet. Too much local traffic." Mia muttered in Italian. Jamie glanced at her, amused. "Ouch. That's some mouth you got on you."

They drove through a series of shopping districts and strip malls. Eventually the road took a turn toward residential. As they drove closer to Millville, with its tony Gold Coast location on the north shore of Long Island, the homes and their plots of land grew larger by the square footage and acreage. Jamie pulled over. "Now you can drive."

"About time," Mia grumbled. "I thought you'd *accidentally* forgotten."

The two got out of the car and switched positions. Mia buckled herself in. She put her foot on the gas and the car shot forward, as it had the first time that she drove it. She slammed on the breaks. "I know, I know. Slowly."

Mia eased the car onto the road, alternating between braking and accelerating. Luckily, traffic was light to nonexistent. She assumed everyone who serviced the mansions they passed was already gardening, butler-ing, or maid-ing. "This is like America's *Downton Abbey*," she said.

"Uh huh." Jamie looked slightly green around the edges. "Make a left at the next gate." He pointed a short distance ahead. "There."

"Already?" Mia protested. "I hardly drove."

"We got you out on the road. Let's consider that progress."

Mia shot Jamie a nasty look but did as she was told. She made a left at an ornate black iron gate framed by tall, gray stone pillars. A road composed of powdered oyster shells split around a guardhouse made of the same gray stone. A uniformed guard motioned for her to stop. "Hi there," he said, his tone not unfriendly but definitely officious. "Name and ID please. For both of you."

"Oh," Mia said, worried. "I'm meeting Larkin Miller-Spaulding. My friend Jamie here drove me. I didn't mention that, so he's not on the list. He's teaching me to drive, and we thought this would be a good opportunity to practice on your beautiful local roads." She followed this with her sunniest smile.

"I don't think he needs your life story," Jamie said under his breath as the guard disappeared into his small stone house.

"Sometimes adding a personal touch helps," Mia said, with a hint of attitude.

The guard appeared in the guardhouse doorway. "You're good to go. The house is about a half mile down."

He waved them along. Mia, trying not to gloat, carefully accelerated. She drove for a while, and then pulled to the side of the road. "I don't want to show up in this junker. I'll walk from here."

Jamie jumped out of the car before Mia could open her door. "No problem. It'll give my stomach a chance to settle. I've never been carsick before. It sucks."

They agreed to meet in the Miller Collection parking lot, and Mia took off, her high heels making it difficult to negotiate the uneven roadbed. After what felt like the longest walk of her life, the Miller mansion finally came into view. Mia stopped and took in the breathtaking sight. The palatial home, a magnificent piece of architectural history dating back to the Roaring Twenties, was designed to look like a castle, and just as large. It was surrounded by manicured gardens that ended at acres of woods. In the distance, Long Island Sound served was the estate's backyard, lapping at the massive compound's shore. To the right of the home was a newer building that mirrored the style of the original house. Mia saw a discreet sign over the building's door and followed a path that led her to it. The sign read The Malcom Miller Art Collection.

Mia took out a compact and checked her makeup. The breeze wafting in from the Sound was far cooler than the muggy air of Astoria, but the walk on the oyster bed had made Mia perspire. She dabbed on some powder and knocked on the door. No one answered. Mia waited, then knocked again. Still no response. *Please don't tell me I got the date wrong,* Mia thought, heart hammering. She peered through a window into what looked like a museum. "Hello," she called out, despite guessing this was fruitless. Left with no other choice, she trudged over to the massive carved wood door of the main house. She was searching for a doorbell when the door opened silently. A young Hispanic woman wearing a maid's uniform gave a slight nod and gestured for Mia to follow her.

They wandered through spectacular rooms boasting carved paneling, beamed ceilings, and antique furnishings, and ended up in a glass-walled conservatory. The room, while beautiful, was claustrophobic with humidity. A middle-aged woman with a helmet bob of platinum hair and the kind of sharp features that were more striking than pretty sat at a wrought-iron, glass-topped table, her pale gray eyes glued to a laptop screen. Across from her sat a man of similar age. Mia could tell he'd once been handsome, but now his face had the florid cast of a heavy drinker. He sipped from what looked like a Bloody Mary. After delivering Mia to the room, the maid departed without saying a word. The woman at the wrought-iron table closed her laptop and stood up. The man didn't. "You must be Mia Carina," the woman said, extending a hand for a perfunctory shake. "I'm Abigail Miller. This is my husband, Spencer Spaulding."

The man responded with an amused smile tinged with superiority, and a little wave. "Hello, there."

Mia had done her homework on the Miller family. She knew Abigail was the CEO of the Miller hedge fund and the brains of the operation. Her husband was retired, although Mia could never track down from what. Whereas Abigail wore a navy pantsuit that reeked of expensive tailoring, her husband was clad in bright-white tennis togs. Mia got the impression he spent more time in a clubhouse than on the court. "It's a pleasure to meet you both," she said, doing her best to tamp down her Queens accent.

"The Collection is really our daughter's bailiwick," Abigail said, the timbre of her voice low and in Mia's mind, boarding school-y. Mia took a guess that "bailiwick" meant area of expertise. "She apologizes for keeping you waiting. She's on the phone with Sotheby's confirming a purchase she made at last night's auction."

"Sotheby's is a famous auction house," Spaulding said.

"I know. I've been there many times." Mia had never set foot in the place and wouldn't be able to tell the superior man where it was if he threatened to hit her over the head with the tennis racket collecting dust in a corner of the fancy room. But no way was she going to give him the satisfaction of knowing that.

Spaulding sipped on his drink. "We had our people research your place. We were a bit concerned about getting involved with the Mob but couldn't resist meeting a real-live mafia princess."

"Spencer, that's rude," his wife scolded. "Don't be an ass."

"I apologize," he said with a mock bow to Mia. "And don't worry, it would never stop us from renting out the Collection and squeezing a few more dimes out of Malcolm's ego fest."

"Ignore him," his wife said. "He gets like this when he's had a few drinks."

It's ten in the morning, Mia thought to herself. "I want to make it clear that Belle View Catering is a completely legitimate enterprise," she said in her most professional voice. "If you're interested in our services, I can provide you with a long list of references from satisfied customers, all of whom are upstanding citizens."

A mousy-looking woman around Mia's age hurried into the room. Her light-brown hair, scraggly at the ends, was half up and half down, a non-hairstyle that telegraphed she'd either run out of time or interest. Given her utilitarian outfit of a shapeless gray jersey tunic over leggings in the same shade, Mia's money was on the latter, an assumption enforced by the woman's footwear, which were the kind of sneakers New Yorkers wore during a transit strike when they had to traipse miles to the office, where they could put on their nice shoes. "Are you Mia?" the woman asked. "I'm Larkin. Sorry I'm late. I had to take a call. It's a long walk here from my bedroom."

In this house? I bet. "No worries," Mia said in a cheery voice. "I had a nice chat with your parents."

Larkin snorted. "Like that's possible."

"Larkin, do *not* start," her mother said with a strained expression on her face.

"There's a waste of family therapy." Spaulding polished off his drink.

Larkin glared at her father, then focused on Mia. "Come on, I'll show you the Collection."

The Collection's director took Mia's hand. Mia found the intimate gesture unsettling, but she was determined to gather clues about the infamous art heist, so she let Larkin lead her out of the house. The oyster shell path crunched under their feet as they walked to the building where the current collection was housed. When they reached the steel front door, instead of using a key, Larkin held her thumb up to a pad under the doorknob. "Fingerprint recognition," she explained, opening the door.

They walked into an expansive space lit by natural light. The walls were bright white, the floors ash, the temperature perfectly climate controlled. Track lighting focused attention on art hung on the walls and sculptures in the center of the room. "My babies," Larkin said, her voice cracking with emotion. She walked Mia through the Collection, jabbering in minute detail about each piece. Mia recognized some names: Picasso, Pollock, Lichtenstein. The rest of the artists meant nothing to her, nor did the convoluted processes they went through to achieve what looked to Mia like the doodling she did when she was bored out of her mind during high school classes.

After half an hour of artistic minutia, Larkin finally, blessedly stopped talking. "So that was our first room," she said.

Mia's heart sank but she tried to cover. "There's more?" she said, hoping to sound enthusiastic. To sell it, she added, "Yay."

Larkin, fired up with excitement, nodded so vigorously she knocked her eyeglasses askew. "We have four more rooms."

I'm gonna be here forever, Mia thought. *Jamie will kill me.*

Larkin's face clouded with anxiety. She nervously adjusted her eyeglasses. "Don't hate me, but two of the rooms are closed because we're hanging a new exhibit. 'AIDS and the Art of the Eighties.' We have several Basquiats and Harings and the work of less well-known artists who passed away before the world discovered them."

"It sounds great," Mia said with sincerity.

Larkin beamed. "It will be. But we have an art installation in the next room I can show you. Wait until you see it. The piece is site-specific and forces you to question everything you know about modern life."

Mia followed Larkin into a pitch-black room, almost tripping over something as they entered. Mia looked down and saw an empty takeout container. "What's this garbage doing here? I'll throw it out for you."

She bent down to pick it up. "No!" Larkin screamed, grabbing her arm. "That's part of the installation." She pushed a button and a row of spotlights illuminated a trail of trash leading to a tombstone. A blow-up sex doll with its head replaced by a globe of Earth had its arm draped over the tombstone. Water meant to be tears, but dyed blood red, streamed down the globe's face, such as it was. An old speaker like the one from the nineteen-seventies that Mia's father still had in his living room, played a soundtrack of moaning and weeping.

"This is called *Earth????* With four question marks." Larkin spoke with reverence. "To make you think. If you want to absorb it, I can leave you in here alone for a while."

"No! I mean, I would love to, but I do need to get back to Belle View eventually."

"Oh," Larkin said, disappointed.

She flipped off the light. Mia followed her back into the main room, blinking and squinting as they transitioned from darkness into sunny brightness. "The installation is wonderful," she lied. "All of the art is. This is a fantastic venue, Larkin. I have, like, a million ideas for what we could serve at an event here." The last part was the truth. Mia could envision fantastic parties in the sleek building. She glanced around the room and noticed a blank spot on the wall. Here was her chance to shift the conversation to the art heist. "I see that spot over there is blank. Someone told me a bunch of paintings were once stolen from here. Is that where one of them used to be?"

Larkin grew rigid. Her face flushed. She worked her jaw as if trying to manage her emotions. Then she gave up and burst into tears. "*Hoop and Boy,*" she sobbed. "They stole *Hoop and Boy.*"

Mia, discomfited, gave Larkin an awkward pat on the shoulder. "There, there." It was a lame response, but she didn't know what else to say.

"Boy was the sibling I never had," Larkin cried. "That painting spoke to me." Given the woman's oddness, Mia wondered if she meant this literally. "And it's lost forever. It was my painting *brother.*"

Mia continued to pat the distraught woman on the shoulder. "That painting was by Ferdinand Vela, right?" Mia impressed herself by picking up a theme to the painting's titles.

"Yes." Larkin fell into a chair that Mia had assumed

was a sculpture and buried her face in her hands. Her body heaved with sobs.

"You know, another one of his paintings just showed up, *Cow and Woman.*" Mia decided not to go into detail with the emotionally fragile art aficionado about the painting suddenly appearing at Belle View. "I heard it was stolen in the big robbery here."

"Yes, the police called about that." Larkin lifted her head. She took a few gulps of air and wiped her eyes with the sleeve of her shirt. "It's ours. We'll get it back as soon as they confirm provenance."

"For that painting to appear out of nowhere after all these years, I bet it's a sign that the other paintings are going to be found, too. Including *Hoop and Boy.*"

"I hope." Larkin stood up. She balled up her fists. "When I find whoever stole that painting," she said, eyes glittering with anger, spitting fury into each word, "I'm going to tie them to the hitch on my mother's Range Rover, drive them over a bed of hot rocks, and have people watch them die like it's an art installation."

"Mm hm," Mia said. "So . . . I'd like to come back and set up a tasting." She pulled a tablet out of her purse-slash-tote bag. "I have photos of some sample arrangements we've created specifically for the Miller Art Collection. Let me show you."

Larkin expression cleared like she had flicked on one of the building's hi-tech light switches. "You don't have to. I can tell you're an art lover. You're in." Larkin was now all business. "Come to the opening of our new exhibit. You'll get a sense of how the space works as a venue and see if you need to make any adjustments for Belle View's offsite catering services."

"I would love that," Mia said, pocketing her tablet.

They left the rarified air of the Collection and emerged from the building. "Thank you so much for the tour," Mia said. "It was . . ."

She pressed her hands together as if praying and looked up toward the heavens. Larkin responded with a knowing smile. "Art. It's a religious experience, isn't it?"

"Yes. An experience."

The two women went their separate ways. Mia checked to make sure Larkin was out of sight, then took off her heels and ran toward Jamie, with the oyster shells that hadn't been ground into dust cutting her feet. "Ow, ow, ow, ow." She jumped into the car and pulled the door shut. "Let's get out of this looney bin."

"Wow. That's a reaction." Jamie tossed the textbook he'd been reading into the backseat and gunned the engine.

"You remember Crazy Teeth Franky? How he got those dental implants and then swore they'd put another person into him who was talking through his new teeth?"

"Sure. He got sent to a place upstate. I hear they take good care of both of him."

Mia gestured with her thumb to the estate they were leaving behind them in a cloud of oyster shell dust. "I just met someone who makes him look sane as you or me. That's the daughter. The father is a lush, the mother a nutcracker. But back to the daughter, Larkin. She loves her art in a way that she'd walk down the aisle with it if she could. And she's *crazy-angry* at whoever stole the missing paintings."

Jamie glanced at her. "Crazy enough to kill?"

Mia contemplated this. She replayed her time with

Larkin Miller-Spaulding. She was off, no doubt about it. But was she all words and emotion? Or might her obsessive passion drive her to action? There was a word for how the disturbed young woman related to her family's artwork. Mia hunted for it. *Anthropomorphic.* When people treated inanimate objects as living things.

"Yeah," Mia said. "I think she's crazy enough to kill."

CHAPTER 11

Jamie dropped Mia off at Belle View. As she came inside, she saw a sight that horrified her: Ravello in the Marina Ballroom, having what appeared to be a friendly chat with *Triborough Tribune* reporter Teri Fuoco. Mia stomped into the room in time to hear her father tell Teri as he gestured to the view through the floor-to-ceiling windows of Flushing Marina, "You won't find a lovelier view at any catering hall in Queens."

Teri seemed skeptical. "I dunno. Versailles on the Park has some pretty lit gardens."

"You won't find a lovelier view anywhere in Astoria."

"That I can buy."

Mia stormed up to the two. She planted her hands on her hips. "Sorry, Fuoco, we don't offer our services to low-life reporters."

"That's discrimination," Teri shot back at her.

Mia scowled at Teri, then addressed her father. "Dad, she's the enemy."

"Calm down, *bella mia*," Ravello said. "I'm giving Miss Fuoco a tour of Belle View. I showed her the whole place. The *whole* place." Mia picked up on the crafty tone in her father's voice. "We even checked for bugs. The kind that spy on you, not the kind you don't want to find in your food. We're good on that score. But not so good on the other."

Ravello reached into his coat pocket. He pulled out a handful of tiny listening devices. Mia fumed. "I knew that Benjy was a plant. No one can be that useless. Those effing Tuteras. They're trying to get in on the catering action here."

"Uh . . ." Teri, embarrassed, broke eye contact. She stared at the floor and pushed the carpet back and forth with the front of her sneaker. "He kinda is that useless. Those bugs are mine."

Ravello looked down at Teri from his six-foot-three-inch height. "Tell us how they got here, dear."

Mia recognized her father's tone, threatening but couched with civility. She'd heard it herself many times when Ravello caught her trying to get away with something. There was no lying to him when he sounded like that.

"I told your new hire I was taking pictures for a wedding magazine and he let me go anywhere I wanted," Teri blurted.

"Argh!" Furious, Mia shook a fist in the direction of Benjy/Cammie's office. "I curse you, Benjy Tutera! No, I curse Vito Tutera for siccing his idiot grandson on us. I curse both of you!" She grabbed her father by his jacket lapels. "Dad, do *something*."

Ravello took his daughter's hands off his jacket and placed them by her side. "I'll talk to Vito and see if he can find another job for him. But we cannot fire Benjy. At least, not yet." He turned to Teri. "Did we miss any bugs?"

"No, sir," she said. "I swear it." Mia relished seeing the brash reporter intimidated for a change.

The three left the ballroom. Ravello returned to his office. Mia put a hand under Teri's elbow and firmly directed her toward the exit. "So long, farewell, *auf wiedersehen*, good-bye."

Evans appeared from the kitchen area. He had on the jeans and white T-shirt he usually wore under his chef's coat and was carrying a motorcycle helmet. "Mia, I found a non-dairy cake recipe for the bar mitzvah. I'm gonna shoot by a kosher grocery store and pick up the ingredients. I'll make one tomorrow, and you can tell me what you think."

"Sounds good."

Teri stared at Evans with a glazed look on her face, then tilted her head and affected an expression that Mia assumed was the reporter's attempt at flirting. "*Hiiii . . .*"

"Hey," Evans said, heading for the door. "See y'all tomorrow."

"Wait, wait!" Teri cried out. She scurried over to him. The reporter smoothed her hair and literally batted her eyes. Mia was transfixed. She felt like she'd fallen into a time tunnel and was watching some dame vamp in the nineteen-fifties. "Are you going anywhere near Ditmars Boulevard? Can I catch a ride?"

"Sure? You okay with riding on the back of a motorcycle?"

" 'Okay?' Uh, *yeah*." Teri flipped her hair back. "Love them. I am all about riding hogs."

Please don't make a motorcycle sound. I may not be able to control myself.

"Vroom, vroom," Teri said, miming motorcycle bars. She winked at Evans. Mia burst into a laugh that she tried to disguise as a coughing fit. Teri shot her an angry side eye.

"I keep a spare helmet here," Evans said, oblivious to Teri's ham-fisted come-ons. "Hold on."

Teri gawked as he went off to retrieve the helmet. "He is *sooooo* hot."

"Catch a ride to Astoria?" Mia fixed her with a look. "Your car is in the parking lot."

"I know. I'll take a Pick-U-Up back here tomorrow to get it. Hey, I've never been on a motorcycle before. Is it scary?"

Due to Evans being Mia's neighbor, he had given her a few heart-stopping rides home on the back of his bike. He drove as if the devil was after him and greeted every pothole with an adrenaline-pumped *whoo hoo*! "No," Mia said. "It's not scary at all."

Evans reappeared. He tossed a helmet to Teri, who grabbed it and eagerly scurried after him.

Mia strode down the hall. She tapped Pete Dianopolis's telephone number into her phone as she walked. He answered with an "I'm picking up Cammie's dry cleaning, whaddya want?"

"I just wondered if you'd followed up on my lead regarding Castor Garvalos, his reaction to Tina's death, and the possible illegal activity at Versailles on the Park." *I sound* so *like one of those TV lawyers*, Mia thought, impressed with herself.

"I'm trying to remember when you joined NYPD as a lead detective. Oh, that's right. *Never*. Son-of-a—I dropped a blouse. Don't tell Cammie. Back to you. It just so happens that I have some news on that Garvalos lead you so helpfully provided."

"You do?" Mia said, her body a-tingle with anticipation.

"Yeah," Pete said, sounding smug. "He has an airtight alibi for the time of Tina Karras's death. He was at a hospitality conference in Washington, DC. For three days. And on several panels."

"Oh." Mia's first reaction was disappointment. Her second—*how do I get on a panel at one of those conferences?* "Thanks for letting me know, Pete. I appreciate it."

"Sure."

Pete sounded a little less smug. Mia picked up a different inflection in his tone. "There's something else. What?"

"Nothing. I gotta go. Cammie needs her dry cleaning."

"For work?" Mia, always hopeful, asked.

Pete burst out laughing. "Yeah, right."

The call over, Mia walked into Cammie's office, where she found Benjy behind the desk in Cammie's office, absorbed in whatever he was typing that she was sure had nothing to do with his job at Belle View. "We need to talk."

Benjy kept typing. "I'll be with you in ten. I'm on a roll here."

Mia stepped into the office and grabbed the keyboard out of his hands, eliciting an outraged yelp. "Look at me, not the computer screen." Benjy fixed her with a sullen glare. Mia decided to try a different tack with him. "Benjy, have you ever had a job before?"

His angry expression faded. "No," he confessed. "At least not outside the family. Grandpop pays me to take care of his computer. You know, updates, get rid of viruses. The stuff that man clicks on, I cannot tell you. I also help him with his smartphone. Oh, man, he's always screaming at the thing. He says it's not working. It works fine. He's just always pressing the wrong buttons."

Mia, thinking of her father and grandmother's adversarial relationship with technology, had to smile at this. "I can relate. Look, you're new to working in a business; my dad and I are new to running one. Let's call a do-over to you starting work here. I'll explain exactly what we need step-by-step, and you tell me whether you can do it. Here's what we can offer: a flexible schedule with a lunch hour and breaks. If you have a conflict—"

"Like an open mic night at a comedy club? Cuz my act's almost ready to try out at one of those."

"Like an open mic night. We'll do whatever we can to work around it. But—and this is huge—during your work hours, I need you to do exactly that. Work. For us. With a hundred percent attention on what you're doing *for us*. Can you do that?"

"Yeah," Benjy said, sounding more resigned than enthusiastic.

Mia handed back the keyboard. "Good. I'll give you a ten-minute break. There are just a few work hours left today. You can spend them doing whatever you haven't done yet that I or anyone else here asked you to do. Got it?"

"Yes, ma'am."

Mia cringed. "Ugh, I hate being called that. Just make it 'Mia.'"

Mia finished her own workday by updating the Belle View website with photos of the setups she'd used to snag a meeting with the Millers. They were such an impressive ruse that they'd now be featured as real options for future customers. She sent out an e-blast to the facility's mailing list to publicize the new additions and within minutes received event inquiries. She set up tours for the interested parties and then powered down.

She left her office and started down the hall. As she passed Benjy, she saw the young man typing slowly and looking miserable, which she took to mean he was finally doing his job. "Quittin' time, Benjy."

Relief flooded his face. "Thank you. I was trying to figure out how many glasses you get from a bottle of wine and then how many bottles you'd need for a hundred people and it's so *boring.*"

This kid is not destined for a career in hospitality, Mia thought. But she gave him a thumbs-up and said, "Good work, buddy."

She found Ravello on the phone in his office. His moony expression told her that Lin Yeung, his girlfriend was on the other end of the call, so she stepped back into the hallway to give her father privacy. When she was positive the call was over, she came into the office. She plopped down in the toile-print upholstered club chair with brass nail trim that faced Ravello's desk. "I'm clocking out soon but wanted to tell you, nice job handling Teri. I think you scared her away for a while."

"I'm not sure if *away* is the operative word here," Ravello said. "I saw her zoom off on the back of Evans's bike."

"Yeah, that's a new one. But at least if she comes around,

it'll be for a different reason than trying to drag our butts through the fire."

"True." Ravello threaded his fingers together and cracked his knuckles. "How'd it go at the Miller place today?"

Mia raised her eyebrows. "*Place* couldn't be a more casual way to describe it. You know those houses on steroids people built when they had buckets of money back in the olden days? This was one of those. And like, three people live there. It's nuts. But," she acknowledged, "it's drop-dead gorgeous."

"Did you find out anything interesting?"

"That if you're super rich, you can act any way you want, which I kind of already know from the place I worked in Palm Beach, Korri Designs, home to the world's most overpriced leather goods. Larkin, the daughter who runs the Collection, is definitely off. Obsessed with the art to the point where I can see how she might kill, either from rage or to protect it. By the way, she invited me to an exhibit opening to see how the Collection functions as an event space. If she's not the murderer, I think we have a shot at getting some work from her."

Ravello pursed his lips as he considered this. "*Bella mia, Mia bella*. I understand why it's important to you to help Linda and Nicole. I'm fond of them, too. But I want to make sure you're taking precautions."

"I am, Dad. Jamie was with me at the Millers, on call the whole time I was there." Mia stood up. She lapped the room as she spoke. "I'm not just doing this for the Karrases. I'm doing it for Belle View. The painting being found, Tina's body being found . . . both of those things happened here. In a way we're lucky Pete thinks it's a crime of passion, ex-wife versus current wife, but still, I feel like we're being used. And that ticks me off."

"Agreed. I don't believe in coincidences."

The two fell silent, each absorbed in speculation about the crime. Mia flashed back to Castor Garvalos's reaction to the news of Tina's death. "There's this guy, Castor Garvalos. He's the G.M. at Versailles on the Park."

"Fancy." Ravello said this with a sardonic smile.

"He had a huge reaction to Tina's death, which I found very suspicious. But Pete just told me that he's got an airtight alibi for her time of death, so the cops won't be digging around for more dirt on him, I guess, at least not right now. In other news, Garvalos is dying to buy Belle View. Says he has an investor, I thought it might be Vito and that he planted Benjy here to run the place down to get a better price for it—" Ravello burst out laughing. He roared until he wheezed. "What?" Mia said, insulted. "It's not like that couldn't have happened."

"I'm sorry." Tears rolled down Ravello's cheeks. He laughed so hard that he stopped making noise. His body simply shook. After a minute, he regained control. "It's thinking of that boy Benjy being part of a devious plot. I have to tell Vito. He'll find it hysterical."

"Don't give him any ideas."

"Good point." Ravello pulled a tissue from a box and blew his nose. "Back to this Versailles guy. Thoughts?"

"Tina threw Nicole's gonzo shower at Versailles. Garvalos almost passed out when I told him Tina died. I don't care what Pete says, there's some connection there, but I don't know what. Ooh, I have an idea. I'll be right back." Mia dashed to her office, grabbed her cell phone, and ran back to Ravello. "I'm gonna call Garvalos and tell him that you and I talked, and you're open to meeting with him to hear his offer on Belle View, but he has to come here. That way we'll get him to the scene of the crime, so to speak. And you can meet him and see what you think."

"I like it."

Mia scrolled through her call history and found the general manager's cell number. She entered it. "Huh. It's like someone answered and then hung up. I'll try again." She reentered the number. "Now I'm blocked."

Ravello put an elbow on the desk and rested his chin on his fist. "From wanting to buy Belle View to blocking you. Hmmm."

"Look up the general number for Versailles," Mia said. "I'll try going through that."

Ravello looked up the number and read it to her. She entered it in her phone. After working her way through the voicemail options, she finally heard a human voice. "Will Longwood, acting general manager. How can I help you?"

"Yes, hi. I'd like to speak to Castor Garvalos. I met with him to talk about Versailles' event packages and I have a few questions."

"He's not here and won't be available for a few days."

Mia raised an eyebrow at this news. "Really? Is he okay?"

"I'm sure he will be. But he's in the hospital."

This news initiated a raise of both eyebrows. "The hospital? Wow. I'm sorry to hear that. I hope it's nothing serious."

His replacement paused, and then said, "Someone conked him on the back of the head. He's got a pretty bad concussion."

"Conked on the back of the head?" Mia repeated this for Ravello's benefit, who responded with an eyebrow raise of his own. "That's terrible." She held the phone slightly away from her ear so Ravello could listen in. "Do the police know what happened?"

"If they do, they're not telling us. Everyone here thinks it was a robbery attempt gone wrong." Suddenly remembering he had a potential client on the phone, the acting G.M. returned to a professional tone, "But I'll be happy to answer all your questions."

"Oh, someone just walked into my office. I'll call you back." Mia ended the call.

"So, this Garvalos character was attacked," Ravello said. "That's an interesting development."

"You know it. And I didn't see it coming." Mia knit her brow. "Hmmm . . . Garvalos takes one to the head. Justine Cadeau, the art dealer at Nicole's shower, turns out to have been a party crasher, and now she's disappeared. Both things happen after Garvalos and Cadeau learned Tina was killed. She seems to have a bad effect on people, both in life and death."

"Hmmm . . ." Ravello drummed his fingers on the desk. "Tina Karras was a flight attendant. I wonder what airline she flew for. And whether she worked international flights."

"Good questions, Dad."

Mia's cell rang. She checked and saw an unfamiliar number. "I wonder if Garvalos is calling back from a burner phone." She answered the call. "Mia Carina."

"Hey," a man responded. "This is Liam O'Dwyer. I hear you have some questions for me."

"Liam O'Dwyer," Mia repeated for her father's benefit. The sole captured member of the Miller Art Collection heist gang had gotten back to her. Ravello gave her a triumphant thumbs-up. "Thank you so much for getting in touch. I'd love to talk to you. When are you free?"

"If it's not too last minute, I can meet tonight. I just got off work."

"That would be great. Where do you work?"

"Manhattan. I'm a security guard at the Rockwood Museum of Art."

CHAPTER 12

"You're a museum security guard?" Mia repeated, stunned.

She immediately regretted blurting this out, but O'Dwyer didn't seemed fazed. "Yeah, believe it or not. The museum figured, who better to keep people out of a museum than someone who broke into one?"

"I can see that," Mia said. "I'm happy to come meet you in Manhattan."

"I live in Queens. I hear you do too, so why don't we meet there?"

"Sure. Do you know the Aquarius Diner on Ditmars?"

"I've been known to take advantage of their early bird dinner specials on my days off. You wanna say seven?"

"Perfect. I'll see you in about an hour."

O'Dwyer signed off. Mia placed the phone on the

desk. "I'm breaking bread with the one guy who went to jail for the Miller heist. *Score*."

"You're meeting at the Karras diner?"

Mia nodded. "I know it and all the people who work there, which gives it a safety factor, like you said before. Plus, I can get some intel from Ron. I want to know how Nicole's doing, of course, but he can also tell me what airline Tina flew for."

Ravello gave Mia a ride to the diner, then drove off to Manhattan for a date with Lin. It was six-thirty, a half hour before O'Dwyer was scheduled to show up. This would give Mia the time she needed to ferret some valuable information out of Tina's widower.

Mia walked into the Aquarius, which ticked off all the archetypal boxes of diner décor. A counter with fake wood paneling on its underside and a light-blue Formica countertop stretched the length of half the room. The counter seats were upholstered in dark blue Naugahyde, as were booths arranged in a sideways u-shape around the room. Four-top and six-top tables filled the center of the restaurant. While the entry and path that ran alongside the counter sported a flooring of tile made to look like fieldstone, the rest of the dining area was covered with carpet featuring an ornate design of seashells and mermaids, in keeping with the Aquarius theme. The air was perfumed with a blend of scents from lemons to oregano.

Ron Karras was behind the counter, dishing out a bowl of rice pudding for a patron. Mia caught his eye and waved. He delivered the pudding, excused himself, and came out from behind the counter. Knowing he was perceived as the bad guy in the breakup of his marriage, Ron responded to Mia with a tentative warmth. She responded with a big hug, and he relaxed. "How's Nicole?" she asked. "I'm trying not to bother her."

"Doing well," he said. "Still on bedrest, but everything is good with the baby."

"I'm so glad to hear that." Mia placed a hand on the diner owner's arm. "How are you doing, Ron? You've been through a lot lately. Nicole . . . Tina's death."

Ron waved to a waitress. "Alexa, watch the door for me," he called to her, then said to Mia in a low voice, "let's talk."

Mia followed him to a tiny office overwhelmed with stacks of paper and old menus. She squeezed in after Ron. He reached behind her and pulled the door shut. "What a nightmare, what a nightmare." Ron repeated this a few times. There was no way he could pace in the tiny room, so he kept turning back and forth. "The police are all over Linda. I lived with that woman for over twenty-five years. Was she upset we broke up? Yeah? Would she kill my wife over it? No freaking way. I don't kid myself. I'm not a guy who'd drive someone to murder, unless it was one of them wanting to kill me for snoring." Ron ran a hand over top of his head. "The police also interviewed me as a suspect, Mia. Twice. They brought me in again today."

This news set off an alarm for Mia. "Ron, I have a question. The guy who runs Versailles where you and Tina threw Nicole a shower—"

"You mean Castor Garvalos?" A dark expression colored Ron's face. "Tina's ex?"

"*Yes*." Mia said, feeling vindicated. "I knew there was a connection."

"Yeah, Tina told me they went out years ago and stayed friends after. God knows why. What a piece of pond scum. You know what he did? He cut Tina a good deal for the party. Then after she dies, he sends me a new bill for twice as much. Condolences and profuse apologies, he writes, but her tragic death voids the original agreement. You know what, calling him pond scum is an insult to pond scum."

Mia chose her words carefully. "Is there any chance Tina and Garvalos . . . secretly rekindled their relationship?"

Ron gave his head a vigorous shake. "He wound up having zero interest in her. Or any women, according to Tina." Ron repeated his nervous habit of running a hand over his head. He checked his palm, then showed it to Mia. She could see a few light-brown hairs. "I'm gonna be bald by the time this is all over."

Mia watched Ron resumed his makeshift pacing. She recalled an image of stunning, vibrant, apparently wealthy Tina. "Do you mind if I'm blunt?"

"Did I mention I was interviewed by the police? I don't think there's anything you can say that would shock or hurt me at this point."

"What did Tina see in you?"

Ron froze. Then he gave a wry laugh. "You weren't kidding. That's blunt. But it's a good question." The diner owner looked past the office wall, out toward his restaurant. "I was comfort to her. Tina's parents ran a little restaurant in Athens. It was a struggle. They sent her here to live with relatives here in the States when she was ten. For a better life. She felt obligated to show them they were right, which made her ambitious. She sent money back to them up until the day they died. But she never stopped being homesick. Being ripped away from everything that meant something to you as a kid—that's rough.

She'd been living farther out in Queens, to be closer to the airport when she flew."

"I was going to ask you, what airline did she fly for?"

"Odyssey. Second biggest Greek airline for years until it got eaten by the biggest airline. Everything was about Greece to her. When she retired, she moved to Astoria because it has such a large Greek population. She'd come into my place pretty much every day. We'd hang out. Things with me and Linda were, I don't know, flat. Like we were friends more than a couple. She knew my stories, my cooking. Tina didn't. We got married in Greece. Had a tiny reception at the restaurant her parents used to own. They both passed away when she was in her teens, long before we ever met. Tina's heart lay in that country. We'd go back a couple of times a year. The plan was to buy a second home there. And maybe eventually make it our first home."

Mia cleared her throat, choking down the urge to cry. Ron wasn't some sad sack lured into the arms of a conniving, beautiful woman. He was a grieving widower, a man who had genuinely been in love. And Tina was no longer a cartoon villainess. She was a lonely woman, desperate for love and approval. She'd made terrible choices along the way; Mia was convinced of that, even without knowing the exact nature of what they were yet. But she now saw Tina Karras as a vulnerable if flawed human being. "That painting. The one that showed up at the shower like it was a gift from Tina. Do you know anything about that? Did Tina ever mention the Miller Collection to you? Did she tell you anything about the painting after she got home from the shower?"

"Very little. All she said was that someone played a very nasty joke on her and she didn't want to talk about it.

But she did change in the short time she was still alive after that. She was nervous and tense all the time. And secretive. She'd make these phone calls where she'd talk in a whisper and then hang up as soon as I came in the room."

Mia was intrigued by these mysterious phone calls. She was about to press Ron to see if he remembered anything specific about them when someone knocked on the door. Ron opened it a crack to reveal Alexa. "Everything okay out there?" he asked.

"Yeah." Alexa poked her head into the office. "Mia, there's a guy here looking for you."

"Thanks, Alexa," Mia said. "Could you seat him at the most private table you have and tell him I'll be right there?"

"You got it."

Alexa gave her a thumbs-up and departed. "I'm meeting Liam O'Dwyer, the only person who did time for the Miller Collection robbery," Mia explained to Ron. "I'm hoping he knows something that can help connect it to what's happening now." She kept her comment vague, not wanting to bring up Tina's murder and cause Ron additional pain.

"Do whatever you can, as long you stay safe. Your grandma told me the FBI was so impressed by how you fought off the killers who kidnapped you in the spring that they gave you a medal and begged you to run the agency."

If Mia had been drinking anything, she would have done a spit take. She slapped her forehead and groaned. "*Marone mia!* That story's more fictional than one of Steve Stianapolis's dumb books. No, none of that is true. I'm not—who's the famous FBI guy?"

"Elliott Ness."

"Right. I'm not him. But I am almost family to all of you, and I'll do whatever I can to try and figure out what happened."

Ron put his hands on Mia's shoulders. "Thank you," he said, his voice husky.

The two returned to the dining area. Mia saw Alexa showing a man to a table in the farthest corner of the restaurant. O'Dwyer was not much more than Mia's five-feet-five-inch height, if he even reached that. He was bald, but had bushy red eyebrows. His face was also red, florid from rosacea, a map of broken capillaries stretching from one cheek to the other. His bulbous nose leaned to the left, which Mia assumed was the result of a fight. But O'Dwyer's eyes had a cheerful glint to them and his whole presence exuded a sense of affability.

Mia joined him at the table. "Liam O'Dwyer?"

"Where?" He faked fear, then gave her a broad smile that exposed a few empty slots where teeth had once been. He extended his hand and give her a hearty shake. "Right in front of you. But don't let my bookie know. I owe him a few Benjamins."

"Wow, you're like, straight out of the Westies," Mia said, referencing the notorious Irish gang that ran Hell's Kitchen on the west side of Manhattan for years. She caught herself. "I'm so sorry."

"Sorry? That's the nicest anyone's said to me in years. I'm flattered. To be honest, I did run with them some. Well, more ran alongside. They were too tight-knit to welcome me full-on. There were only about twenty of them. They had a big presence for a small group." O'Dwyer sounded wistful. Mia knew he was privately thinking, *those were the days*.

Alexa appeared, armed with a couple of beers and two plates featuring Greek salad and giant slabs of moussaka. "I told her my favorite Greek dish," O'Dwyer explained to Mia. "And ordered a coupla beers. You want one?"

"Thanks, but I'll stick to water, at least for now."

"Ah, keep your wits about you. Smart girl." O'Dwyer closed his eyes and inhaled the fragrance of eggs, beef, and spices. "Bee-you-tee-ful. Alexa, will you do me the honor of being the next Mrs. Liam O'Dwyer?"

The waitress, seventy if she was a day, flashed her left hand. "Sorry, handsome. Somebody put a ring on it fifty years ago. Plus, if you want cooking like this, you'll have to propose to our chef, Constantine. But I don't think you're his type."

She left and O'Dwyer dug into his meal. Mia, nervous about bringing up the crime that put him behind bars, speared a chunk of cucumber, then put it back on her plate. "I really appreciate you meeting with me, Mr. O'Dwyer."

"Lee to my friends."

"Lee. I know that the subject I want to talk to you about might be a sensitive one—"

"You want dirt on the Miller heist on account of how that ugly painting showed up and then Tina bought the ranch."

Mia stared at him, open-mouthed. "Mr.—Liam. Lee. You make it sound like you knew Tina."

"That's cuz I did. She's the one who got me into the whole effed up mess." O'Dwyer shoveled another forkful of moussaka into his mouth.

Mia's pulse raced. It was like one of those pictures that

was only a bunch of dots until you connected the dots and brought an image into view. O'Dwyer was a dot. Or a line. Or both. "Just so you know," she cautioned, "Ron, who owns the diner, was married to Tina."

"Did he whack her?"

Mia gasped. "No, no. Don't even think that."

"No worries, I wouldn't blame him if he did. She was . . . what's the new way you say bad news? Toxic, that's it. She was one toxic broad."

"How did you meet her?"

"Before all these Millennial types were tootling around town with their rideshare gig jobs, there were gypsy cabs in this city. Remember them?" Mia nodded. "I could never pull together the scratch for a taxi medallion, so I used to drive a gypsy sometimes. We were only supposed to respond to calls and not cruise looking for passengers. Yeah, right. Anyway, I picked up this chick Tina Iles one night. She was working an international flight and running late. She was a stew for this airline called Odyssey. Hasn't been around for years. Anyway, I got her to JFK so fast that she took my card and used me all the time after that. On one ride, she starts telling me about how her family was rich before World War II and had all this great art, but the Nazis stole it and they ended up broke. She said this Miller Art Collection had a bunch of her family's paintings but refused to give them back. She asked if I could help her right this wrong and get back the paintings. I'm not gonna lie. It helped that she was hot. It also helped that she offered me five grand and I had gambling debts to pay off. Which reminds me, say hello to your father. I played in a couple of his games before I went away."

"I'll do that." O'Dwyer was friendly and forthcoming,

which calmed Mia's nerves. Her appetite returned with a vengeance. She inhaled a few big forkfuls of her meal, alternating between salad and moussaka. "Did you believe Tina's story? From what Ron's told me, her family was poor. They owned a tiny café in Athens and struggled to keep it going. I doubt they were big art collectors or collected any art at all besides those wall calendars with pretty pictures of the Greek islands."

"Did I mention Tina was hot? That's all the research I needed to do into her story."

"Noted." Mia scraped her plate for errant scraps of moussaka. "Can you tell me about how the heist worked?"

"I can say what I know. The operation was planned for the night before a new security system was being installed. The one they had sucked."

"How did you learn the exact date the system was going to be changed?"

O'Dwyer shrugged. "Got me. I was pretty much kept out of the loop except for what I was supposed to do. First up was knocking out the guard, which was easy since the guy was about a hundred and always half-crocked. Then I grabbed the paintings I was told to grab, loaded them into my car, and drove them to a location near Sunken Meadow Beach."

Mia put an elbow on the table and rested her chin on her fist. She studied O'Dwyer with a thoughtful expression. "I know Tina was hot, like you say. But you're the only one who ever did time for the job. Doesn't that make you angry? You knew she was involved. Why didn't you finger her?"

O'Dwyer rested his fork on his plate. He lifted the napkin from his lap and dabbed the corners of his mouth. "Cloth napkins. That's classy. So many places, even pricey ones, use paper now. It's a crime, you should pardon the expression." He returned the napkin to his lap. "Like I said, I played in card games run by your father. Boldano games. And Tutera games and Gambrazzo's and Abruzzo's. Once news about the heist got out, TV and the papers kept saying the Mob might be behind it. For all I knew, they were right, and Tina was only the front woman for the job. I figured I was safer in jail. I didn't have nothing better to do anyway. My car died and I couldn't afford to replace it. I'd already lost the five grand from Tina on cards." O'Dwyer grew nostalgic. "The heist was all over the news for weeks. I gotta say, it was kinda exciting knowing I was part of something that big. When one news guy said, 'This was a crack operation," I got a swell of pride from knowin' I was part of that." The ex-con's dreamy expression turned to a scowl. "Then I had to open my big mouth at the bar to a snitch. That's what landed me in jail. But"—he brightened again—"I got a career out of it." He showed off the Rockwood Museum of Art logo on his lapel. "A lot more boring, but a lot more stable."

Alexa reappeared at their table holding a tray laden with Greek desserts ranging from semolina cake to baklava to Honey Phyllo Rollups, a sweet treat that was an Aquarius diner specialty. "From the boss. With a message that dinner is on the house." Mia started to protest, but Alexa interrupted her. "He also said that if you squawk about it, I'm allowed to take you down. I took a self-defense class for seniors, so I know how to do it, and I don't mind showing off."

O'Dwyer stared at her in awe. "Your husband is a very lucky man."

"He knows it. Or at least he says he does, cuz he also knows I'm stronger than him."

Alexa placed the dessert tray on the table. She poured them each a coffee. O'Dwyer took a sip of his. "It's missing something. Like Ouzo."

"You're not the first person to tell me that." Alex pulled a small bottle of Ouzo out of a pocket in her apron and poured a shot into O'Dwyer's coffee. "Mia?"

"Why not?"

Mia held out her coffee cup to Alexa, who juiced it up with a slug of Ouzo, and then moved on. O'Dwyer began assembling a sampler plate of desserts. "You want me to make you one?"

"No thanks, I'm full. I'm going to take mine to go. Is there anything else you remember about the heist?" Mia pressed O'Dwyer. "Anything at all? Even a small detail. You never know what could be important."

O'Dwyer stopped what he was doing and shot Mia a canny look. "I've been so busy eating and talking that I never asked why you want to know all this. I thought you ran a catering hall. Are you some kinda P.I., too?"

"No." Mia lowered her voice. "You know how you wondered if Ron killed Tina? He didn't, but the police think his ex-wife Linda might have. I grew up with this family. Their daughter Nicole is one of my best friends. She's about to have a baby. The stress is terrible. I want to help them. I also want to make sure that everyone knows Belle View had nothing to do with what happened, even though the painting and Tina's body both showed up there."

"Does not look good for anyone," O'Dwyer acknowledged.

"NYPD is a great law enforcement agency—except when they're arresting one of my relatives, of course— but they also got a lot going on. I figure if I can be boots on the ground and pick up stuff I can share with them, it's not the worst thing in the world."

"I'm guessing people have told you to be careful."

"Yeah, I hear that a lot."

O'Dwyer, pensive, sipped his doctored coffee. "Thinking . . . thinking . . ." His face brightened. "Yes! I remembered something. Tina was having a fling with one of her airline's pilots. I even remember his name because it's so classy. Hugo Herold Hartley. Elegant, huh?"

"Uh huh," Mia said, distracted, her eyes on the diner's front door. Pete Dianopolis and his partner Ryan strode in, the expressions on both their faces telegraphing that they were on duty. Pete flashed his badge at one of the restaurant's younger waitresses, who looked scared. The girl pointed to Ron, who was ringing up a customer's check. Mia stood up. "I'll be right back, Liam. I need to check on something."

O'Dwyer turned to see what was going on. "Oh, boy. That looks familiar. And not good."

Mia hurried over to the counter, the ex-con on her heels. They arrived just in time to see Ryan pull out a pair of handcuffs and Pete say to Ron, "Ronald Karras, you're under arrest for the felony assault of Castor Aegeus Garvalos."

CHAPTER 13

There was a clatter as the diner's patrons dropped their silverware. The entire restaurant fell silent. They listened to the officers recite Ron his Miranda rights and watched him be cuffed and escorted out of Aquarius.

"What the f—" waitress Alexa said, breaking the silence.

Mia shook off her shock. "Alexa, you've been here the longest. Take charge of the others. Tell them to act like everything's normal. Finish serving everyone here. When anyone asks what's going on—and they all will—tell them you have no idea."

"Which is the truth," Alexa said, gaping in the direction of the building's front door.

"Put out the CLOSED sign so no new customers come in. As soon as the last one leaves, lock up. But tell everyone it's business as usual. I'll call my dad. We'll get our lawyer on it. If Ron's not out by tomorrow, run the place yourself. I'll make sure Ron knows and promotes you to assistant manager."

Alexa waved a hand dismissively. "I don't need that. I'm old. I got one foot out the door of this place. I'll do it for Ron. He's a good guy. The only thing he'd ever murder is a slice of our foot-high chocolate layer cake."

The waitress took off. Mia turned her attention back to her meal mate, Liam. "Sorry about all this. Thank you so much for talking to me."

"Sure, no problem. You got any other questions, just give me a call." The ex-con stood up. "You never forget your first arrest."

He sounded more sentimental than traumatized.

Mia spent the cab ride home alternating between texts and phone calls. Ron's ex-wife burst into tears at the news. His ex-mother-in-law responded with a triumphant, "I knew it!" Both women agreed that this latest dire development should be withheld from Nicole unless telling her became absolutely necessary. Mia contacted Mickey Bauer, the defense attorney the Carinas kept on retainer. Since the fees laid out by her family had paid for the lawyer's summer place on the Jersey shore, his instant response was, "I'm on it." She followed this with a group text to her father and grandmother alerting them to the development, and a plea to Cammie to find out whatever she could from Pete about the charges against Ron.

When the cab dropped Mia off, Elisabetta and Ravello were there to greet her at the front door. Mia gratefully accepted the glass of wine Elisabetta handed her. "*Che incubo.*"

"I know," Mia said, following the others into the living room. "A total nightmare." She collapsed onto the multi-colored crocheted blanket that covered Elisabetta's couch and kicked off her shoes.

"What happened?" Ravello asked. "What did Ron do that got him arrested?"

Mia threw up the hand that wasn't holding a glass of wine. "No idea. At all." Her cell rang. "It's Cammie. I asked her to flirt any intel she could out of Pete." She answered the call. "Hey. Any luck?"

"It took a little more work than usual, but I got something."

"I'm with Dad and Nonna. Can I put you on speaker?"

"Sure. Tell them to ignore the noise. I'm in the middle of a mani-pedi, and Kanya is drying my tootsies with a fan."

"Now? It's like, nine o'clock at night."

"Messina, dear." Cammie adopted a patronizing tone. "If anyone you know was gonna track down the one twenty-four-hour beauty salon in Queens, who would it be?"

"You, Ms. Dianopolos," Mia said in the sing-songy rhythm of a schoolkid. She pressed the speaker button on her cell phone. Elisabetta and Ravello moved closer to hear Cammie over the fan and the nail salon chatter in the background. "Ron went over to Versailles and got into a screaming match with this Garvalos guy," Cammie reported. "A few hours later, one of Garvalos's coworkers found him on the ground outside, unconscious, a bad gash on the back of his head like someone hit him with something. Since you pointed a finger at Garvalos, the police were already looking into him. They know he and

Tina used to go out, and think they started seeing each other again behind Ron's back. He found out, which led to him confronting Garvalos. And possibly Tina's murder. The spouse is always the number one suspect."

Mia felt sick to her stomach. "I put Garvalos on Pete's radar. Ron's arrest is my fault."

"Mia, you have two guys going at it, and one of them is found knocked out. The cops would have picked up Ron no matter what, given the circumstances. Plus, different judge, different prosecutor than when your dad was arrested in the spring." Mia glanced at her father, who grimaced at the memory of his false arrest. "They're both new and looking to make their bones on a high-profile case. It is in no way your fault."

"Thanks, but I still feel like I'm at least partly responsible." Mia recalled Linda's confrontation with Tina prior to the latter's death. "Although it would help if the Karrases would stop being in the wrong place at the wrong time."

"Good point. I gotta go. Kanya needs my hands. She's painting little leaves on my fingernails. I'm hoping it'll send the universe a message to lose the hot weather and send us an early fall." With this, Cammie signed off.

"I need more wine," Mia said.

She got up and padded barefoot into the kitchen. "Don't blame yourself," her father called. "You heard Cammie. This was a gimme."

Mia filled her glass and returned to the living room with the bottle. Nonna held out her glass. "*Ecco.*"

Mia topped off her grandmother's wine, as well as her father's, then sat back down. "I talked to Ron tonight. I never got any sense at all that he was threatened by Garvalos's relationship with Tina. He basically said the guy plays for the other team." Mia mulled over the conversation. "But he was definitely ticked off at him. Garvalos used Tina's death as an excuse to hustle more money out of Ron for that insane baby shower Tina threw." Her phone pinged a text. Mia read it, then announced, "Mickey was able to arrange Ron's arraignment for first thing in the morning. You can bet I'll be having another convo with Ron after that."

Lunch the next day found Mia at the Aquarius Diner where, after posting bail, Ron had been welcomed back like a war hero by his staff. Given Ron had never received so much as a traffic ticket, the judge set the bail amount at twenty thousand dollars, despite the assistant DA's posturing and demand for a much higher figure. Ron was able to post the ten percent of the bail amount required to release him, but the restaurateur was still recovering from his night in jail. "It's an ugly, ugly place, Mia. I don't know how your father and brother survived."

"I guess if you're there enough, like them, you get used to it."

Ron's hand shook as he lifted his coffee cup to his mouth. "I didn't touch Garvalos. Believe me, I wanted to. But I didn't."

"Why did you go see him at Versailles?"

"I had to. He blocked my calls."

Mia curled her lip. "Yeah, he does that."

Ron cast a pleading look at her. "I went to see him because of that stupid bill he sent me. That's what we got into a fight about. Not a fight, an argument. I never touched him. I swear. He was fine when I left. His same old obnoxious self."

"I believe you."

"Yeah, but will a jury?" Ron motioned to Alexa. She came over, took out her flask, and added a splash of Ouzo to his coffee. "I don't usually—"

"No worries, Ron. I get it." She thought of Spencer Spaulding, who appeared to drink for a living. That wasn't Nicole's father. Except for plighting his troth to a questionable second wife, Ron had led a blameless life, although his one veer off track was turning out to be a doozy. "The question is, if you didn't attack Garvalos, who did? And why?"

"That's for the police to figure out."

Which they won't do, Mia thought, *as long as they think you're the culprit.*

After finishing with Ron, she checked in with work. "Everything's good here because Benjy the idiot's got the day off," Guadalupe said, her tone venomous.

Mia felt a miniscule of sympathy for Benjy. Being in the chef's crosshairs was a scary proposition for anyone. She told Guadalupe she'd be at work by three, then hailed a cab. "Versailles on the Park, please."

The cab deposited her at Versailles' palatial front entrance. She was about to skitter up the steps when saw a truck from Queens Quality Linens, the same service Belle View used, parked at the banquet hall's side entrance. She took a brisk hike to the truck. Avron, a Queens Quality employee who often did Belle View's linen runs, pushed a laundry bin out the Versailles side door to the truck. She called to him. "Avron, hi."

Avron glanced her way. His face lit up when he recognized Mia. "Miss Mia," he said, the greeting tinted with a Middle Eastern accent. "Hello. Nice to see you."

"You, too." Mia approached him. "I didn't know you did Versailles' service. I thought they used Quality Control."

"Quality Control? I have never heard of them. And believe me, I know all of our competitors."

Confirming for me that they don't exist. "Avron, can I ask you a professional question?"

Avron, flattered, beamed. "Of course."

"Do you service Versailles on a regular basis and if so, have you ever done a nighttime pickup here? That was two questions, even though I tried to pass them off as one. My bad."

"Please, do not worry about that. To answer the first, yes, we're contracted with Versailles to handle their linens. And to answer the second, are you kidding? These cheap S.O.B.'s pay overtime? It will never happen."

Again, confirming what I thought. I'm on a roll here. "Thanks a ton. I'll see you at Belle View."

"A lot more of me, thanks to so many more parties there now. How do you say it here? Way to go? And bumping fists?"

"That's right." Mia held up a fist and Avron bumped it with his own fist.

She left the Queens Quality employee loading the laundry bin into his van and entered Versailles through the side door, heading straight for the kitchen. She wanted to get Sandeep's take on what happened to Garvalos and had come up with an excuse for the visit that she hoped would fly with the chef. Mia pushed open one of the kitchen's swinging doors. She found Sandeep sitting on a stool next to one of banquet hall's massive stoves, absent-mindedly stirring a large pot with one hand while he used the other to scroll his cell phone. His demeanor reeked of exhaustion. There was a gray cast to his skin and dark shadows under his eyes. Intent on his multi-tasking, he didn't seem to hear Mia enter, so she gave the doorframe a light tap. "Sandeep?" He stopped stirring, lifted his head from his phone, and gave her a blank stare. "Mia Carina. From Belle View Banquet Manor."

A polite expression replaced the puzzled look on his face. "Ah, yes. Castor's friend. Hello."

He'd given her the miniscule opening she needed. She stepped inside the room. "Yes. I heard what happened to him. Horrible. I was on my way back to work after lunch and thought I'd stop in to see how you're doing and if you've heard anything else about what happened to him."

Sandeep shrugged a single shoulder. "I'm all right. Cooking settles me."

Mia sniffed the air, redolent with a familiar blend of herbs and meats. "Ragu sauce. Beef and pork."

Sandeep smiled. "Well done."

Mia pointed to herself with an index finger. "Italian girl. If I can't ID a sauce, I get kicked out of the tribe." She closed her eyes and inhaled. "A hint of nutmeg. Nice touch."

"Thank you."

There was a tinge of dismissal in his response. Mia ignored it. "The hospital wouldn't tell me anything about Castor's condition since I'm not family," she boldly lied, hoping Castor was still even in the hospital. "How is he?"

"Conscious, which is good, but disoriented. At least

they got the guy who did this to him, although he's out on bail, which is an outrage."

"The thing is, I know him—Ron, the man the police arrested—and he swears he was only arguing with Castor about a big increase he threw into the bill for the baby shower that Ron's late wife Tina threw, and that Castor was fine when he left."

The chef blew a derisive *pfft* with his lips. "You believe that? Please. What else is he going to say?"

"Unless Castor officially identifies Ron as his attacker—*and I pray he doesn't lie and do that*—the evidence is pretty circumstantial."

"If the police arrested him, they must think they can make the charges stick."

"You're probably right." Mia affected a thoughtful pose. "Although I keep wondering if there might be another reason for the attack. Something that involves Versailles."

Sandeep's eyes narrowed. "Like what?"

There was a belligerence in his voice that made Mia nervous. She hurried to finish her thought. "This is gonna sound crazy, but we've had some weird stuff happen at Belle View. What if someone's targeting local catering halls? You know, doing things that would get them the wrong kind of attention and chase away customers."

Skeptical, Sandeep said, "Why would anyone do that?"

Mia had decided that if her father didn't buy her theory about Vito using Benjy to devalue Belle View, it might come in handy with Sandeep. "To bring down the value of our halls and then buy them at a cheaper price."

This was a lightbulb moment for the chef. "Oh, I see what you're saying. Yes, that makes total sense. If the case against this Ron person falls apart, you should run that by the police."

Mia picked up a note of relief in his voice. The man was eager to embrace any theory where Versailles played the victim. He made a show of checking his phone. "I didn't realize how late it is. I have to host a tasting. If you don't mind . . ."

"I'll get going. When you see or talk to Castor, tell him I send my best."

"I will." The chef resumed stirring the ragu, his back to Mia.

Dismissed, Mia made her way to Belle View, accomplishing a few blessedly Benjy-free hours of work. She left Belle View for home, where she fed Doorstop and Pizzazz, and cleaned Doorstop's litter box. The parakeet buzzed around the room chirping cheerily while the cat lay prone on the floor batting a toy mouse between his paws with a modicum of interest. Around seven P.M., Mia changed into an all-black outfit from sneakers to headband. Her long-sleeved tunic was problematic for a hot night but perfect for someone trying to blend into the evening's darkness, like Mia. She opened the Pick-U-Up app and typed in Versailles' address. Moments later, she was in a sub-compact sedan heading back to the catering hall. "Come back for me in half an hour," she told the driver after he dropped her at the top of the entry road to Versailles. "I'll meet you here."

Mia knew from her family's past that when running a recurring illegal activity, continuity was key, so she timed her visit to the exact moment she'd seen the Quality Control linen truck pull up previously. She got off the road and traipsed through woods so no one would see her, then assumed position in a clump of bushes that gave her an eyeline to the establishment's side door while hiding her from view. The front of the building was aglow with lights. A choreographed water ballet sprayed from the facility's two fountains, although Mia noticed that one of the enormous half-clothed statue goddesses was missing a middle finger. *Nice prank,* she chuckled to herself. The parking lot was filled with cars, indicating an event in progress. This didn't concern her. Rather than interrupt any nefarious doings, a party allowed for extra cover. Expelling soiled linens would seem a perfectly normal, event-oriented task. Minutes ticked by. Finally, Mia heard the rumble of a vehicle. She craned her neck to see where it was coming from. A van trundled down the road. As it passed, she saw the now-familiar Quality Control logo on the van. It pulled up to the building's side door and the driver hopped out. Mia turned off the sound on her phone and snapped photos of him and the van. The side door opened, and Sandeep emerged, pushing a laundry bin. Mia continued shooting pictures. The van driver transferred the bin effortlessly, once again indicating it contained a light load.

Mia's phone lit up. Her Pick-U-Up driver was not far away. She muttered a curse, then ran through the brush back to the top of the Versailles road. She was out of breath and dripping with perspiration by the time she got there. She checked the main road. Seeing no sign of her driver, she took a minute to run through the photos she'd taken and text the best of them to Pete with a brief explanation. Her heart pounded. Now that she was done spying, her goal was to make a quick getaway. She tapped a foot, impatient, then released a sigh of relief as her ride appeared down the block. Mia waved to the driver. Suddenly, an engine roared. Mia turned and cried out as the Quality Control van barreled down the Versailles road, gunning for her.

CHAPTER 14

Mia threw herself out of the van's way, taking in a mouthful of dirt when she landed at the road's edge. The van's tires screeched as it made a sharp right turn, almost colliding with her Pick-U-Up driver, who hit his horn and screamed a string of profanities out the window. The driver pulled over, got out, and ran to Mia. He helped her to her feet. "Holy crap! You okay?"

Mia spit out dirt. "I'll live."

"That sonuva could've killed you."

Guessing that was the plan, Mia thought but didn't say.

She and the driver walked back to his car. "He should've stopped," the man said. "But maybe he didn't see you because you're wearing all black. My wife wears all black when she walks the dog. I say it's dangerous and she ignores me. I'm gonna tell her what happened tonight. Maybe scare some sense into her."

"Happy to be a cautionary tale." Mia let out a groan as she maneuvered herself into the back seat. She'd hit the ground hard and would have the bruises and aches to show for it.

"You might wanna report that guy to the police," the driver said, concerned.

"There's no point. I didn't get a license number and I can't prove he's anything but a bad driver." She checked her phone. Despite the cracked screen, it was functioning. The photos she'd sent Pete had gone through. "What I needed to happen, happened. That's the most important thing."

Mia refused the driver's offer for a free trip to urgent care. He dropped her off and she made her way up the stairs to her apartment as quietly as possible. She was covered with dirt and scratches and not in the mood for a grilling from her grandmother. Doorstop, sensing she wasn't completely herself, meowed his concern when he saw her. "It's okay, bud," she said, petting his silky golden-orange fur. "All I need to do is to lie in a hot bath until my entire body prunes up."

Mia washed her face in the bathroom's tiny sink. Then she filled the tub and added a bath bomb. The room filled with steam and the smell of lavender. Mia stepped into the tub and submerged her aching body up to the neck, re-laxing into the water's warmth. Doorstop parked himself on the worn bathmat to keep an eye on his human. From her position in the bathtub, Mia noticed that the corner of the dated, rosebud-patterned wallpaper that abutted the tub was peeling. Her home, like her place of business, needed updating. *I have to stop spending time in these high-end locations like Versailles and the Miller estate.* At least the bathroom was hers and hers alone. She didn't have to worry about her would-have-been-ex-if-he-hadn't-died husband, who spent more time primping than she did, banging on the bathroom door yelling at her to hurry up.

Mia closed her eyes and mulled over the day's events. Short of hiding in a laundry bin and getting herself wheeled into the Quality Control van at Versailles—a step she considered but wisely passed on—she'd done everything she could to sic an NYPD investigation on them. It was time to move on. But to what? A memory niggled at her; a possible clue that had been buried by the drama of Ron's arrest. Liam O'Dwyer had brought up Tina's affair with an Odyssey pilot. Mia searched her brain for the man's distinctive name. It suddenly came to her. "I know what my next step is, Big D," she said to Doorstop. "Track down a pilot with the classy name of Hugo Herold Hartley."

Mia woke up early the next morning, determined to do whatever it took to find contact information for Tina's former lover . . . which ended up taking all of one minute. If that. The pilot—now retired—had a page on a popular social media site where he posted regular updates, mostly of him gardening at his lovely home in a posh Connecticut town. Mia decided to try messaging him. She debated how best to explain why she wanted to talk to him, then went with an honest-but-doesn't-hurt-to-drop-the-Boldano-name approach. She shared the details about how *Cow and Woman* unexpectedly reappeared at a Belle View event, Tina's reaction to it, and her subsequent murder. *Here's hoping he reads it and gets back to me*, she thought as she stood up to go take a shower. An alert sounded from her computer and Mia glanced down to check it. To her surprise, it was an instant response from Hartley: "How soon can you get here?"

Mia sat back down. A flurry of typing led to Hartley's address and instructions on how to get there. Now all she had to was find a ride to Lowingfield, Connecticut. She pulled her cell out of her purse and speed-dialed a number.

"What's up?" Jamie sounded groggy.

"I'm sorry, did I wake you?"

"Nah. I was lazing in bed. Finished a final yesterday and celebrated last night. I have to whisper, though. Madison is still sleeping."

Much as she didn't want it to, Mia's heart gave an involuntary clutch at the image of Jamie and his girlfriend spooning. A moment like this was a painful reminder that despite assuring herself she was okay with being in the Friend Zone with Jamie, a part of her still clung to a dream of transitioning him into the Boyfriend Zone. She inhaled a deep breath through her nose and centered herself. "Are you by any chance free today? I need to go to Connecticut to do some snooping."

"What's going on? I heard Ron Karras was arrested."

"And released, although the charges are still pending." Mia updated Jamie on the recent events, including the results of her Versailles stakeout. She decided not to mention almost being run down by the fake linen company van, fearful it would engender a bout of mansplaining about how she needed to be more careful. "Whatever's going on at Versailles is in Pete's hands now, so we'll see if it goes anywhere. But meanwhile, there's one lead I haven't followed up on yet." She shared her conversation with Liam O'Dwyer and how it had led to Hugo Herold Hartley.

"You're in luck," Jamie said. "I'm free. Mads and I were going to hit the beach, but she felt like she was getting a cold last night and decided to take it easy."

Maybe it'll be fatal, Mia thought, followed by, *Bad Mia! Stop it!* "Awesome. That you're free, not that Mads has a cold." *Did that sound snarky? Do I care?* "Come over as soon as you're ready. We can leave early. We're going against traffic."

"See you in half an hour."

"Oh, and Jamie, I want to drive."

Mia ended the call before he could protest. She called Cammie and explained the situation. "Do you mind staying at Belle View for a few hours past your usual five minutes of work?"

"Oh, honey, I would except that I'm in Connecticut myself at a women's empowerment retreat. It's really just a bunch of us getting spa treatments and complaining about our husbands or bosses or both. They're all so jealous of my cushy job."

Mia rubbed her brow. "Oh, boy. This means I'm left with Benjy minding the store. He's been a tiny bit better, but it's still a terrifying proposition. Who knows, though? Maybe being in charge will motivate him."

Cammie burst out laughing. "You have the best sense of humor."

"Yeah. God forbid there should be a drop-in potential customer. Benjy might see them as an open mic night for his comedy routine and send them running to book their event at Versailles. I better make sure Dad's there."

"Sounds like a plan. Oooh, they just put out a platter of

chocolate-dipped strawberries to go along with breakfast. I *love* this place! Bye-yee."

Mia next called her father to alert him to the day's plans. The call cut out and she tried again. "Mia?"

"Yeah, it's me, Dad." She heard a subway roar behind him. "Where are you?"

"Coming back to Queens from Manhattan."

Ravello sounded embarrassed and it dawned on Mia why. He'd spent the night at his girlfriend's place. "Did you have a nice time with Lin?" she teased.

"Yes, what's up?" Ravello said, quickly changing the subject.

Mia told him about the sleuthing trip she and Jamie would be taking. "Can you keep an eye on things at Belle View until I get back?"

"Not a problem. When was the last time you had a day off, anyway? I can't remember."

"Neither can I. Let's call this a sick day. As in, I'm sick of all the drama we keep getting sucked into, may it end soon, and I get to take a genuine vacation day."

Mia ended the call. *How come the men in my life have no problem getting into relationships but I do?* she brooded. *Posi even got a girl's number during a prison work program.* The closest she'd come to dating since the assumed drowning of her adulterous husband was with an archetypal bad bet who put her life in danger. Her family, blue collar by nature, generally dismissed therapy, instead going with the get-over-it approach to problems. *But maybe it's time for me to check it out,* Mia thought. *Otherwise, I may end up either a lonely cat lady or walking down the aisle with another deadbeat.*

She filed the self-examination away for when she could accompany it with a few glasses of wine and focused on getting ready for her day trip to the suburbs. She examined her wardrobe, debating what kind of outfit would play in the Connecticut suburbs, a place she'd spent zero time despite it being New York State's next-door neighbor. A half hour later, her bed covered with rejections, Mia had to accept that she had no idea what would be deemed an appropriate look for the Constitution State. She settled on wide-leg off-white linen pants that she paired with a teal scoop neck top and sedate neutral sandals. As she was applying makeup, she heard the front door open. Mia followed the sound of the footsteps below into Elisabetta's kitchen, where all roads led in an Italian household. She headed downstairs and found Jamie in the kitchen being plied with food by her grandmother. Elisabetta motioned for Mia to take a seat at the room's decades-old dinette set. "You need a good breakfast for the long drive north."

"It's a forty-five-minute drive, Nonna. We're not exactly setting out on a pioneer trail."

"Eat," Elisabetta commanded.

Mia knew a losing battle with her grandmother when she saw one, so she sat down to a plate of sausage and cheese frittata, along with sides of polenta and fried potatoes. "I'm not sorry she's making us do this," Jamie said. "Mads is vegan. I don't know what half the stuff in her refrigerator is. All I know is it doesn't taste like this." He held up his plate. "May I please have some more potatoes?"

Elisabetta cast an affectionate smile at him and pinched his cheek, leaving a red mark. "*Va bene.* You can have all the potatoes you want, *bello ragazzo.*"

Mia waited impatiently while Jamie powered through three more servings of Elisabetta's fried potatoes. He finally forced himself away from his plate after Elisabetta packed up the leftover potatoes in an old, worn ricotta container for him. The two bid her good-bye and headed out to the car. Mia held out her hand. "Keys, please."

Jamie shook his head. "Nuh uh. You're not ready for this drive. I'll get us to Connecticut. You can take over on the local roads."

"Way to have faith in me," Mia groused as she got in the car.

Once on the road, however, she was grateful for Jamie's stellar driving skills as he wended his way out of Queens, across the Whitestone Bridge onto the Hutchinson River Parkway, and eventually onto I-95. She'd underestimated the length of the drive. By the time they reached the exit for Lowingfield, they'd be on the road for well over an hour.

Jamie exited the interstate and pulled into a mini-mall parking lot. "Your turn. I'll navigate."

They got out of the car and exchanged places. "Make a right out of the parking lot and then a left at the first light," Jamie instructed.

Mia, feeling tense, gripped the wheel and followed his instructions. Within minutes, they'd traded the suburban sprawl of Lowingfield's main artery for a New England landscape of gently rolling green hills and Colonial-style homes. An old stone wall hugged the curves of the narrow country road they traveled. Mia relaxed and enjoyed the view, so different from the cement stoops and rowhouses of Queens. "It's major league pretty out here."

"I know," Jamie said, gazing out his window. "I want to live in Connecticut someday."

This was news to Mia. And a shock. She'd never

imagined Jamie anywhere but on their current home turf of Astoria. "You do? Why?"

"*Why?*" Jamie gestured to the view. "Look around. It's incredible. All the grass and trees and flowers. And smell that the air." He inhaled the breeze wafting in from his open car window. "You know, Madison grew up not far from here. Her parents still live there. Their place goes back to the nineteenth century. There's a stream in the woods behind it. It's like, if heaven was a house, it would be theirs."

He's met the parents, Mia thought, her heart sinking. *They're serious.* Jamie's relationship with Madison mystified her. 'Mob boss's son meets upscale sorority girl' would make a great movie meet-cute, but how could it possibly last long-term? She couldn't picture the couple having enough in common to stand the test of time. Now she and Jamie, growing up together in the Life—*they* had a lot in common.

"Why would anyone *not* want to live here?" Jamie continued.

"Oh. I dunno," Mia said, forcing herself to stay on topic. "I don't think it's the place for me. I'd always be the girl with the accent."

"You could lose it, like I did."

"How did you do that?"

"I copied how people on TV sounded. I wanted to be different from my family. It felt like the first step was to sound different. Whoa." Jamie gripped the dashboard. "You need to slow down around the curves on this road, so you take them more smoothly."

"Yes, sir." Mia adjusted her speed around the next curve. As she drove, she thought about what Jamie had said.

While she was self-conscious of her accent, she would never shed it to differentiate herself from her father and brother. But then, she didn't have the issues with her family that Jamie did. She stopped at a red light. A woman came out of the house on the corner. She wore khaki shorts and a polo shirt. Her silky blonde hair was pulled back in a headband. She held a toddler by the hand and carried a baby in the crook of her other arm. The flaxen brood walked across the home's verdant front yard to a gleaming minivan in the driveway. *These are not my people,* Mia thought.

"The light changed," Jamie said.

"Right, sorry."

The two drove along in silence for another mile. "Left at that mailbox," Jamie said.

Mia made the left and they bumped along a hard-packed dirt road. Jamie pointed to a stately home with white columns and black shutters. "There. That's it."

She pulled into the home's circular driveway and parked next to an older-model Jaguar. She and Jamie got out of the car and headed up the stone front steps. Mia was about to ring the doorbell when the front door opened, revealing a distinguished-looking man who appeared to be in his late seventies. He was dressed in boat shoes, perfectly pressed chino slacks and a crisp white button-down shirt. A tan and a sea of creases that spoke of much time spent outdoors decorated his face. Overall, the man exuded an overall glow of health and self-confidence. "Hullo. I heard you pull up out front."

He said this with a British accent. Mia had watched *Downton Abbey* enough times to know his accent was what they called "upper crust." *Now here's a guy who fits in here,* she thought. "You must be Mr. Hartley," she said.

"Hugo, please. Come in." He ushered them into a capacious center hall decorated with Early American antiques. "I've got tea and pastries in the morning room."

Hartley led them through the living room, dining room and kitchen, each decorated to perfection. "Your home is stunning," Mia said.

"Unbelievable," Jamie added. Mia could tell he was picturing himself living there.

"My late wife had marvelous taste. In fact, she dabbled in interior design. Here we go." They were in a glass conservatory off the kitchen. A silver tea set and china plate of pastries sat on a wrought-iron table. Hartley distributed plates. "Dig in, as you Americans like to say." Mia placed a few petites fours on a plate and Jamie helped himself to a selection of sweets while Hartley poured them tea. "So," he said, "you want to know about that bitch Tina Iles."

Mia almost dropped the cup of hot tea the retired pilot had handed her. Jamie choked on the pastry he'd bitten into. "Yes," Mia managed to say. "If you don't mind sharing whatever you think might help us find her killer."

"Mind? My dear, nothing would make me happier than to identify whoever did the deed, and reward them with a hearty clap on the back." Jamie shot Mia a furtive "Is this guy crazy?" glance. She gave her head a tiny shake to indicate Hartley wasn't. "I was a pilot for Odyssey Airlines when Tina was a flight attendant. She was flirtatious, I was full of myself, and one thing led to another. We hurtled into an affair. I must say the sex is the only positive memory I have of the whole ordeal."

Mia heard Jamie mutter "TMI" and kicked his ankle under the table. He flinched but shut up.

"Little did I know that my inamorata was sneaking illicit prescription pain pills into my carry-on luggage, which she'd secretly remove when we met at a hotel for our assignation."

Hartley took a sip of his tea. Mia noticed he crooked his pinky finger as he drank, so she did the same. "Tina assumed no one would suspect a pilot of my stature to be a drug mule," Hartley said. "That plan went south when a random search of employee's luggage yielded her stash— in *my* luggage. I insisted I knew nothing about the pills and demanded the bottles be dusted for prints. Mine weren't on any of them, needless to say. Since the airline couldn't prove I was involved, they allowed me to retire rather than fire me. Oh, how I wanted to point every single finger at Tina, but I was afraid she might accuse me of sexual harassment. My job ended and my marriage broke up. Fortune smiled upon me when I met Marissa, my late second wife, at a seniors' singles mixer. The last ten years were the happiest of my life." Grief clouded the pilot's face for a moment, then he regained self-control. "When I read in the paper that Tina was dead, I celebrated. I'm still celebrating." Hartley pulled a towel off a standing wine bucket behind him, revealing a bottle of champagne on ice. He removed the bottle from the bucket and popped the cork. "Champagne, my friends?"

Mia and Jamie both declined. "Do you know anything about the robbery at the Miller Art Collection?" Mia asked.

"I'm afraid not. That came after the biggest mistake of my life."

Mia and Jamie finished their tea and the pilot offered them a tour of his garden, which Jamie instantly jumped on. Half off the large property was a riot of flowers emulating an English country garden. The other half was arranged in a graph of half a dozen vegetable beds. "The soil here is rocky but once you extricate the stones, it's rich."

"I can see that," Jamie said with enthusiasm. "Your tomatoes are awesome."

"Thank you. I'll give you some to take with you."

"Between them and Nonna's potatoes, you've got dinner," Mia joked to Jamie.

"Uh huh," he said, distracted by the garden's wonders. "Are you growing snap peas? I love them."

By the time they left Hartley's company, Mia and Jamie were weighed down with bags of the retired pilot's homegrown produce. "You can drive," Jamie said. "I want to take pictures of everything to send to Mads."

Jamie focused on trying to photograph the vegetables as they bumped down the uneven dirt road onto the main road. "What did you think of Hartley?" Mia asked after a while.

"I think he's got the life."

Mia managed not to release an annoyed grunt, although she did roll her eyes. "I mean, as a suspect."

"If I was trying to hide the fact that I killed someone, celebrating by offering champagne to strangers is a pretty odd move," Jamie said. "This zucchini is huge. I need to use the panoramic setting on my phone."

"It is strange. The champagne, not the zucchini, although that thing is scary-big. But Hartley could also be one of those people who thinks he had every right to knock someone off, isn't sorry, but will wait until the police figure it out and come to him."

Jamie snapped a burst of zucchini pictures. "Talk about a small sub-group of people."

"Smuggling drugs, artwork . . . that Tina was a busy

lady. I wonder if Ron knows exactly how busy she was. She came into their relationship with a lot of money for a former flight attendant. But I think he was too in love to ask questions. He's kind of a face value guy in general. Ah!" Mia swerved as a squirrel darted across the car's path.

"Whoa." Jamie once again grabbed the dashboard. The tomatoes he was trying to photograph rolled into the car floor. "Careful."

"There was a squirrel. I didn't want to hit it."

"I love animals, too. But safety first, Mia. Sometimes it's either us—"

A chipmunk scurried into the middle of the road and froze. Mia swerved to the left of the tiny animal with a screech of tires. She felt herself losing control of the car and fought to regain it. She turned the wheel to the right, but over-corrected. The beater sedan flew into a ditch next to the side of the road, half in and half out of it, the wheels on the car's left side spinning helplessly several feet of the ground. Jamie's entire vegetable stash lay scattered at his feet.

"—or them."

CHAPTER 15

"I'm so, so, so, sorry," Mia repeated to Jamie while they sat on the curb outside a service station a few hours later, waiting for Jamie's older brother, Donny Junior, to retrieve them. Jamie's car had been towed and declared a total loss.

"For the millionth time, it's okay. You're a new driver. I stopped paying attention to take pictures of vegetables. This is on me."

A brand-new black Cadillac Escalade with tinted windows pulled up in front of them. The driver's window lowered, and Donny Junior stuck his head out. "Howdy, idiots. Get in the car."

Mia and Jamie exchanged a look. They picked up their bags of vegetables and climbed into the SUV, Jamie in the front, Mia in the back. "This car is ridiculous," Jamie said to Donny. "You look like an airport limo driver."

Donny Junior turned off the engine and folded his arms in front of his chest. "You want a ride back to Astoria or you wanna walk?"

Jamie slunk in his seat and muttered an apology. Mia felt terrible for him. "Thank you so much, Donny. This is all my fault. Jamie was being such a good friend, teaching me how to drive, coming all the way to Connecticut with me. I'll pay for the car."

Donny waved a hand to dismiss the offer and began to drive. "Don't worry about it. The car was a junker we picked up at a repo lot. And hearing Dad say a few choice words about his favorite son for a change, I woulda paid *you* for that."

Jamie slumped down even further in his seat.

Donny put on a satellite radio station and spent the two-hour-thanks-to-traffic drive home singing along to eighties hits when he wasn't yanking his little brother's chain. "Dutch oven!" he yelled at one point after passing gas in the sealed-up vehicle.

"Real mature," Mia muttered under her breath. The thirty-four-year-old, who was belting out "Livin' on a Prayer," didn't hear her.

It was early evening by the time the Boldano brothers dropped Mia off in front of Belle View. "I think it's best if I take a break from driving lessons for a while," Mia said to Jamie as she exited the SUV.

"Maybe longer than a while," was Jamie's quick response. "We've got a great transit system in New York. And there are cabs, rideshares. Who says you even need to learn how to drive?"

"Yeah. Good point."

Disheartened, Mia closed the car door. "See ya 'round, Mia," Donny Junior said. He fixed his brother with a smug smile. "I got instructions from Dad to bring you to him. He wants to have a 'little talk' with you." He elbowed an unhappy Jamie in the ribs. "Your turn to get torn a new one, bruh."

Mia heard Jamie groan as his brother chortled and peeled out of the parking lot. She pressed a number into her phone, using her free hand to pull open one side of the heavy glass double doors to the catering hall. The call went to voicemail, so Mia left a message for Donny Boldano Senior explaining exactly what happened, taking full responsibility for the accident, and hopefully exonerating Jamie.

As she headed to her office, Mia glanced into the Marina Ballroom, where the Women of Orsogna Club was scheduled for their monthly get-together. Her eyes widened. She froze for a second and then walked backward to making sure she wasn't seeing things. An opera singer had been booked by the club as their entertainment. She was nowhere to be seen. Instead, Ravello, wearing a black plastic apron that covered him from neck to knees, presided over a long table covered with flowers. "When you're starting out as a floral display artist, it's best to choose a limited color palette," he explained to the group of around thirty women, who were an attentive audience. "Either one or two colors." He gestured to the array of flowers on the table. "For our lesson today, you've got a choice of using pink or white as your primary color. Green will be the secondary color for everyone. Each table is going to work together to create an arrangement that we'll donate to the Astoria Senior Center."

A woman held up her hand. "What we will use for vases?"

Ravello held up an empty industrial-sized mayonnaise jar. "We have five condiment jars that were destined for the recycling bin. Instead, they'll be the perfect vessel for your creations. You can keep the labels on the jars to give your displays a countrified feeling or use this solvent to remove them for a more streamlined look." He held up a spray bottle of adhesive remover that Mia assumed he dug out of the bowels of a Belle View supply closet. "Divide yourselves into five groups of six and then come pick out your flowers."

The women chattered among themselves with enthusiasm as they gathered up armfuls of lilies, hydrangeas, carnations, snapdragons, and an assortment of greenery. Ravello saw Mia and came to her. "I pulled this one out of my kiester," he said to her sotto voce.

"I'm impressed. You sound like a floral design expert. 'Perfect vessel for your creations.' Nice, Dad. But what the heck happened? Where's the singer?"

"Laryngitis. Benjy tried to cover with his comedy act."

"Oh, boy. That must've gone over well."

"It could've been worse."

"Compared to Cammie's reaction to his act, that's high praise."

"But he's only got about ten minutes of material. None of it great. Luckily, Lin called in some favors with her suppliers and got me all this." Ravello motioned to buckets of flowers.

"Pays to have a girlfriend in the floral business."

Ravello gave a vigorous nod. "How was your trip to Connecticut?"

"Informative."

Mia relayed what she'd learned from Hugo Hartley. Ravello raised an eyebrow. "Sounds like a man with a motive. But why now? If he was gonna get revenge, you think he would've done it years ago."

"Exactly. Unless something came up that we don't know about yet. I'll clue Pete in on what we found out. He can do some digging into Hartley's recent activities, if I can get him to stop looking for ways to pin Tina's murder on Ron." Mia's stomach growled. She hadn't had anything to eat since the pastries at the retired pilot's house. "I'm starving. I'm gonna go to the kitchen and scrounge around for leftovers."

"*Si, figlia mia.* I better get back to the ladies. They went through a lotta wine tonight." Ravello cast a critical eye at a lopsided arrangement being futzed with by a nearby group of giggling women who were clearly inebriated. He plastered on a smile. "*Bellissima*, ladies. Let me make a few small adjustments."

Ravello left to salvage the arrangement and Mia made her way to the catering hall kitchen. She found an unhappy Guadalupe wiping down the prep station. "Uh oh," Mia said. "The look on your face is the kind of look I'm guessing you had after an IED went off back in Iraq."

"I would've welcomed a homemade bomb tonight," the former Army cook grumbled.

"Whatever went wrong, the ladies seem okay now." Mia opened the refrigerator to hunt for leftovers. She pulled out a container filled with a meat sauce and sniffed it. "Why does this smell like taco meat?"

"Because that's what it is."

"I thought the Orsogna ladies always ordered Italian food."

"They do and they did. But it's hard to make lasagna without lasagna noodles." Guadalupe glowered in the direction of Cammie and Benjy's office.

Mia, appetite gone, put the container back in the refrigerator. "They weren't ordered? That's a rhetorical question. Of course they weren't. If they had been, I'd be eating leftover lasagna right now." She sighed. "The time has come, Lupe. The time has come."

Guadalupe brightened. "You gonna give the kid the ax? Can I be there?"

"No, you cannot," Mia said, her tone reproachful. "Annoying as Benjy is, there's no pleasure in this. And we better pray it doesn't tick off his grandfather."

"If you want my opinion, Grandpa knows exactly what that kid's about. That's why he palmed him off on us."

"Is Benjy still here?"

"Far as I know. I was all set to yell at him after he did that act of his for the Italian ladies, but he said he needed to make some notes about his performance while they were fresh in his head." Guadalupe brandished a metal spatula. "I'll tell ya what *I'd* like to get fresh in his head."

Mia made a settle-down motion with her hands. "Take a breather. I'll handle this."

She left the kitchen to find Benjy, checking out the Marina Ballroom on her way. Ravello was engrossed in creating his own flower arrangement, so rather than run what she was about to do by him, she decided to act now and explain later. This was a sure case of the old saying that it was better to beg forgiveness than ask permission.

Mia heard typing coming from Cammie's office. She rapped on the door to alert Benjy, then opened it. He lifted a hand from the keyboard to wave hello. "I came up with a tagline for my act. 'Comedy you can't refuse.' Like the line from *The Godfather* movies. It never gets old."

"It's old, Benjy. Like, almost fifty years old. Although we have been known to use it here at Belle View ourselves." Mia no longer had the patience to be polite. "This job isn't working out. I'm gonna have to let you go."

Benjy pushed away from the desk and hung his head. "I know. Thanks for letting me stay this long."

Mia's annoyance evaporated. She felt sorry for Benjy who, despite his desire to become a comedian, struck her as a lost soul. "I'm sorry it didn't work out."

"You tried," he said. "I appreciate that. I tried, too. But . . ." he gave a small shrug and didn't bother finishing the sentence. "If it helps, I'll tell Nonno you didn't fire me, I quit."

"That would help," Mia said, relieved.

Benjy opened a desk drawer and retrieved a notebook and some odds and ends. He pulled his backpack out from under the desk and began packing up. "I wish I could figure out what I wanna do with my life. Nobody but me thinks I should be in comedy."

"From what I've read, it takes years to put together a good act," Mia said. "If you're passionate about doing that, give it time. But whatever support job you get, make sure you like it more than this one."

"Yeah. I guess." Benjy zipped his backpack shut and stood up. A scrap of paper fell from the desk and Mia retrieved it. What she saw surprised her. Benjy had doodled a cartoon strip of mobbed-up jungle animals. The bubble over a mobbed-up lion read, "I'm not lion to you." He was saying this to a pretty tiger who was rolling her eyes and closely resembled Mia. Benjy looked stricken. "You're not supposed to see that."

He reached for the paper, but Mia held on to it. "Did you draw this?"

Benjy blushed. "Yes," he said, mortified.

"Did you draw a lot of them?" Benjy, unable to look Mia in the eye, cast a glance downward and nodded. "Benjy, this is adorable. And funny."

Benjy lifted his head. "Really?"

"Yeah, really. Can I see some others?"

"Sure."

Benjy unzipped his backpack and pulled out a notebook. He handed it to Mia, who thumbed through it. The book was filled with cartoon strips featuring the same anthropomorphic cast of animal characters. Lines that were groaners in Benjy's act were endearing coming from a goombah hippo or a gazelle drawn like something out of *The Real Wives of the Serengeti Plain*. "Benjy, you have a talent for this. I know someone who might be interested in your work. Would you be cool with me checking it out?"

"Seriously? Uh, *yeah*."

The twentysomething's normally hangdog expression disappeared, replaced by a beaming grin. It was the first time Mia had seen him radiate anything besides misery and boredom. She photographed several strips with her phone and forwarded them to Teri Fuoco with this message: **How would you like to buy a cartoon strip for the Tri Trib that's drawn by Benjy Tutera of the Tutera Family?**

The response was an instant **YES!!!!!!!**

She showed this to Benjy. "Here's the response."

The budding cartoonist beamed. "Best. News. *Ever*."

"I'll forward Teri's contact info."

"I'll call her first thing in the morning." Benjy grabbed one of Mia's hands and shook it vigorously with both of his. "Thanks, man. You're awesome. I owe you."

"You don't owe me anything," Mia said. "Although I wouldn't mind a signed copy of your first published cartoon."

"Wait until I tell Nonno. He'll be so happy he may cry."

Mia thought of Vito Tutera's fruitless attempts to launch his grandson. "I'll bet he does."

She followed Benjy as he bounded out of the office into the foyer, almost colliding with Ravello, who was carrying a giant floral arrangement. "Bye, Mr. Carina. Thanks for letting me work here and good luck."

Benjy practically skipped through Belle View's front doors. Ravello placed the arrangement on the foyer's gilded console table. "I'm guessing there's a story here but I'm tired, he looked happy, so let's save it for tomorrow."

"Let's just say I averted an inter-Family war and found Benjy a possible career. I'll help you clean up the ballroom."

"Nothing there that can't wait until tomorrow."

"That also goes for the hunt for Benjy's replacement. No more 'connections.' We'll go the usual route and post to employment websites."

"*Si, bella.*" Ravello motioned to the door. "*Allora, andiamo.* I'll drive you home."

The two started toward the parking lot. Mia's cell phone rang. She saw the caller was Teri Fuoco. Usually she declined the pesky reporter's calls but since Teri had just done her a favor, Mia answered, albeit grudgingly. "Thanks for giving Benjy Tutera a shot. What's up?"

"I'm calling *you* with thanks. Tutera's cartoons are genuinely adorbs and his being connected on top of that'll make me a hero with my publisher."

"You're welcome."

Mia went to sign off but heard Teri yelling, *"Don't hang up, I have news."* She held the phone back up to her ear. "News? Like, what?"

"I'm repaying you for the Tutera get with a little intel I pulled out of my law enforcement sources. You know that art dealer who was at your friend's shower? Justine Cadeau?"

"Yeah? Did the police find her?"

"You could say that. She just turned up dead. In Switzerland."

CHAPTER 16

"Dead?" Mia repeated, stunned. "How? What happened? Do you know anything else?"

Ravello tugged at Mia's sleeve. "What? Who's dead? What's going on?"

Mia motioned for her father to be quiet. She listened to Teri, who said, "That's all I know. Since it's on international soil and may or may not be crime-related, Interpol's involved, and they are super tight-lipped."

"If you hear anything else," Mia said, "can you let me know?"

"Will do. And when you see Evans, tell him I have the book. He'll know what I'm talking about."

Teri signed off. Ravello tugged on Mia's sleeve again. "Who died? What happened?"

"Jeez, Dad, chill. You're like a gossipy tween." Father

and daughter got into Ravello's Lincoln Continental. "Teri called with news about Justine Cadeau, the art dealer at Nicole's shower who it turns out that nobody knew. You know how I went to talk to her at her gallery in Manhattan, but she'd disappeared? They found her dead in Switzerland."

"*Marone.*" Ravello made the sign of the cross.

"Teri didn't have any more information than that. At least Ron can't be a suspect in this case, which is a little good news. As soon as I get home, I'm gonna see if I can find out anything about it online."

But when Mia got home, her internet search was delayed by an unwelcome event. It was almost nine P.M. Since Elisabetta's target bedtime was usually eight P.M., she was surprised to find her grandmother and neighbor Philip sitting at the kitchen table, deep in conversation. Elisabetta wore a dress, not her go-to apparel of velour tracksuit, and her best wig. "Hi. Were you guys at another wake?"

Elisabetta, a sober expression on her face, shook her head. "We were about to leave for one, but Minnie called me with bad news. The man from Versailles who got hit on the head got all of his memory back. He said Ron tried to kill him."

"The charge against your friend was upped to attempted murder," Philip said.

"Oh, no." Mia fell into the chair across from Elisabetta. "He's lying, I know he is. Did Minnie call Mickey Bauer? He's our lawyer," she added for Philip's benefit.

"Your grandmother told me. Mr. Bauer left today for a three-week river cruise of France's chateau region."

Mia pursed her lips. "Paid for by our retainers."

"In my pre-parent life, I was a partner in a law firm," Philip said. "I still take on cases sometimes. Mostly pro bono. Like this one."

Elisabetta clutched his hands in hers. "He's a saint, he is. God made you the way he made you, but oh, if you liked girls . . ." She couldn't finish the sentence, much to Mia's relief.

"Back to Ron," Philip, eager to change the subject, said. "After Minnie called Lizzie—"

"Whoa," Mia said. "She lets you call her Lizzie? She hates that name."

Elisabetta mimed a lip zip to her granddaughter. "Messina, *silenzio*."

"Sorry. Philip, you were saying?"

"After Minnie called Lizzie, Lizzie called me in a panic. Thanks to a 1991 State Supreme Court ruling that mandated a twenty-four-hour deadline for all arraignments, I was able to get Ron's case handled tonight."

"That's how good he is," Elisabetta said. "Mickey made poor Ron rot in jail for a night."

"I got lucky," Philip, all modesty, said. "But they upped Ron's bail to five hundred thousand dollars."

Mia held a hand to her heart. "*Marone mia.*"

"He posted ten percent and put his restaurant up as collateral, so he's out on bail. But he had to surrender his passport and wear an ankle monitor."

Mia digested this. "Now that we're at ankle monitor," she said, "I don't think we can keep what's going on from Nicole anymore."

"She knows," Elisabetta said. "Linda had Ian tell her."

Philip sighed. "So sad. *Così triste.*" He turned to Elisabetta. "Finn insists we speak only in Italian for an hour every day. He's such a *pisane* wannabe. How's my accent?"

Elisabetta made the half-and-half gesture with her hand. "We'll work on it."

Mia retreated to her apartment, where Doorstop greeted her with a demanding meow. She gave him a few tiny treats, then texted Ian to see how Nicole was handling the news about her father. Seconds later, her cell phone rang. "My father didn't do this," Nicole wept.

"I know, sweetie."

"They're going to try and say he killed Tina, too."

"They can't bring a case against him without proof, and they have squat."

"Oh, Mia. This is the worst time of my life and it should be the best."

Mia's heart broke for her friend. "Honey, you need to stay calm and focus on that precious baby of yours. Trust me, people who love you are doing everything they can to find out who's really responsible for what happened."

"Like you."

"Like me."

Nicole ended the call with a stream of thanks. The instant she signed off, Mia grabbed her laptop and booted it up. "That dirtbag Garvalos is totally full of it," she said to Doorstop as she deposited herself on the bed. "While the police are figuring that out, we're gonna follow some actual leads."

Mia let Pizzazz out of her cage. The parakeet perched on her shoulder as she typed "Justine Cadeau Switzerland" into the search bar on her laptop. No links to news about the art dealer's death appeared on the screen. Mia assumed Teri was right and Interpol was withholding in-

formation on it. "She was either murdered or they must
have found a connection to the art theft," she mused to
Pizzazz, who pecked at her shoulder. "Otherwise, why
would they care?" Mia canceled the Justine Cadeau
search and instead sent Pete Dianopolis an email detail-
ing what she'd learned from Hugo Hartley about Tina's
drug trafficking ruse. She added a "you probably already
know this" at the end of the email with the news of
Cadeau's death. With Ron on top of the attempted mur-
der/possible murderer suspect leaderboard, she didn't
want to risk insulting the detective. She got a quick response back from Pete. It was a thumbs-up emoji, which
she took as a positive sign. He followed this with a question: "Is Cammie working tomorrow?" Mia wrote back
that she hoped so, considering Benjy was gone, but she
couldn't predict anything Cammie might or might not do.
To which Pete replied, "TELL ME ABOUT IT!"

Doorstop yawned, inspiring a yawn from Mia. The
day had been a long, fraught one. She placed Pizzazz
back in her cage and covered it for nighttime. Then she
changed into a large sleep tee and crawled under the covers. Doorstop curled up in the crook of her back. Mia
loved feeling him snuggled up against her. "You're my
support animal, buddy. Did you know that? You and Pizzazz." Mia stroked the cat's orange-gold fur. "So much
happened today. So much. I can't believe I'm only back
from Connecticut about five hours. It feels like I was
there weeks ago. It's pretty, that's for sure. Could you see
us living there?" Doorstop responded with a light snore.
"I know. Neither can I. Why is that? It's quiet. It's more
than pretty, it's gorgeous. What's wrong with me? I could
learn to love it, I guess. I didn't like Florida when I first

got there. Actually, I didn't like it much better when I left. But that was more about the whole Adam disappearing thing and me being a suspect."

"Mia!" Elisabetta called from the foot of the stairs. "I hear you talking to someone. Who's up there with you?"

"No one, Nonna. I'm talking to Doorstop."

"*Marone.* You're turning into one of those crazy cat ladies. You need a boyfriend. *Buona notte.*"

" 'Night." Mia turned off the light on her nightstand. "I don't need a boyfriend. I'm doing great on my own. Then again . . . I'm still talking to a cat."

In the morning, Mia did another search for details about Justine Cadeau's death and again found nothing. She showered and readied for work, then carried a yogurt downstairs, where she found her grandmother using a sturdy pasta machine clamped to the dinette table to crank out homemade fettuccine. "Dinner tonight?" Mia asked.

"*Sì,* with meatballs I'll make later."

Mia opened a drawer and took out a spoon. She removed the lid of her yogurt and stirred the contents. "You're in your housecoat. No funerals this morning?"

"No," Elisabetta said with a sigh. "The way things are going, poor Gugliemo's gonna be barefoot the rest of his life."

"Technically, his life's over. You mean for eternity."

"That sounds even worse."

Mia finished her yogurt, rinsed out the container, and placed it in Elisabetta's small recycle bin. She bent down and kissed her grandmother on both cheeks. "I gotta get going. I'm biking to work today."

"I'm sorry things didn't work out with Jamie—"

Mia, defensive, interrupted her grandmother. "He's got a girlfriend, Nonna. I'd never interfere with that."

Elisabetta shot her a look. "I was gonna say, *with Jamie and the driving.*"

"Oh."

"Posi can teach you when he gets out. That's not gonna be too long from now."

"I don't think anyone can teach me," Mia said, resigned. "The universe has sent that message in a big way."

The bike ride to Belle View proved rejuvenating. The day dawned cooler than previous days, which Mia hoped was a harbinger of fall weather. She noticed Evans's motorcycle in the Belle View parking lot, which reminded her of the message Teri requested she pass on to him. Mia locked up her bike and made her way to the catering hall kitchen, where Evans was washing out a mixing bowl. Mia inhaled the scent in the air, which was a delicious blend of melted butter and chocolate. "Whatever you're making, I think I gained weight just smelling it."

Evans smiled. He wiped his hands on a dish towel. "Flourless chocolate cake. That's the recipe I wanted to try for the bar mitzvah. I already made one. Here."

The chef cut a slice from a cake cooling on the counter, plated it, and handed it to Mia with a fork. She took a bite and swooned. "*Marone. Delizioso.* The Wittenbergs are gonna love it." She cut off a larger forkful. "I talked to Teri Fuoco last night. She wanted me to tell you that she has the book. She said you'd know what she's talking about."

"Yeah. Her grandmother's from Malta and Teri's gonna lend me the journal where she wrote down all her recipes. Guadalupe and me are talking about putting together menus from countries whose cuisine we don't get to try too often. She'd do appetizers and the main dishes. I'd do desserts and drinks. Maybe put it out to the community as a monthly event or something."

"I love this," Mia said, instantly warming to the idea. "We can partner with local merchants who sell stuff from those countries, like wine and crafts. They can publicize the dinners to their customers."

"Great." Evans tended toward the monosyllabic, but his enthusiastic expression spoke volumes.

But I did want to mention one thing." Mia grew sober. "Be careful with Teri. She seems to have a crush on you—"

"No *seems* about it. It's for realz." Evans couldn't help preening a bit.

"Even so. My take on her is that she's a reporter first and a woman second. Which means that crush or not, her number one goal would be to wheedle dirt on us from you. We kind of have a truce but she's still the enemy."

"I know." Evans cut another slice of cake and placed it on Mia's plate. She didn't stop him. "My plan is to make the crush work for us. You know, feed her the right dirt when we need to and wrong dirt when we need to. It's like that saying, keep your friends close and your enemies closer."

Mia polished off her second slice of cake. "Wow, thanks. That's some sneaky thinking right there, and I like it. But don't get too close, if you know what I mean. When it comes to taking one for the team, there's only so far you should have to go."

"Noted, boss," Evans said with a grin.

Mia hurried to her office before she succumbed to the urge for a third piece of Evans's cake. Wary of her father's hiring practices after the Benjy debacle, she listed the job opening on a handful of websites. That task accomplished, she tried another search for intel on Justine Cadeau, which led to yet another a dead end. She decamped for the Marina Ballroom to finish cleaning up the flower detritus left over from the previous night's event.

She found her father in the ballroom corralling errant flowers into a bucket filled with water. "I did a general sweep of the place already," he said. "Nothing left behind."

"I'll pull the tablecloths and napkins." Mia began removing the yellow linens, placing them in a pile in the center of the room. "Which reminds me, I haven't had a chance to share what I think is going on at Versailles."

"Anything that might put it out of business?" Ravello didn't bother to try hiding this under the guise of a joke.

"Could be." She detailed her suspicions about the Quality Control van being used for illegal transport, once again editing out the part where the van tried to run her down. Ravello was less over-protective than the average Italian father, but he was still an Italian father. "I'm sure it ties in with the attack on Garvalos, and maybe even Tina's murder. Although after my meeting with Hugo Hartley, I thought that might have more to do with the one-woman drug smuggling operation she had going."

"There's no such thing as a one-person drug operation," Ravello said as he absent-mindedly arranged the leftover flowers. "If you're a courier, there's got to be someone at each end of the chain. A supplier and a buyer."

Mia stopped what she was doing and stared at her father. "Do I want to know how you know this?"

"*Figlia mia*, please," Ravello said, wounded. "I know because it's simply common sense. The same protocol would apply to the movement of any goods. Take these tablecloths and napkins." He motioned to the yellow mound. "Let's say you wanted to smuggle them. You'd get them from a supplier, say, a corrupt company employee. You'd then sell them to a connection looking to buy black market linens, and list them as 'lost' or 'damaged; replace' on the inventory list. I'll be honest, I know that part because back in the day, the Family had a couple of fingers in the linen supply business."

"Way to make the rentals for the Women's Club of Orsogna sound sketchy." Mia yanked a tablecloth and sent it flying onto the pile. "But you're right. That's why I know something's going on at Versailles, I don't care if Pete keeps dismissing it. Too much laundry funny business." She faced her father. "None of it related to us or the Family, *corretto?*'

"*Corretto.*" Ravello put one hand on his heart and held up the other. "I swear."

"*Va bene.* Alright then." Mia resumed gathering linens to be cleaned. "Given what you just laid out, that adds two more suspects to the list, the drug supplier and buyer. Ron said he and Tina went back and forth to Greece a lot. Maybe she took up her old sideline and brought Garvalos and his chef, Sandeep, into it to help smuggle the drugs, which would explain the Versailles connection."

"Possible, but I doubt it," Ravello said. "Remember, she was running that scam before 9/11. Much, much harder to transport anything internationally now, even if you work for an airline. Remember the flight attendant who got busted a couple of years ago for trying to smuggle cocaine in her carry-on luggage?"

Mia nodded. "If they're not smuggling drugs, they could be moving stolen artwork, at least domestically. Which brings us back to *Cow and Woman.*"

"Dumb name for an ugly painting."

"But one worth a ton o' money. I can't prove it, but it's obvious Justine Cadeau crashed the shower to drop off that painting and send a message to Tina. And now she's dead. Tina didn't know her. I could tell that. Justine was a lot younger, like about my age. But there *has* to be some connection between them. They're both dead under what the police would call mysterious circumstances."

"Any updates on what happened to this Justine in Switzerland? Like, how she died?"

"Internet radio silence. It's aggravating."

"Our city does have a pretty crack police department, sweetheart. I should know. They nailed me enough times."

"I get it, I should leave the detective work to NYPD. But I can't. I'm too close to this."

Ravello eyed his daughter with affection, but also concern. "You need more to do than work here and go home."

Mia dumped the last armful of linens on the pile. "You too with the *you need a boyfriend*?"

"Did I say that? I did not. But you need something else in your life. What that might be is up to you." Ravello added the last flower to his impromptu arrangement. "Although a few dates and maybe even a relationship wouldn't be the worst thing in the world."

Mia released an exasperated exclamation and marched out of the ballroom to her office. She slammed the door shut. Her cell rang. "What?" she snapped into the phone.

The caller was Teri. "Hello to you, too. I was gonna give you some fresh intel on Justine Cadeau but forget it."

"No, wait! I'm sorry." Mia rubbed the bridge of her

nose. Needing to vent, she blurted, "I'm not having a great day. Everyone's pressuring me to date and I'm sick of it."

"Hah! Been there. I tried to get my mother off my back by telling her I was gay. You know what she said? *So, bring home a woman.* I was like, *seriously? Now you're suddenly politically correct?*" Mia had to laugh at this. "Just keep doing you. When they get that you're happy with the life you're living and don't need a boyfriend or husband to define you, they'll back off. Or maybe not. They're Italian."

"Thanks. I hate to admit it, but that's good advice. And I'm glad to know I'm not alone."

"Hey, look at us. We had a conversation like we're friends."

Mia stiffened. She did a one-eighty back to professional mode. "You called with news about Justine. What is it?"

"Right, that. She died in a single-driver car accident. Went flying off the road somewhere in the Swiss Alps."

Mia pondered this development. "Interesting. Do the police think she was run off the road?"

"No one's sharing any theories. I'm waiting to get some pix of the crash site. When I do, I'll email them to you."

"That would be fantastic. And Teri—thank you."

"No worries."

Mia was about to end the call when she remembered her conversation with Evans. "Oh, I almost forgot. I gave Evans your message."

"You did?" Teri sounded girly and breathless. "Awesome. Did he say anything?"

Mia picked up on the hesitancy in the reporter's usually confident attitude. "He was excited. He's looking forward to making some of those recipes."

Mia swore she heard Teri jumping up and down. "Oh, that is so cool."

"So much for not needing a man to define you."

"I don't. But it's been a long time since I even had a hook-up. And it's fun to have a crush."

She signed off. Mia spent the rest of the workday checking her email for the pictures from the *Tri Trib* journalist and plowing through resumes for the retail manager position. All the candidates seemed to possess the necessary qualifications, but no one stood out. She created an online folder where she saved the resumes of the best potential candidates.

Mia was about to sign off when a pop-up on her screen indicated a message from Teri. Mia opened it. Attached were several photos of a European-model sportscar on its roof at the bottom of a ravine off a narrow two-lane road ringed by mountains which were so tall they had snow on their peaks, despite the fact it was August. Mia studied the photos from every angle. She blew them up and shrunk them. In the end, she gleaned nothing more than what Teri originally told her: Justine Cadeau met her end on a remote road in Switzerland. "Why were you there, Justine?" Mia murmured to the screen. "And where were you going?"

Mia closed the email and left her office. The silence indicated that she was the last employee still at Belle View, so she locked up the building and unlocked her bike. As she rode home, the photos of Justine's car accident haunted her. *Maybe I'm better off not driving,* she thought as she deftly negotiated her way around a large pothole.

Mia reached home. She dismounted the bike and parked it in the freestanding garage off the alley behind the house. She entered Elisabetta's kitchen through the back door and headed down the hall to her upstairs apartment. She passed Elisabetta, who was in her bedroom putting on gold earrings. Her grandmother was dressed in black head to toe. "Hi, Nonna. Going to a viewing?"

"Yes," Elisabetta said. "Go upstairs and put on a black dress. You're coming with me."

CHAPTER 17

Mia rubbed her brow and closed her eyes. Then she opened them. "Nonna, I love you beyond words but if you asked me for a list of two million things I'd like to do tonight, attend a stranger's viewing wouldn't be on it."

"Philip can't go. He's working on Ron's defense in case he needs one. No one else can go either. I went to another viewing this morning and got strange looks because I was alone. Like I was one of those old harpies who goes to funerals for kicks."

"No, you're going to wakes and funerals for a *sane* reason."

"I don't need sarcasm, *nipotina mia.*" Elisabetta finished putting on her earrings. "I need company. You know how I've been nagging you about going to church? There'll be a priest there tonight, so I'll count it as that."

"You will?" Mia asked, now intrigued.

"Yeah. For this week."

"And next."

"*Meh, dammi una pausa!*" Elisabetta protested. "Give me a break."

"And next," Mia repeated.

Elisabetta started to issue another protest, then threw her hands up in a gesture of surrender. "*Va bene.* Next week, too."

"*Va bene,*" Mia said. "So, who died?"

"Arturo Medaglia. He was ninety-seven and a *pisane* I knew from the church senior center. He liked the ladies and tried to make time with me once."

"Like, recently?" Mia, imagining a nonagenarian hitting on her octogenarian grandmother, couldn't keep the stupefaction from her voice.

"Yes, recently," Elisabetta said, insulted. "Young people like you think everything shuts down when people get old. Let me tell you, once they stuck a coupla stents and a pacemaker into Arturo, he got fresh with a lot of us. I wouldn't even be going to his visitation except word on the street is that it's an open casket."

"Yippee." Elisabetta shot her granddaughter a look. "Sorry," Mia said. "I'll go change."

Mia trudged upstairs. She'd yet to take her black dress to the cleaner, so she had to settle for black pants and a black silk V-neck tee shirt. She pulled her long, dark hair into a high ponytail and freshened her makeup. She headed back downstairs, where Elisabetta, holding a tote bag along with her purse, was waiting for her by the front door. "The cab is here," Elisabetta said. "*Andiamo.*"

As the cab drove through Astoria to the Lugano Funeral Home on Steinway Street, Elisabetta laid out her plan. "We'll take turns paying our respects. I'll go first.

Gugliemo's shoes are in here." She patted the tote bag. "When no one's looking, I'll drop one in the casket. Then I'll pass the bag to you, and you'll do the same. We need to do it right before they close the casket. We don't wanna give anyone time to look and go, hey, what are those shoes doing in there?"

"Honestly, Nonna, I don't think anyone does much lingering at these things. You kneel, you pray, and you make tracks."

"You never know these days. What if someone takes a selfie of themselves with Arturo?"

"Oh, dear lord," Mia said, appalled at the thought.

"They could see the shoes that way. They could be in the picture, like proof. Maybe go . . . what's it called, when something goes everywhere around the world?"

"Viral."

"*Si*, viral. It's a different world now, *cara mia*."

"You're not wrong there."

"We're almost at Lugano's. Put on a sad face."

The cab pulled up to the front of the Lugano Funeral Home, a nondescript, mid-century brick building wisely located between a flower shop and a home for the elderly. Mia paid the cab driver and helped Elisabetta out of the car. "You look more annoyed than sad," her grandmother said.

"Sorry." Mia made a sad face. "Better?"

"Now you look like someone grabbed the purse you wanted from the sales table. Think of something that would make you cry."

Mia forced herself to imagine Jamie living in Hugo Hartley's house in Connecticut. She pictured Madison, Jamie's girlfriend, pulling into the driveway and parking, then reaching into the back to remove an infant from a car

seat. A tear rolled down Mia's cheek as she sank into a
sad fantasy of herself alone and sobbing as she wrapped a
housewarming gift for the happy family.

"*Perfetto*," Elisabetta said. She rubbed her hands together. "Let's do this."

The two women walked into the funeral home lobby,
which was crowded with people paying their respects.
The minute they stepped inside, Mia and Elisabetta were
assailed by an overwhelming smell. The air wasn't perfumed with the blend of fragrances produced by Ravello's lovely floral arrangement. Instead, there was only
one note: lilies. "I've been to so many funerals lately, and
it's the same at all of them," Elisabetta said to Mia under
her breath. "This is what death smells like to me now.
When I go, promise me, no lilies."

"I promise."

Elisabetta eyeballed the attendees milling around the
lobby. "Let's split up and work the room. You know what,
there might be some single young men here."

"That would be a great story to tell our children.
'Mommy, how did you and Daddy meet?' 'Oh, honey, it's
such a sweet story. I was at a visitation for an old guy I'd
never met so we could send shoes in his casket up to
heaven for another old guy I never met, and your great-
grandmother told me to troll the room looking for
dates.'"

"*Hai una bocca per te, lo sai?*"

"Yeah, I know I got a mouth on me. But only when
pushed to it."

Mia and Elisabetta circled the lobby from opposite directions, maneuvering around the massive, space-clogging
floral displays so prevalent at Italian funerals. Mia's front
as a mourner was helped by the fact that she saw many

familiar faces in the crowd. She was welcomed as a fellow Perpetual Anguish parishioner. Mia avoided making eye contact with the parish priest, embarrassed that she didn't remember his name even though Elisabetta had introduced her to him several times. She felt guilty for using Mass as a negotiating tool with her grandmother and vowed to make it to church . . . eventually.

Her phone pinged a text. Mia checked and saw a message from Elisabetta: **It's go time.** She turned toward the room where the viewing was being held and bumped into another woman. "Sorry."

The woman turned around and Mia's heart sank. Standing in front of her was Alicia Medaglia Cohen, leader of her high school's mean-girl pack. Alicia, sleek-haired, rail-thin, and dressed in a stylish black wrap dress, gasped with baldly faked delight at the sight of Mia. "OMG!" Alicia threw her arms around Mia yet barely touched her, as if it was a mime routine. "I heard you were back in town. It's so good to see you."

"You too, Alicia," Mia lied. "How've you been?"

Alicia made the universal sign for crazy, twirling both fingers at the sides of her impeccably made-up face. "*Pazzo*. My husband's in finance in the city, so he works like a dog, poor man. Which leaves only me and the nanny with the twins. Luckily, she's a live-in—legal, of course, I think—so that helps. But with our babies starting private school this fall, and the boards I'm on and the boards he's on, it was like our lives were on steroids, so we splurged on a weekend place on the Vineyard. The Hamptons are so last millennium."

Mia knew whatever she said in response to this humblebrag would come out fully loaded, so she simply said, "Mm hm."

"Thank you for coming tonight." Done with lamenting about the trials and tribulations of her one-percent life, Alicia brought the conversation back to the vigil. "It means a lot to us."

Mia panicked. Alicia's "us" meant she was related to the deceased, but Mia had zero idea how. "I couldn't *not* come," she tap-danced. "Arturo was such a wonderful man. So beloved in the community." *Somebody help me out here.*

"Yes." Alicia extricated a tissue from a small black purse that Mia recognized as a top-of-the-line item from her obscenely expensive former Florida employer, Korri Designs. Alicia dabbed at her dry eyes. "Losing the patriarch of our family has been brutal."

Grandfather, that's it! But different last names. Must be on her mother's side.

"At least I got to say good-bye before he passed. *A dio, Prozio Arturo.*"

Great-uncle, not grandfather. Thank God I kept my trap shut. "Heaven is a better place for Arturo's arrival there," Mia said. She inwardly cringed at this ham-fisted response, but Alicia seemed to appreciate it, rewarding her with another faux hug.

"Thank you. So . . ." Alicia's tone did a one-eighty from lamenting to avaricious gossip. "I heard about all your troubles. Your husband disappearing in Florida, the murders at the place where you work . . ." Alicia placed a hand on Mia's arm. She made a *tsk tsk* sound and shook her head, doing her best to look sympathetic—and failing. "How are you holding up with all that?"

Mia made a fist and did a small air pump, mostly to remove her arm from Alicia's touch. "I'm doing so good. It hasn't been easy getting over my husband's presumed death." *I will never let her know that I hated the cheating S.O.B.* "And my dad and I did hit a rough patch at Belle View, but that's behind us now."

Alicia inhaled through her teeth, then blew out a breath. "I'm glad you think so."

"Oh, I know so. Belle View is rocking it."

"That's wonderful." Alicia put a modicum of effort into sounding supportive but couldn't keep a patronizing inflection from her voice. "We're having a memorial for *prozio* Arturo and thought about holding it at your place. But with all the drama there, we thought we'd better go with Versailles on the Park."

"Good choice. To be honest, we're so booked up we probably couldn't have fit you onto the schedule," Mia lied again. Her phone dinged. Elisabetta had texted a series of exclamation marks. "It's been great catching up, but I haven't paid my respects to Arturo yet."

"Go, go." Alicia made a shoo-ing gesture with her hands, then checked her smart watch. "This thing's almost done, thank God."

Mia made her escape from Alicia's company into the room where Arturo lay. Fortunately for her and Elisabetta, the room was empty save for a bored funeral director who Mia noticed was playing a game on his cell phone. Her grandmother approached Arturo. She kneeled, crossed herself, and mumbled a prayer. Then she stood up and surreptitiously glanced around the room. She made eye contact with Mia, nodded, pulled a men's shoe out of her tote bag, and dropped it into the coffin. Mia walked down the aisle between folding chairs. As she and Elisabetta passed each other, Elisabetta handed off the tote bag. Mia followed her grandmother's actions, kneeling, praying, standing, and dropping the second shoe in with

Arturo. She completed this just as people began filling
the room for the vigil's final prayer. The funeral director
snapped to attention, guiding the family to the front
rooms and indicating everyone else take a seat behind
them. He motioned to the priest. "Father Joseph, if you
will lead us in the prayers."

Mia repeated the priest's name in her head, hoping to
finally memorize it. Elisabetta pulled a rosary out of her
purse. Father Joseph took center stage in front of the coffin and began the service. Mia followed along with the
prayer's call and response, but her mind drifted. Alicia's
mention of Versailles brought to mind the image of the
laundry bins. They might be handy for local illicit transportation, but not beyond those geographic parameters.

"I'd like to invite Arturo's family to pay their last respects," Father Joseph said.

Elisabetta clutched Mia's arm. "If anyone sees the
shoes," she whispered. "We don't know anything."

The women waited, hearts thumping, while a seemingly endless line of the late man's relatives passed by the
coffin, stopping to kneel and pray. Elisabetta fingered her
rosary like it was a chain of worry beads. "What a bless-
ing that we Catholics kneel," Elisabetta whispered. "If
this was one of those religions where you stand and pray,
we'd be doomed." The line of mourners finally ended,
and the women exhaled their relief.

Father Joseph led the room in the Lord's Prayer. The
funeral director made his way up the aisle. "That's a
fancy-shmancy casket," Elisabetta said to Mia under her
breath. "Very roomy. Too bad Annette didn't know. We
could've fit a coupla pair of shoes in there for Gugliemo.
Maybe even some slippers."

The funeral director reached Arturo. He made the sign

of the cross, then pulled down the lid of the coffin, which rested on a gurney, and secured it. He and several men Mia assumed were Arturo's relatives slowly pushed the coffin down the center aisle toward the door toward the limo that would carry it to church for the morning's funeral service. Mia had a sudden vision. The stolen paintings and Tina's position as a flight attendant melded together into one clear picture in her mind with such force that it propelled her out of her seat.

"I know how they did it!"

CHAPTER 18

There was no way to explain Mia's outburst to the stunned mourners, so she and Elisabetta left the funeral home as fast as possible. "*Marone mia, che notte.*" Elisabetta blotted her forehead with the edge of her sweater. "What a night. You almost gave me a heart attack with that crazy scream of yours. They could've dropped me right into that casket with Arturo."

"*Mi dispiace*, Nonna, but I had a brainstorm about the Miller Collection paintings." Mia pulled out her cell phone and speed-dialed her father, who answered on the first ring. "Dad, hi, I know it's late, but can you see if Donny is free? I need to talk to you both."

"You want to talk to Donny?" Ravello sounded concerned about his daughter's sudden need to confab with the Family's *capo di tutti capi.*

"Yes. Don't worry, I just want to run something by

you. I wouldn't ask if it wasn't important. Trust me on this."

"Okay, I'll check with him. It's only a little before eight. Donny's a night owl. Gimme a minute." The phone went silent. Mia held on. A moment later, Ravello came back on the line. "He's free. Have the cab drop you at my house. We'll drive out to his place. But first, you have to stop at La Guli and pick up a cookie platter."

"*Meh,* of course," Mia said, insulted. "Arrive empty-handed? What kind of Italian do you think I am?"

"You spent a lotta time in Florida, *figlia mia,*" Ravello said with a chuckle. "I don't know how Italians do things there."

"It's not the same as here, for sure, but they know enough never to show up at a friend's house without a hostess gift."

Mia ended the call and directed the cab to the Family's favorite pastry shop. They arrived at the decades-old establishment moments before it closed for the evening. "Look who's here, two of my favorite people," Julie, the zaftig saleswoman behind the burnished wood counter, said. "What can I get ya?"

"I need a cookie platter," Mia said. "We're taking it out to the Island to Donny."

"Donny Boldano?" Julie said, impressed. "I better make it extra special."

Five minutes later, Mia and Elisabetta emerged with a massive pastry arrangement, plus a bag of free treats they shared with their happy cab driver.

"I don't know what's going on, but whatever it is, be careful," Elisabetta said as the cab dropped Mia off in front of Ravello's home, the house where she grew up that was only blocks from her grandmother.

"I always am, Nonna."

The cab drove off. Mia scurried up the front steps with the cookie assortment in her arms. Like her place, her father's was an unassuming two-family home. When she was a kid, Mia and Posi lived upstairs while their parents lived downstairs. Mia didn't mind the separation. It dimmed the noise from Ravello and Gia's operatic arguments. Since his annulment years prior, Ravello had lived alone. Mia wondered if there was a time in the future when her father would share the home with his girlfriend, Lin Yeung.

Mia rang the doorbell and Ravello opened the door. He was dressed in his version of off-the-clock: perfectly pressed gray trousers, a white polo shirt, and a black blazer. He took in Mia's outfit. "Your grandmother drag you to a viewing?" Mia nodded. "Gugliemo's shoes?"

"Mission accomplished."

She followed her father through the first floor, past the nondescript furniture and leather reclining couch, all of which dated back to her childhood. The only new addition was a large flat-screen TV. "We need to update this place."

"Why? Everything still works. All I need is my recliner, a remote, and a working microwave."

Mia shook her head. "Spoken like a confirmed bachelor."

They exited through the kitchen backdoor to the freestanding garage. Mia waited while her father pulled his Lincoln into the alley—she knew from experience there was no room for her to get in the car, which was a tight fit in the decades-old garage—and got in on the passenger side. Ravello pulled onto 21st Avenue and headed toward the Boldano family home.

Mia scribbled notes on a small pad in her purse while her father drove. "You wanna clue me in on what's going on?" Ravello asked.

"I'd rather wait and talk to you both at the same time."

Ravello acknowledged this and left Mia alone. A half hour later, they pulled up to a gated, white-columned home in Stony Harbor, a suburb on Long Island's South Shore. Mia glanced up from her notes. She took in the tree-lined street, with its lovely Colonial and Tudor homes. Her thoughts drifted to Jamie and she had a revelation. *Of course he wants to live in the suburbs. It's where he grew up. It's what he knows.* Life was sending Mia and Jamie in different directions. He had a girlfriend he cared about and a plan for his life that was news to Mia. It was time to stop daydreaming about a future with him. Yes, they dated in high school, but the relationship flamed out. Mia had always chalked it off to teenage immaturity. Now she began to wonder if there was a deeper reason the two never moved beyond a brief romance.

Ravello slid down his window and pressed a button on the security pad. After a short beep, he said, "Giant shrimp." The gate swung open.

"Giant shrimp? That's the code?"

"Donny Junior set it this time. He thinks it's funny. You know, because shrimp means small, but giant means big."

"Yeah, they call it an oxymoron. And Donny fits the moron half of that word."

Ravello drove onto the property, parking in front of the main house. Aurora Boldano, Donny's wife, waved from the front door. Aurora was in her late fifties. She was dressed simply in navy slacks and a light-blue, boat-necked top, and wore her dark hair, streaked with white, in a chignon bun. With her high cheekbones and aquiline nose, Aurora always reminded Mia of the elegant Italian women who browsed the upscale shops of Rome.

Ravello and Mia met her halfway up the steps. She gave them each a warm embrace. "*Ciao, amici.* What a wonderful surprise—dear friends dropping in on a quiet summer night." Aurora had come to America as a teenager and still bore a faint hint of an Italian accent.

"I hope we're not imposing, Mrs. B," Mia said.

Aurora, taller than Mia by half a foot, took Mia's chin in her hand and gazed down at her with affection. "*Bella*, you're like a daughter to us. A visit from you is always a joy and never an imposition." She kissed Mia on both cheeks, then motioned to her and Ravello. "*Vai.* Donny's waiting for you in his office."

Aurora, whose good taste was the envy of other Family wives, led them past the home's perfectly appointed dining and living rooms to Donny's office. The room was large and sumptuously paneled with burled cherry wood. The furniture and oriental rugs were all antique. Donny's large desk filled one-half of the room. The other half was set up for casual meetings, with a sofa and two wingback chairs encircling a traditionally styled coffee table. Mia placed the cookie assortment she'd bought next to an even larger one the Boldanos had laid out. An espresso set sat next to it, filling the room with the scent of strong, fresh coffee. "Donny will be here in a minute," Aurora said. "If you need anything, please let me know."

Aurora left, pulling the door shut behind her. Not even a minute later, the door opened, and Donny Boldano Senior came in. He was a few years older and a few inches shorter than his wife, but Donny owned any room he walked into with his confident, commanding presence.

"*Ciao, miei amici*," he said, accompanying the greeting with kisses on the cheeks of both his visitors. He sat in a large armchair facing the couch, where Ravello and Mia each took a seat. The three made small talk while Donny distributed demitasse cups of espresso and helped himself to cookies from the Carinas' offering. He bit down on a chewy *pignolo*, a popular southern Italian cookie made with almond paste and dotted with pine nuts. Donny smiled. "*La Guli?*"

"*Ma certo*," Ravello said. "Of course."

Donny held up the half-eaten cookie. "This is when I miss the old neighborhood." He finished it and clapped his hands to remove crumbs. "So, Mia. You called the meeting. Talk to us."

Mia pulled her notes out of the front pants pocket where she'd stuffed them. "This is about the Miller Art Collection heist."

Donny stiffened. "We had nothing to do with that."

"Oh, I know," Mia, eager to mollify him, said. "But I think I know how the thieves pulled it off. I wanted to run my idea by people who are in a position to tell me if I'm on to something or not."

"Because of our past experience," her father said, getting it but also making sure to emphasize the word *past*.

Mia glanced at her notes, then spoke to the men. "There was someone on the inside for sure. Who, I don't know, but someone who had a connection to Tina Karras. Tina was a flight attendant. This was right before 9/11, when everyone was way more loosey-goosey about security. Dad, remember that teen tour I took of Europe the summer before my senior year in high school? I brought home a carving knife I bought in Germany as a present for Nonna in my carry-on bag."

"I know that knife," Ravello said. "Your grandmother loves it."

"It was *molto* different in those days," Donny mused. "Sometimes I'd forget I had a pistol in my jacket pocket, or a knife tucked away in one of my socks. Nobody paid no never mind then. If an airport cop happened to notice the bulge in my jacket, I'd just get a scolding." He spoke with a sense of nostalgia.

"So," Mia continued, "you have a flight attendant who flew trans-Atlantic flights twenty years ago. You have stolen paintings. I was at a viewing tonight with my Nonna—"

"Did she get the shoes to Gugliemo?" Donny asked.

"You know about that?" Mia asked, astonished.

Her father nudged her. "Mia, it's Donny's business to know things. Don't insult him."

"*Mi dispiace*, sir," Mia said, apologetic.

Donny waved a hand. "*Fa niente*. It's nothing. Go on."

"Dropping the shoes inside the casket got me thinking. What if the robbers smuggled the artwork to Europe in a coffin that was in a plane's cargo area on a flight Tina worked? I did a little research. Collecting art is a big thing with Eastern European oligarchs. And it's way easier for them to buy on the black market over there than here."

Ravello and Donny considered this. Ravello spoke first. "You said that O'Dwyer guy only got the artwork as far as the beach, where it was transferred to men in masks. They could have loaded it into a coffin and driven it to JFK."

"And who says it was just men in masks?" Donny said. "Maybe one of them was this Tina broad."

"Good point," Ravello said. "They get to JFK, this Tina changes into her stewardess outfit—"

"Flight attendant, Dad. Stewardess is a dated word."

"Whatever. She changes, pretends that the family of the 'loved one' in the coffin has asked her to oversee delivery. She gets on the flight and as soon as it lands, she makes sure the artwork gets to the fence on the other side of the pond."

"It's a good plan," Donny said. "A very good plan."

"A great one," Ravello seconded.

The mobsters looked at each other. Mia caught the gleam in their eyes. "No, no," she cried out, waving her hands in front of their faces to snap them out of it. "Don't even think it, *Goodfellas*. It's a new world, remember? Security everywhere. So, *so* much security."

This brought the men out of their reverie. "Right. Fu—" Donny, who was old-fashioned enough not curse in the presence of ladies, caught himself. "Fu-lippin' security everywhere. You can't ring a doorbell without your face ending up on the news. Back to you, Mia. I think your father and I would agree that the plot you laid out makes a lot of sense. If anyone should know, it's guys like us."

"That's why I came to you. Also, because I could use some help. Mr. B, I know you have . . . connections . . . at JFK. This all happened twenty years ago, but can you find out what flight or flights Tina flew the day after the heist? And maybe how Castor Garvalos was involved? Because I know he was. What about his chef, Sandeep, who I saw transferring laundry bins to the fake linen service van?"

"Linens?"

"Yup. Linens." Mia wasn't surprised that Donny sparked to the Mob buzzword. As Ravello had mentioned while they were breaking down the Women of Orsogna event, Families often utilized linen service businesses for both legitimate and illegitimate gain, with the occasional capo jailed on a racketeering or extortion charge related to operations. She steered the conversation back on track. "And what was Justine Cadeau's part in this whole thing? She's the art dealer who showed up at Nicole's shower and I'm sure dropped off the painting that freaked out Tina. Justine died in a suspicious car crash in Switzerland a couple of days ago. She was closer to my age, which means she would've been a kid when the heist took place. So why was she involved now?"

"And what was she doing in Switzerland?" Ravello said.

"Exactly," Donny said. "And who was the brains behind the whole operation?"

Ravello gleefully slapped his thighs. "This is fun. We get to solve a crime instead of committing one for a change."

"And earn points with NYPD," Mia said. "You can share any inside info you dig up with them that could help ID suspects. And offer the whole story to Pete Dianopolis as the 'ripped from the headlines' plot of his next Steve Stianopolis mystery."

Donny got up and crossed the room. He pressed on a burled wood panel. It slowly opened, revealing a full wet bar. He took a bottle of expensive whiskey off a shelf and poured shots into three shot glasses. He handed one to Ravello and another to Mia. "A toast to America's newest crime solvers. *Salute!*"

"*Salute!*" Ravello and Mia chorused. The three downed the shots.

Mia placed her empty glass in the bar's small sink. "Thanks so much for jumping on board with this," Mia said. "My task will be attending an installation opening tomorrow night at the Miller Art Collection. This girl Larkin who runs the place thinks I'm coming to see how the space works as an event venue. Which, to be honest, isn't a bad idea. But I'll really be there to learn whatever I can about the robbery, the Miller-Spaulding family, and their employees."

"Except," Donny said. "There's no way you're going alone."

"But Mister B—"

The Mob boss held up his hand. "No argument. I'm sending Jamie with you."

CHAPTER 19

Larkin Miller-Spaulding had messaged Mia that the dress code for the exhibition opening was "dressy casual," which Mia considered an oxymoron on a par with Donny Boldano's annoying "giant shrimp" gate code. But she knew exactly what to wear. She left work early to pick up her unassuming black dress from the cleaner. It would allow her to fit in with the hip art crowd—as well as she could with her heavy Queens accent—but also disappear into the woodwork if she wandered off to do some snooping.

Jamie texted that he had arrived. Mia put a hand on the wall to balance herself as she navigated the stairs and then the steps in her four-inch, black platform heels, an impulse buy she didn't regret except at times like these.

"You look nice," Jamie said, opening the passenger door of his Prius for her.

"You, too." He was clad in a black leather jacket over a tan tee shirt and jeans, and his brown hair, usually wayward, had been tamed with product. "You like my hair? Madison jujj-ed it for me."

"She did a good job," Mia hated to admit.

"So, what's the plan?" Jamie asked as he drove toward Millville.

"I need to look like I'm scoping the place out as an event venue. This'll give me an excuse to explore the whole property looking for the best 'party sites.' I'll talk to guests and people working the event, and check out the catering prep area, the staff, the food displays, the whole nine yards. But I'll really be hunting for clues about whatever took place during the heist and whatever might be going on now. Because something is. A missing painting doesn't suddenly reappear, and two people don't die for no reason."

"No, they do not. What am I supposed to do besides keep an eye on you?"

"Your cover is that you're my boyfriend and you're there as a favor to me. You're bored by the whole thing, which is why you're gonna spend your time floating around looking like you wish you were somewhere else."

"Oh, so I'm playing myself."

"Hah. Funny stuff. If Benjy was still doing a live act, I'd tell you to pass that on to him. But what you really need to do is suss out the Collection's security system."

"And keep an eye on you."

"Yeah, you said that." Jamie's over-protectiveness bordered on macho, annoying Mia. "I'm a city girl with a mobster father. I was trained to trust nobody and have eyes in the back of my head. I can take care of myself.

I'm not some suburban fainting flower like—" Mia stopped herself.

"Like Madison." Jamie said this with a frown and pursed lips.

Mia felt terrible. "I didn't say that."

"Oh, please. You were about to."

The two fell into an awkward silence. "I'm sorry," Mia finally said.

"She's a good person, Mia. You need to get to know her."

"Okay."

"Wow. Try to control your enthusiasm."

"I'm being terrible, I know. It's just . . ." Mia decided that Jamie deserved honesty. She took a deep breath and dove in. "When I came home and before I knew you had a girlfriend . . . I felt like there was something between us. Like . . . a sexual energy. On both our parts."

"There was." Jamie paused. "I almost broke up with Madison."

"You did?" Mia tried not to sound pleased.

Jamie nodded. "But something stopped me. I've given this a ton of thought over the last few months. I've seen how your passion and drive have turned around Belle View. And I started thinking . . . what would our future look like? If we could live our dream lives, what would mine be? What would be yours? What I finally came to is . . . it feels like we have very different goals."

Mia took this in. The truth might hurt—but it was now impossible to deny. Mia had fantasized about a relationship with Jamie because it was safe. With their unique shared history as Family offspring, the two were comfort food for each other, and Mia had made herself believe this was enough to base a romance on because it was easier and less painful than dating outside the box. But the reality was that Jamie had more in common with Madison than Mia. And he had just articulated a feeling Mia sensed herself but resisted accepting. "I want to grow a business," she said. "You want to grow tomatoes."

Jamie couldn't help laughing at this, which broke the tension. "And zucchini and cucumbers and beans and lettuce."

"Hey, maybe you can be one of Belle View's suppliers. If I throw in the words 'locally sourced' to a client, it instantly ups the price of a package."

This earned another laugh from Jamie. "I do love you, Meems."

"I love you, too."

They fell silent again, but instead of being awkward, it was a silence borne of a lifelong friendship. After a few minutes, Jamie peered at the sign above the expressway. "Shoot, our exit's the next one. I almost missed it."

They exited the expressway and followed the route to the Miller compound. The entire place glowed like the world's classiest amusement park. Huge oak trees lining both sides of the road to the mansion and Collection were threaded with tiny fairy lights. The estate home twinkled and sparkled, almost blindingly so, as they drew closer. Music and a murmur of voices filled the air with a sort of party white noise. Knots of well-dressed event attendees clustered outside the art collection, continuing their conversations and taking champagne glasses from trays while ignoring the waiters who served them.

"They have valet parking," Jamie said.

"Not for us," Mia said. She pointed in the opposite direction. "Park in the space over there, the one closer to the road. If we need to get out of here fast, we don't want some valet searching through a box of keys and fobs to find yours."

"Noted."

Jamie started to make a left-hand turn but stopped to let a dark van go by. Mia caught the profile of the van driver's face and clutched Jamie's arm. "You're not gonna believe this, but I swear that van driver was Liam O'Dwyer. He's the guy who went to jail for the art heist."

"You're kidding." Jamie turned to check out the van, but it had disappeared. "That's interesting."

"Yeah, a *little*. What is he doing here? We have to find out."

"Put it on the list."

Jamie parked in the secluded spot Mia had noticed. They got out of the car and walked toward the party. Jamie gaped at the Miller-Spaulding mansion. "Wow. This place is . . . I don't even know what to say."

"A stunning piece of architecture? A gross example of too much disposable income?"

"Yes."

They passed by the estate's private dock where a few high-end speedboats were moored, indicating some guests had boated over from their own palatial homes. Mia and Jamie arrived at the Collection building and were instantly set upon by waiters offering champagne and passed hors d'oeuvres. "Good service," Mia commented. She helped herself to an hors d'oeuvre. "Beef carpaccio on a tiny piece of toast with horse radish. I need to remember this."

"Also, these little potato pancakes," Jamie said, his mouth filled with one.

"They're blinis with caviar," the waiter said, managing to sound polite and disdainful at the same time.

"They're blinis with caviar," Jamie mimicked as soon as the waiter moved on to other guests. "La di flippin' da."

Mia had to laugh at this. "For once I'm not the embarrassing, low-class guest."

"Gee, thanks," Jamie said with a wry face.

Mia glanced around. She saw Larkin Spaulding-Miller and gave a small wave. The Collection director's face lit up and she scooted over. She threw her arms around Mia. "You came. That makes me so happy."

Mia caught Jamie's eye and bemused expression. "Of course. I can't thank you enough for inviting me." She gentled wriggled out of Larkin's grasp. "Larkin, this is my friend—my boyfriend—Jamie."

"Uh huh," Larkin said. She grabbed Mia's hand. "Guess what's back in the Collection? You have to see."

Larkin pulled Mia into the Collection's main room. A nonplussed Jamie brought up the rear. Larkin grabbed Mia by the shoulders and positioned her in front of a painting. "*Cow and Woman*," the young woman said. "It's home."

"You got it back," Mia said. "That's wonderful."

Larkin's face darkened. "But *Cow and Woman* isn't *Hoop and Boy*. I want all of the paintings back, *all* of them, and I don't care what it takes to get them!"

Her voice rose to a screech. Guests in the room quieted and turned to see what was going on. Jamie instinctively pulled Mia away from the Collection's director.

"Larkin dear, simmer down." Abigail Miller materialized by her daughter's side, along with husband Spencer, who held a champagne glass in each hand. "Have you taken your meds?"

"No," Larkin said in a sulky tone.

"I didn't think so. Open up."

"I don't wanna," the thirtysomething whined.

"I said, open. *Up.*"

Cowed by her mother's tone, Larkin opened her mouth. Abigail pulled a small bejeweled gold pillbox from a pants pocket and dropped a couple of pills down her daughter's gullet. She took a glass of champagne from her husband, who yelped a protest. "Wash your meds down with this, Larky." Abigail handed the champagne to Larkin, who downed it. Abigail noticed Mia and Jamie staring at the family, transfixed by the bizarre scene. "Hello."

Mia snapped out of it. "Hello, Abigail. Larkin was showing me *Cow and Woman*. I'm glad it's back where it belongs."

"Yes," Abigail said. "So are we."

She took the empty glass from Larkin's hand and strode off. Spencer lingered. He motioned to a waiter, who hurried over with a fresh glass of champagne. "We owe you a thank-you for the return of *Cow and Woman*," Spencer said to Mia. "Given your family's history, there was every chance you would have tried fencing the painting instead of turning it over to the police. We're grateful you chose to do the right thing. It was a pleasant surprise."

Jamie's mouth dropped open. He was about to respond but Mia kicked him in the shin to make sure he stayed quiet. She didn't want to risk being evicted from the property. Spencer left them to schmooze other guests, and Mia seized the chance to escape from Larkin's presence. "Jamie and I need to look around and get a sense of how we might utilize the space for different types of events."

"Uh huh." Larkin gave Mia a loopy smile and wandered off. Either the meds or champagne—or the combo—appeared to have had an instant effect on her.

Jamie grabbed Mia's arm. "These people are *insane,*" he said in a panicked whisper. "We have to get out of here."

Mia yanked her arm away. "No. Spy first, make a run for it after. Now, go. See if you can find any clues. I'll do the same."

Jamie reluctantly separated from Mia. She made her way from room to room, eavesdropping on conversations to see if anyone was gossiping about the art heist. No one was, so Mia tried another tack. Figuring older partygoers were more likely to remember the Collection's dark day, she sidled up to a well-dressed, middle-aged foursome.

"My broker's not a fan of talent agency IPOs," a man attired in a perfectly tailored suit said to the other three, all of whom nodded vigorous agreement. "He says the big agencies are generally a bunch of bottom feeders who live to poach each other's clients, which makes their stock value volatile."

Mia sidled up to the foursome. "I couldn't help overhearing your conversation." Trying to corral her accent, Mia over-annunciated, which made her sound like she came from a foreign country. Luckily, this seemed to work for her. She had the group's attention. "I've come into a bit of an inheritance and am debating how to invest it. The stock market makes me nervous these days. I'm drinking in all the magnificent art around us tonight and wondering if that might be a sounder investment."

Mia feared she'd gone too far with her florid imitation of a wealthy young heiress but to her relief, the others bought her act. "You've got good instincts." The compliment came from a woman wearing a diamond pendant Mia pegged at ten karats. "Art is a smart investment, although you *must* use an advisor who has great word of mouth recs."

"Oh, yes. Absolutely. But then again . . ." Mia hesitated. "There's the danger of theft. Like what happened here a while ago. I heard many priceless works of art were stolen from the Collection."

The woman shrugged. "That's what insurance is for."

Insurance. Mia's mind raced. Considering most of what decorated her family's walls were paintings of Jesus and old, yellowed portraits of John F. Kennedy, art insurance was such an alien concept she'd never considered it. Was that the heist's ultimate payday? *But the money would have gone to the Millers,* Mia thought, *so why would Tina or anyone else be involved? Unless they were promised a chunk of it.*

"Although," the other woman said, "I remember Abigail saying her father refused to file any claims because it would mean surrendering ownership in exchange for the insurance company's current determined value versus its future value once it was recovered. And she agreed with him."

"Pro move on her part," the fourth man said. "Look how they got back *Cow and Woman.* That one painting is worth more now than the whole stolen lot was worth twenty years ago."

So much for my insurance theory, Mia thought, deflated.

Mia continued to listen in on conversations for the next half hour, but while she picked up tips on what mega real estate broker to use when buying a Tribeca triplex, and which multi-hundred-dollar facials were "absolutely worth every penny," she gleaned no additional insight into artwork hinky business. She filled a plate from one of several buffets laid out by the event's caterer. Impressed by the creative, high-quality offerings, she took a break from heist investigations to check out the competition, traipsing through the grass to two prep tents located a discreet distance from the Collection. Mia peered into the first and saw several chic young women filling the party's goodie bags assembly-style. She stepped inside to take a closer look at the giveaways. "I'm in the event business," she said to one of the women to justify her presence. "Finding the perfect favor for a guest is one of my favorite parts of the job. We've done some pretty high-end stuff. We once gave out wine bottles where the labels had pictures of the bride and groom, and their wedding date."

The women, who exuded the warmth of one of the estate's marble statues, gestured to a finished bag. "Look inside."

Mia pulled open the magnetic closure of the giveaway tote, which a label told her was made from imported Fair Trade African cotton. Inside the tote rested a bottle of

aged whiskey, a box of expensive chocolates, a Mont-
blanc pen, a Tiffany's keychain, a boxed candle she recognized as being from one of the priciest brands available,
and a slew of brochures. She removed one and examined
it. The gorgeous brochure offered a free weeklong stay at
a Tahitian resort featuring luxury bungalows built over
the pristine water of a private cove. "Not bad," Mia said,
mustering a laissez-faire attitude to cover her embarrassment. She replaced the brochure and slunk away.

She crossed to the second tent. The spongy, scented
warmth emanating from it indicated this was the caterer's
prep tent. She pulled back the entry flap a few inches and
peeked in. What she saw sent a shock wave through her.
There, supervising the flow of food, was Versailles' executive chef, Sandeep Singh. Even more shocking, helping
him was a wan-looking Castor Garvalos. Versailles on
the Park had been hired to cater the Miller Art Collection
exhibit opening. Like her father, Mia didn't believe in coincidences. What she saw in front of her was a physical
link from Tina to Versailles, and finally to the Miller Art
Collection.

Garvalos turned in her direction, and Mia jumped
back. She scuttled behind the trunk of a large tree. Then
he turned away, revealing a large bandage on the back of
his head. Mia positioned herself to spy on the men without being seen. She turned off her cell phone's ringer and
texted her discovery to Jamie, then resumed her surveillance. Sandeep added garnish to a tower of literal giant
shrimp and placed the platter in a cater-waiter's hands.
Garvalos pushed the cater-waiter toward the exit. He
checked his watch, a nervous expression on his face. Perspiration dripped from his forehead. He grabbed a napkin

and wiped it away. Garvalos tapped his foot and glanced toward the back of the tent, where kitchen staffers stacked plates in crates for the trip back to Versailles and its dishwashing facilities. Sandeep focused his attention on a large table where cater-waiters were assembling plates of petites fours, brownies, lemon bars, pecan bars, and an assortment of handcrafted chocolates for the dessert buffet. A waiter picked up one of the dessert trays and carried it toward the tent's exit. Garvalos followed him out, heading right toward Mia.

She dashed down the lawn to the estate's dock and pretended to be taking in the view of Long Island Sound. Garvalos passed behind her and she released the breath she'd been holding. She turned slightly and noticed one of the beautiful young things from the gifting tent heading toward the Collection with her arms full of gift bags that each sported a bow made from sparkling silver ribbon. The ribbon jogged a memory for Mia. But before she could place it . . .

"Beautiful view tonight, isn't it?" a man's voice slurred, startling her. Spencer Spaulding staggered to her side.

"Yes. Very." Mia inched away from him.

Spaulding gestured across the Sound with the champagne glass he was holding. Champagne sloshed from the glass. The inebriated man swayed so much Mia feared he'd topple into the water. "So very Gatsby."

"Is he a guest tonight?"

"Nooo . . ." Spencer spoke to her as if she was mentally challenged. "That's a book. *The Great*—"

"*Gatsby*," Mia interrupted. "I know. I read it in high school. I was kidding. I could never forget that last line. 'So we beat on, boats against the current, borne back ceaselessly into the past.' It's like tonight—how people are still thinking about the paintings that were stolen twenty years ago."

This snapped Spencer out of his drunken stupor. He eyed Mia with suspicion. "One of my friends told me about this heiress he was talking to who was interested in buying art but worried about it being stolen. Because of what happened here."

Mia fought to quell her panic. *The best defense is a good offense.* "Makes sense to me. If I were her, I'd be worried too. These boats are gorgeous. Is one of them yours?"

She prayed he'd take to the change of subject. Spaulding drained the last of his champagne and used the empty glass to point at a sleek, black speedboat. "That beauty. I used to fly around the Sound on her. Westchester, Connecticut, the far end of the Island. Then I got a BUI—boating while intoxicated—and Mommy took away the keys. It's her baby now. And she tied the purse strings even tighter. By the way, when I say 'Mommy,' I mean my wife Abigail."

"I got that."

Spencer gazed at the boat disconsolately. "I need a refill."

He stumbled, regained his balance, then staggered away. Mia watched him go. She wondered if he'd always had a drinking problem or if being a supernumerary to the star of the show, his wife Abigail, drove him to it. Thoughts jumbled in Mia's head. Spaulding referenced Abigail being tight with money. The police always assumed the Miller theft was an inside job. What if Spaulding came up with the plan to supplement his paltry allowance from "Mommy," and farmed out its implementation to others, like Tina, O'Dwyer, and possibly Garvalos? The plan failed and he turned to booze. *This makes sense*, Mia thought, excited. But she needed to run the theory by Jamie. She remembered that she'd turned off the ringer on her phone. She removed it from her purse and checked for Jamie's response to her text about Garvalos. He hadn't gotten back to her. Concerned, she telephoned him. The call went to voice mail. "Jamie, where are you? We need to talk. I have an idea I want to run by you. Call me or find me. I'm by the dock."

She ended the call and gazed out at the Sound while she waited for Jamie's response. Water lapped at the shore's edge and the Millers' speedboat gently and rhythmically thumped against the dock. She checked behind her to see if Jamie might be heading her way. Sandeep stepped out of the prep tent. He said something into his headset. Mia ducked down, out of sight. Garvalos appeared from the direction of the Collection building. He strode to the middle of the lawn and scanned the area. Mia combat-crawled down the dock, intent on reaching the speedboat. She maneuvered over the boat's side, trying to create as little movement as possible, and hid in its bottom, where she texted Jamie a warning to keep an eye out for Garvalos and Sandeep.

As she lay waiting for the coast to clear, Mia flashed on something Spaulding had said. "I used to fly around the Sound on her." If the boat could traverse the Sound, getting from Millville to Flushing Bay would be easy. And a convenient way to transport a body. Mia laid out the events that had brought her to this moment. *The painting appears at Nicole's shower. Tina freaks. She confronts someone about it. Maybe Spaulding? He kills her. Tosses her in the boat and powers back to where the painting showed up.*

Mia had no idea where the police were in their investigation. For all she knew, they had already scoured the boat for clues. Then again, she knew from Pete's complaints to Cammie that he and his brothers in blue were often constricted by laws regulating search and seizure. And if anyone was going to put up a fight on this topic, it would be a family like the Miller-Spauldings, who had the wealth to lawyer up and block an investigation. Mia, on the other hand, was free to take her go-to "better to beg forgiveness than ask permission" approach. She crawled to the boat's edge and peeked over the side. Garvalos and Sandeep were gone. Making sure to stay low, she began combing through the boat's interior.

Mia shaded her phone's flashlight with her hand to keep from being caught as she scoured every nook and cranny. She heard voices and the sound of cars. The party was ending, which meant she was running out of time. Mia peeked over the boat's side again and saw the group of one percenters she'd chatted with in the Collection making their way to the valet stand. Each carried a goody bag. Mia gasped, then clapped a hand over her mouth. She suddenly realized why the bows on the bags looked familiar. They were made from the same distinctive ribbon that decorated the gift-wrapped *Cow and Woman* at Nicole's shower. It was hard to imagine Spaulding wrapping a package so beautifully. Mia replayed something else the soused man had shared. "I got a BUI and Mommy took away the keys." His wife had commandeered the boat. *Abigail,* Mia thought. *She's got brains, financial brawn, and the boat keys.*

Mia searched the boat with renewed determination, but it appeared to be spotless. Disheartened, she was about to give up when she saw a glint under the phone's light in a crevasse between the boat's two leather seats. She wriggled her hand into the crevasse until she felt something cold and metallic under her fingertips. Mia grunted as she worked to dislodge whatever it was. After a few minutes, she extricated a glittering rainbow brace-let—exactly like the ones Tina wore and Mia coveted. Elated at finding a significant clue, she photographed the bracelet and typed a text to Jamie. She was about to press Send when she heard a familiar voice.

"Hand over your phone," Abigail Miller said. "And no sudden movements or you're dead."

CHAPTER 20

Mia looked up to see the Miller heiress holding a petite, but what she assumed was effective, pistol. Trapped, she turned over her phone. Abigail pocketed it. "You've been snooping around ever since *Cow and Woman* showed up again and I'm sick of it."

The Miller mogul handed her a fob. Mia stared at it, confused. "What is this?"

"It's how you start the boat, you low-rent ignoramus. Untie it from the dock and start driving."

"I can't even drive a car," Mia said. "I have no idea how to drive a boat."

"No time like the present to learn. But first, give me the bracelet."

"What bracelet?" Mia asked with an innocent expression.

"The one I'm going to kill you for finding."

"Any chance you mean that as a figure of speech?" Mia said, praying that if she stalled long enough, someone would notice what was going on. "You know, like, *you ate the last cookie. I'm gonna kill you.*"

"None. Now move." Abigail motioned to the boat's moorings with her gun.

Left with no other recourse, Mia undid the ropes. The boat began to float away from the dock. Abigail kept the gun trained on her. "Use the fob to turn on the motor," the woman instructed. Mia did so. "Gently nudge the throttle forward, then steer the boat to port."

"Huh?" Mia responded, genuinely clueless.

"Left. Port is left, starboard is right. Sorry you had to learn that on the last day of your life."

"Not as sorry as I am," Mia muttered. She turned the wheel to the left as she carefully accelerated. Her heart beat wildly. She wasn't sure which was more terrifying, the threat of death or handling the sleek racing boat.

"Straighten the wheel. Straighten it!" Abigail yelled this as they headed toward a manmade jetty. Mia adjusted course, gripping the wheel so hard that her knuckles turned white. "Go slowly," Abigail instructed. "People will get suspicious if we zoom out of here." She gave Mia's back a hard poke with the gun. "And don't get any ideas about zooming out of here to knock me off balance."

"It never occurred to me," Mia said, depressed that Abigail had thwarted her plan. She held tight to the wheel as the boat slowly motored through the estate's cove toward the Sound. To circumvent the terror threatening to overwhelm her, Mia started to talk. "I know the heist was an inside job."

Abigail gave a mirthless laugh. "Bravo. You're a genius. From day one, everyone from reporters to law enforcement to our estate staff, legal and illegal, figured that out. But no one could never figure out who the insider was. My money made sure of that."

"Spencer."

"And his mistress."

Another link in the chain. "Tina."

"Spencer wasn't always a drunk. But he *was* always a philanderer." Abigail spit out the word like it was toxic. "They met on one of her flights to London. He was on his way to visit another mistress. Instead, he hooked up with Tina. My British security team outed him to me. My father had just moved me up the Miller ladder. I didn't want the distraction of a divorce, so instead I let Spencer stay in the marriage but cut his allowance to a pittance. If he wanted to finance his sluts, he'd have to do it on his own."

"That sucks."

"I know."

Abigail sounded hurt and aggrieved. *Show her sympathy*, Mia told herself. *If we're like girlfriends sharing stuff, maybe she won't off me.* "I'm sorry he put you through that. My husband cheated on me, so I know how painful it is." Mia adjusted her body just enough to block Abigail's vision of the boat's throttle, then lowered the speed imperceptibly. The longer they stayed in the cove, the better her chance of escaping. "So, Spencer came up with a plan to steal some of your father's paintings and sell them to pay for other women? Wow. That is cold."

"Stone cold."

"Humor me," Mia said, praying Abigail would. "I want to see if I can figure this out. Spencer steals the paintings with Tina's help—"

"And with the help of her mercenary ex-boyfriend, Castor."

"Right. The paintings are stolen and sent to a fence in Europe. But somehow, they disappear. Spencer doesn't get the money he banked on, then finds out his girlfriend Tina kept one painting to herself that she managed to sell. He gets depressed and starts drinking."

Abigail, amused, rested her back against the side of the boat. Her casual attitude in the face of the deadly deed she intended to commit reminded Mia of the entitled uber-wealthy clientele at Korri Designs. They were a class of citizens who blithely breezed through life as if buckets of money gave them a free pass on all of the world's horrors. If nothing else, it enabled a deeply embedded state of denial. And a great commission on the company's name-droppy status products. "You're sharper than you look and sound," Abigail said. "This is fun. Keep going."

Mia lowered the boat's speed another imperceptible notch. "We're at *Cow and Woman* reappearing. Let me think . . . let me think. You've got lots of money. You track it down and buy it back."

"Bingo!" Abigail raised her gun and shot it into the air. It didn't make a sound. "Silencer."

"I know. I've seen them before."

"Of course you have. Continue."

"The next step would be exposing the painting to Tina, which had to involve Justine Cadeau."

"Her father, Pierre Cadeau, was the original fence in France, another fact uncovered by my security team. Unfortunately for Spencer, Pierre, who was something of a gourmand, died of a heart attack before he could reveal where he'd squirreled away the paintings until it was safe to move them to market. Even my team has been unable to track them down."

"Ah. I never would have guessed the part about the fence being Justine's father."

Abigail shrugged. "That one was a toughie. I'll give you a pass on it."

The moon emerged from cloud cover and a shaft of light illuminated Abigail's silvery hair. *Let someone see us, please let someone see us,* Mia thought as the boat drew further and further away from the shore. The irony that she was facing a watery death like the one that felled her husband Adam wasn't lost on her. "What I don't get," she said, stalling, "is why you used the painting to scare the hell out of Tina."

Abigail gave a snort. "That's not obvious? I did it to send a message. *You don't know me, but I know you and I know what you did. And I'm watching you.*"

"Why wait twenty years to send that message?" Mia wondered.

"That's how long it took me to track down the painting and buy it back. Those Russian oligarchs can be tough negotiators." Abigail, impatient, poked Mia in the side with her gun. "Okay, now I'm bored. Let's move this along. I know you've been slowing the boat down. That's over. Time to pick up the pace. Gun the motor."

Reluctantly, Mia obeyed the order. The boat left the relative comfort of the cove for the open Sound. "One last thing," Mia said, desperate. "What's Castor Garvalos's connection to all this? Why did you hire him to cater the party tonight?"

Abigail's smug self-confidence disappeared. The news was apparently a revelation to her and not a good one.

"What-how-what do you mean?" Dumbfounded, she tripped over words.

"You didn't know he's here? How about that." Despite the dire circumstances, Mia couldn't pass up the chance to gloat.

"The party was Larkin's baby. I forced Spencer to make himself useful and help—" Abigail stopped mid-sentence as something dawned on her. Anger mottled her face, twisting it into a malevolent expression. "Spencer," she spit out. "He brought on that snake."

"Wouldn't he be afraid you'd notice?"

"Of course not," Abigail said scornfully. "He knows I'd never commingle with the help."

You wouldn't, you sick, obnoxious snob. "He's obviously up to something," Mia said, grasping at the chance to use the unexpected twist to her advantage. "I'll turn around so you can deal with him before it's too late."

"No, keep going!" Abigail shouted. "First you, then him."

It was too late. Mia had already yanked the boat to starboard toward shore. But she cut the turn too sharp and the boat whipped around in a circle, bouncing hard back and forth as it cut against its own wake. "I don't know what I'm doing!" Mia screamed.

"Slow down and straighten the wheel!" Abigail screamed back as she fought to keep her gun focused on her captive. Mia reduced the thrust and managed to straighten the boat, pointing it toward the dock. "The other way," her captor yelled. "And gun it!" Mia did so. The lightning-fast boat shot out of the cove into the Sound so fast it terrified her. She instinctively pulled back on the throttle. "We're finally getting somewhere," Abigail said, exasperated. "Head to starboard."

"What's that again? I already forgot." Mia wasn't lying.

"*Right.*"

"Why can't they just say left or right? It's nuts."

Abigail gave a guttural grunt. "Lord help me. Dumping you in the ocean cannot come soon enough. Then I can move on to Spencer."

"About that," Mia said, seizing a possible opening. "What do you think he's up to?"

Abigail furrowed her brow. "Hmmm . . ."

It was the brief moment of distraction Mia needed to put a final plan into action. She threw the throttle into reverse and gunned the engine. Abigail cried out as she flew backward. Her gun also went flying, into the depths of Long Island Sound. The crazed woman let loose a stream of vile language.

"I'd rather die in a crash than let you kill me," Mia, holding tight to the steering wheel, yelled back at her.

"Too bad that's not going to happen."

Out of the corner of her eye, Mia saw a crazed Abigail coming toward her, hands extended, ready to wrap around Mia's neck and choke her to death—the same way Mia assumed Tina had met her fate. She thrust the throttle into forward, praying the act didn't strip the boat's gears. The boat shifted direction so sharply it lifted Mia off her feet, but she managed to maintain her grasp on the steering wheel.

Abigail wasn't so lucky. The force of the direction shift caught her off balance. "Aghh!" she screamed as she tumbled off the side of the boat into the Sound.

Mia quickly put the boat in neutral. Her plan had worked but she spiraled into panic. She couldn't bear the thought of leaving Abigail to drown. On the other hand—

rescue her potential killer? Not a great idea. Mia decided to split the difference. She grabbed a life vest and threw it to Abigail. "Here. When I get to shore—without you, you murdering psycho—I'll send help."

Abigail swam toward the boat, ignoring the life vest. "No need," she called to Mia, an evil grin on her face. "I'm a *great* swimmer."

As the murderous mogul swam toward the boat with strong, sure strokes, Mia hurried back to the steering wheel. She engaged the throttle, gunned the engine, and sped away.

Well, will you look at me, Mia thought as she raced back to the Miller dock. *I guess I do know what I'm doing.*

CHAPTER 21

An hour later, the Miller estate glowed even brighter.
But now the illumination came from police flood-
lights, not fairy lights, although they gamely continued
twinkling in the trees.

As soon as Mia crashed the speedboat into the estate's
dock—*gotta work on my braking*—she'd stumbled onto
land, grabbed a cell phone out of the hands of a cater-
waiter taking a cigarette break, and summoned law enforcement. It turned out they were already on the
premises. Mia *had* spotted Liam O'Dwyer driving past
her and Jamie. He'd been hired by Larkin to confirm that
the second security system she'd installed was working
properly. His presence led to a comedy of errors that
doomed the second robbery attempt. "Garvalos and
Spaulding both thought the other one hired me to work
the heist," he told Mia as they watched officers load the

two handcuffed men in the back of a patrol car. "I played along and alerted the authorities."

"You're a hero," Mia said.

"Nah," the guard said, waving off the compliment. But he looked pleased.

Mia turned her attention to Jamie. An officer had discovered him bound and gagged in the back of Castor Garvalos's personal Versailles van. "Are you sure you're okay?" she asked, concerned.

Jamie nodded. He touched a spot on the top of his head and grimaced. "I didn't get knocked out. I just saw stars. I'm more embarrassed than anything. I guess I'm not great at snooping around. That Garvalos guy totally figured out what I was doing."

"But you went down fighting," Mia said, trying to bolster his ego. "It took him *and* Spaulding to tie you up."

Jamie, unconvinced, gave a halfhearted shrug. Liam pointed toward the cove. "Talk about going down fighting."

Mia followed the direction of his finger. Several officers were struggling to subdue a drenched Abigail Miller-Spaulding, who'd been retrieved from the water. "Do you know who I am?" she screamed at them, following the question she deemed rhetorical with a stream of insults and invectives. "Spencer, where are you? Call my lawyer!"

"Yeah, that won't be happening," Mia said as the officers finally dragged her out of the water and into custody. "Spencer is otherwise engaged. Hey, you know who I don't see anywhere? Sandeep. The Versailles chef."

"Oh, he zoomed out of here as soon as the police pulled up," Liam said. "The cater-waiters are trying to figure out how to close the party with one boss arrested and the other on the run. For what, I don't know. He wasn't involved in the old or new heist."

Mia searched the crowd of looky-loos and law enforcement officials. "Do you see Larkin anywhere? I feel bad for her. It's gotta be hard watching both your parents be carted off to jail."

"Or not," Jamie said.

He gestured toward the estate drive, where Larkin chased after the patrol car driving away with her father and Garvalos. "Where are the paintings? *Where are the paintings?*" she screamed as she ran, along with a panoply of profanity that would have made her foul-mouthed mother proud.

"This is one cuckoo crazy family," Liam said, shaking his head.

Mia watched Larkin chasing after the patrol car, shaking a fist at it as the vehicle disappeared down the long, manicured drive. Mia switched her focus to Abigail, who was spewing bile at her arresting officers, unable to shake a fist because her hands had been cuffed behind her back. "It's like what F. Scott Fitzgerald said about the rich. They're different from you and me."

Jamie, surprised, favored her with a smile. "Look at you, quoting F. Scott."

"I liked his book, *The Great Gatsby*," Mia said. "It stayed with me."

She gazed at the Millers' palatial estate, probably built around the time Fitzgerald wrote his classic novel. Maybe he'd stayed at this very home. Who knew? It might even have been the mansion that inspired Gatsby's. Mia then thought about the massively dysfunctional family it now housed—or did house, until two members were accused of heinous crimes. The compact two-family home she shared with her grandmother, which would forever smell like marinara gravy because the scent was imbedded in the walls, looked pretty good to her at the moment. So did Belle View. The humble banquet hall might be a work in progress, but at least it wasn't a superficial beauty hiding a "laundry" list of criminal activity, like Versailles on the Park.

"I think the police are done with us," Jamie said. "You ready to go?"

"Yup." The snobby gifting tent employees had bailed on their duties when the police showed up, leaving behind a clutch of gift bags. Figuring she'd earned them, Mia had claimed a bunch for her family and friends. She filled her arms with as many as she could, then motioned to the others with her elbow. "I'll get these. You get the rest."

"Yes, ma'am."

Jamie grabbed the bags Mia couldn't carry, and the two marched off to his car.

Mia spent the following week recapping her story to the police and monitoring updates. A call from Pete vindicated her insistence that Versailles was a hotbed of suspicious activity. "We picked up Sandeep Singh as he was about to board a flight to Mumbai," he told her. "That was some smuggling operation he had going."

"More art?"

"Nope. Saffron."

"The spice?" Mia said in disbelief.

"The *expensive,* in-demand spice. There's less of it thanks to global warming, and international gangs figured out it's easier to smuggle than drugs. Your friend

Ron Karras is off the hook by the way. When Garvalos was giving up his chef's little operation to us in hopes of a plea deal, he admitted that when he uncovered the saffron smuggling, he demanded Singh cut him in on the profits. They had a fight, Singh pushed him, he fell backward and hit his head on the hand of one of those lady statues in front of Versailles."

"That's why she's missing a middle finger."

"Yup."

Mia ran through the events of the last few weeks in her head. She had one last question. "Garvalos said he had an investor with deep pockets. I thought it might be Singh, but since Garvalos only found out about the saffron smuggling a few days ago, that doesn't time out. It had to be either Spencer Spaulding or Tina. My money's on her."

"Ding, ding, ding, you answered correctly. Yeah, in his blathering about how he wasn't a crook, he was merely an ambitious businessman, he brought up his plan to expand the event business, with funding by his late ex-girlfriend."

"Who liked the idea of buying Belle View because she knew it—and us—are dear to Minnie and Linda's hearts, thus providing a big eff-you to them."

"Given that she's passed on, we have no way of knowing what she was thinking, but I can see the twisted logic in that," Pete said. "This whole thing's gonna make for a great Steve Stianopolis mystery. I already got the title. *Con Artist*."

"Good one."

"Thanks. Do me a favor. Tell Cammie I'm up for a promotion. Which'll come with a raise."

"Will do."

"And Mia . . ." Pete paused. "I have to say, you got some real insight into the criminal mind."

"I understand the criminal mind," she said, "because I grew up with it."

Mia managed to dodge all media requests except for one. She allowed Teri Fuoco an interview. Thanks to the reporter's crush on Evans, Teri was open to presenting Belle View in a less Mob-by light. Even better, Donny Boldano proved to be the hero of the day. Through his JFK connections, he managed to locate a manifest from long-defunct Odyssey Airlines that confirmed Tina Iles-Karras worked a flight twenty years prior where a casket was flown from New York to France—and signed for by Justine Cadeau's father, Parisian art dealer Pierre Cadeau.

Teri's story was picked up by multiple outlets, which made Mia happy because it meant Teri owed her. And in both their worlds, favors were currency. Feeling magnanimous, she invited the journalist to an off-the-record small event at Belle View celebrating the birth of Nicole and Ian's baby boy, Lucas. New grandfather Ron, celebrating his freedom as well as his grandson, provided a feast from his diner. This allowed Guadalupe and Evans to join the party, although Evans insisted on trying his hand at baking a cannoli cake, which won raves from the most skeptical Italians in attendance, including a "*molto deliciozo*" from Elisabetta.

Mindful of the new parents' exhausted condition, the event was a casual afternoon get-together for friends and family. Philip and Finn brought their little ones, six-month-old Justin and eighteen-month-old Eliza. "We have so many pre-owned baby clothes from our little guy that we'd love to pass on to you for Lucas," Finn told Nicole as he bounced Justin on his lap, adding, "I'm not a fan of the term, 'hand-me-downs.' Sounds kind of Great Depression-y."

"Whatever you want to call them, we'll take them," Nicole said.

"I see a lot of playdates for our kids," said Philip, who was wiping off the cannoli cake that Eliza had smeared all over her tiny, adorable face.

Ian put an arm around his wife's shoulder. "So do we."

"And Philip, I don't know if Dad's had a chance to tell you this, but after the way you helped Ron, he wants to make you our regular lawyer," Mia said. "You're part of the family now. With a small 'f.'"

Ron held up a glass. "To Philip. And to Mia. And to family. *Opa!*"

"*Opa!*" everyone chorused with raised glasses.

After a couple of hours, most guests departed, leaving only the Karras-Whitman clan and Carina–Belle View crew, who decamped from the Bay Ballroom to the second-floor bridal lounge, where they sprawled out on the room's comfortable couches waiting for additional updates on the Miller goings-on from Mia. Even Cammie stuck around, "provided you don't rope me into doing any work, remember, hashtag coasting." Mia's phone pinged a text. "Dad sends his apologies for missing the party," she told the others. "He had a meeting." She saw wary expressions on a few faces and an intrigued look on the reporter's mug. "A meeting about Belle View business, not . . . other business."

"Oh," Teri said, disappointed.

"Mia, fill us in on what exactly happened at the Miller place," Ian said, chomping down on one of the chocolate "It's a Boy!" cigars he and Nicole had distributed to guests. "I was busy helping my wife give birth."

"And by that he means yelling, 'Oh, my God, it's coming!' and trying not to faint," his wife tossed out while rocking the baby carriage that held their sleeping infant.

"Hey," her husband protested. Then he sheepishly added, "She's right."

Mia helped herself to another serving of cannoli cake, which Evans had moved into the lounge from the ballroom, then settled into her seat. "Here's the deal. Versailles on the Park is high-end in Queens, but it's way low-end for the Miller crowd, which made me suspicious about why Castor Garvalos, a guy who it turns out was part of the original heist team, was catering such an upscale event. When I was in the boat with Abigail, I caught a lucky break. The Miller family had a serious issue with communication, as in there was none. Abigail had no idea her husband was planning a second art heist. Her husband had no idea their daughter had installed a backup security system. In the one second Abigail was putting all this together and picturing a total disaster, I was able to mess around with the boat just enough to save myself."

The group responded with cheers and relief that Mia had managed to escape her captor. "But why did she kill Tina?" Ron asked, his tone plaintive.

The group quieted, out of respect for the widower. Nicole cast a glance at her mother. Linda gave a slight nod to indicate she was okay. Whatever animosity existed between the exes had dissipated with Tina's death. Mia chose her words carefully. "From what the police have been able to put together so far, it looks like Abigail has been planning this for a long time. It all depended on getting back *Cow and Woman.*

"Stupid name for a stupid painting," Minniguccia muttered. Elisabetta nodded vigorous agreement.

"Abigail hired a private investigator, a sketchy guy she paid a fortune to hide what she was doing and who immediately blabbed everything to the police when they confronted him. He did some digging. He tracked down Justine Cadeau. He also learned about the . . . issues . . . between Tina and Linda. The painting showed up in time for the shower here, and Abigail paid Justine to crash the shower and plant the painting. Justine used the money from Abigail to pay for the trip to Switzerland. She had an idea where her father might have hidden the paintings and wanted to check it out."

"Was she murdered, too?" Teri asked, sniffing out a possible new story.

Mia shook her head. "No. She splurged on renting a super pricey sports car and was driving too fast on a mountain road. Anyway, after the painting scared the you-know-what out of Tina, Abigail called her pretending to be you, Linda."

"Like I told the police," Linda declared.

"And then she called Tina pretending to be *you*. She got you both here to meet and argue with each other so she could set you up as Tina's killer. She couldn't have predicted Ron taking over as the prime suspect, but I don't think that was an issue. All Abigail cared about was punishing Tina, and the heat for it being on anyone but her."

"How did she"—Jamie, trying to be sensitive to Ron, finished the sentence with—"you know."

"The P.I. Abigail hired picked up contact between Spencer and Tina. She assumed they were seeing each other again, but they weren't. They were laying out a game plan for the second heist. After a meeting at a coffee shop in Millville, Abigail followed Tina and knocked her out. She got her on the speedboat and did the deed out in open water so one would see her, wrapping the same ribbon around Tina's neck that she used to wrap the painting. I recognized it as the bows on the goody bags. The P.I. scoped out where the security cameras at Belle View and the marina are focused so she could dodge them when she dumped—brought Tina here." Mia's phone pinged a text. "Another inquiry into Belle View's avails. Now that Versailles is shut down, we're sloppy seconds for a bunch of people whose events got axed. A little insulting. But I'll take it."

"Yo!" a voice called from the first floor. "Anyone home?"

"That's not Dad," Mia said, puzzled. She got up and called out the open door, "We're upstairs. Who is it?"

"Liam O'Dwyer. On my way up."

Moments later, the security guard strode into the room. Mia greeted him and introduced the others. "I'm sorry you couldn't get here earlier, but we can make you a plate of leftovers."

"I'll take it. But first . . ." He glanced around the room. "Great, a nice, big TV. Can you hook it up to WiFi?"

"Yup," said Evans, who was something of tech whiz in addition to his culinary skills.

O'Dwyer pulled a tablet out of his briefcase and the two men got to work. A live feed popped up on the TV screen of what appeared to be police officers and officials in a cemetery surrounded by mountains. "Those guys are Interpol," Guadalupe said. "What's going on?"

"You'll see," Liam responded.

A young woman stepped into the scene. There was no sound, but she appeared to say something to two men who were shoveling dirt off a gravesite. "That's Larkin Miller," Mia said, excited.

"The Swiss police found directions to this burial plot in Justine Cadeau's belongings," Liam said. "Her car went off the road only a mile from the cemetery. Where no Cadeaus are buried. According to Interpol's sources, she discovered the information when she was going through a storage space filled with stuff that belonged to her father. She'd only found out about the space when the company contacted her before auctioning off the contents."

"Mia, Dad told me your theory of how they got the paintings out of the country." Jamie said, as excited as she was. "On a plane, in a casket."

"Larkin flew over as soon as the authorities contacted her," Liam shared. "She asked me to make sure you saw this because she thinks you were right."

Everyone watched in silence, tension in the room ratcheted up to the nth degree. The cemetery workers stopped digging. It took some doing, but using a complicated system of levers and pullies, they extricated the casket from its resting place. The group held its collective breath as the men wrestled with the casket lid until they finally threw it open. "If that's not paintings, I do *not* wanna see what's in there," Cammie said in a low voice.

On screen, Larkin peered into the casket. Then she appeared to scream and began jumping up and down. She reached in and pulled out a painting that she hugged to her, weeping for joy. "It's paintings," Mia said, releasing the breath she'd been holding. "And that's gotta be *Hoop and Boy.*"

Larkin jumped up and down a few more times, kissed the painting, and then held the painting out to the camera. "Mia," she mouthed, "I owe you." She waved and the picture cut out.

"Well," Mia said, "I think Belle View's got a lock on catering the next Miller Art Collection opening." Her phone alerted her to a new text. She read it. "Dad's on his way back. He says he's got good news for me."

CHAPTER 22

Cammie stood up and stretched. "If Ravello says any-thing interesting, text it to me. I've been here so long I almost put in a full workday."

"You were here for a party," Mia pointed out. "There was no work involved. At all."

Cammie, affronted, put a hand on her hip and struck a pose. "Oh, really? Who packed up the leftovers?"

"You. Mostly *for* you."

"Hey, a gal's gotta eat. And if I bring a little something to Pete, he'll owe me, which is always good."

The group made its way downstairs to the Belle View foyer. "I gotta get back to the diner," Ron said. "Tell your dad I say hi. And thank you, Mia. You cleared my name. And gave me answers I needed."

He kissed Mia on both cheeks and walked away. Linda

threw her arms around Mia in a warm embrace. "I owe you thanks, too. You were a pit bull, *bella*."

"The police would have figured things out eventually," Mia said. "All I did was move it along."

"And for that, I will always be grateful." Linda gazed after her ex-husband, who was making an exit after showering his newborn grandson with kisses. "Ron's gonna spread Tina's ashes in Greece. I'm going with him."

Mia, surprised, raised an eyebrow. "You are?"

"Yes. I don't think he should do something like that alone."

"Do you think you two will get back together?"

Linda gave a small shrug and held up her hands. "Meh, *chi sai?* Who knows? This whole horrible business has given me a much clearer picture of my part in our breakup. I've been feeling like a wounded victim ever since we split up. My mother's no help on that score."

"No, she is not," Mia said, recalling Minniguccia's diatribes against Ron and Tina.

"But I wasn't blameless. Instead of working through problems in our relationship, I ignored them. What do therapists say? I was in denial. I can't predict the future, but I do see Ron and I being in each other's lives. Especially now that there's Lucas."

Linda cast a fond glance at her grandson. Nicole noticed and with Ian in tow, pushed the baby stroller toward her mother. The family said their goodbyes to Mia. "We need to have a conversation about you being Liam's godmother," Nicole said.

"Oh, Nicole." Mia, tearing up, placed a hand on her heart. "I'd be honored."

"And Nicole can do the same for you when you have babies," Elisabetta declared.

"Had to throw that in, didn't you, Nonna?" Mia said, with an amused eye roll.

Minniguccia patted her old friend on the arm. "Be nice to your nonna, *bella*. She's the only one of us old ladies who ain't a great-grandma yet."

"Rub it in, *perché non si,*" Elisabetta muttered, which Mia understood to be a loose translation of "rub it in, why don't ya?"

"You know what I heard?" Minnie, ever the gossip said. "I heard Gianna Vachaletto might be becoming a great-*great*-grandma."

Elisabetta released a frustrated moan. "A great-great-grandma," Mia said, amused. "Ah, the white whale of Astoria seniors."

Nicole and her family decamped, with a promise to drop Elisabetta off at home. Evans came out of the kitchen holding two motorcycle helmets. "I'm gonna take off." He offered a helmet to Teri. "Want a ride back to Astoria?"

"Mia said her father is on the way. And he has news." Teri's face contorted as the reporter and woman in her duked it out for dominance.

Mia felt a pittance of pity for the *Triborough Trib* journalist. "I'll let you know what Dad says, if it's anything worth sharing."

Teri's face lit up. "Thanks." She turned to Evans. "I'm all yours."

Evans handed Teri a helmet and she happily bounced from the building. As he passed Mia, he winked at her. She mouthed a "thank-you" for extricating the nosy woman from the premises.

Jamie and Liam came down the stairs from the bridal lounge. "I helped Liam put the TV back the way it was," Jamie said.

"Thanks. Liam, you're a rock star. If we ever need security for an event, we're calling you."

"I'll be pretty busy with my new gig as head of security for the Miller Art Collection," the ex-con said. "But if I'm free, you got it."

"I'll meet you outside," Jamie said to him. "Be there in a minute."

Liam acknowledged this with a salute and headed out the front door. Jamie put a hand on Mia's shoulder. "Will you do me a favor?"

"Of course," she said. "Anything."

"Will you get together with Madison?"

But that.

"Get to know her?" he persisted. "For me? She could use a friend in the family. And the Family."

Mia tensed. She flashed on her history with Jamie. The fun childhood escapades. The less fun bond of having parents who ping-ponged in and out of prison. The brief high school romance. The hope for something more that had settled into friendship. One that she could see lasting for a lifetime. Mia relaxed. "Of course. Text me her number. We'll go out for drinks."

Jamie beamed with relief. "Great. Thank you." He kissed the top of her head. "Love ya."

"Love ya, too."

As soon as Jamie was gone, Mia retreated to her office. She was responding to emails when Ravello gave the door a light rap and then opened it. "Hi, Dad. You missed the whole party."

"For a very good reason." Ravello gleefully rubbed his meaty hands together. "I found our new Retail Manager."

Mia shot her father a wary look. "Is he with the Tutera Family?"

"Nope."

"That's a relief."

"He's a Gambrazzo."

Mia let out a loud groan. "Dad—"

Ravello motioned for her to calm down. "Don't worry, he's clean. Another kid who doesn't want to go into the Family business. Even better, he has experience in the service industry. Lots of it." Ravello pulled a folded-up piece of paper from the inside pocket of his jacket and handed it to Mia. "Here's his resume."

"He's got a resume? I guess that's something."

"Yeah, exactly," Ravello said, eager to impress her with his current candidate.

Mia skimmed the resume for thirty-two-year-old Shane Gambrazzo. A list of jobs showed that he'd worked his way up from waiter to either Retail Sales or Operations Manager at several respectable locations. "This isn't bad. I'd be willing to meet with him."

"Good." Ravello took Mia's arm and pulled her up from her office chair. "Because he's in the foyer."

"*Dad . . .*" Mia protested as he dragged her down the hallway.

"I'm telling you, he's our guy. And the sooner we hire him, the better. If we don't make a move, someone else will. Trust me on this."

They arrived in the foyer. A man in a suit with his back to them was in the doorway of the Marina Ballroom, checking it out. "Shane," Ravello said. "Come meet my daughter, Mia."

Shane Gambrazzo turned around. Mia's jaw dropped. Literally. Her mouth actually fell open. Standing in front of her was the most gorgeous man she had ever laid eyes on. Jamie Boldano was cute. Her brother Posi was handsome. This guy was an Adonis. He had naturally blond hair, but his complexion was olive, which made his pale, sea-green eyes stand out like peridot gemstones. He had a small cleft in his chin, high cheekbones, and stood eye-to-eye with Ravello, which put him at around six feet, three inches. Mia could tell that under his well-fitted suit jacket, Shane's torso formed a perfect inverted triangle, broad of shoulder, small of waist.

He held out his hand. "Hi, nice to meet you," he said in a voice as low and sexy as a nighttime radio DJ with the merest hint of a Queens accent. The greeting came with a smile that exposed perfect teeth.

"Hey-hi-ho-hey . . ." Mia found herself unable to form a complete sentence.

Cammie emerged from the short hallway that led to the kitchen area. She carried two full plastic bags. "I got my leftovers, so I'm gonna—"

Cammie froze in her tracks. The plastic bags fell from her hands. She gaped at Shane. "Whaaaa . . ."

Shane gave an exasperated grunt. "Great. Here we go again." He held up his hands in a defensive gesture, with palms facing out. "I got a mirror. I know what I look like. Lemme just say that hashtag-me-too goes both ways, ladies."

This snapped Mia out of her besotted stupor. "Yes. Right." She extended a hand to him. "Nice to meet you too, Shane. Welcome to Belle View."

Shane relaxed. He took Mia's hand and gave it a businesslike shake. *How is his hand so firm and yet so soft?*

she wondered, then scolded, *Stop it!* "So far, I'm impressed," he said.

By me? Are you flirting? Oh, please be flirting. Mia, no! Fermare! Stop! He means Belle View! Or does he? She forced herself to listen to Shane, focusing on a spot on the wall over his shoulder to avoid being lured into his magnificent, manly beauty. ". . . And the views here are killer," he was saying. "I do have some ideas about your website, though. I thought I might mess around with it a little. Kind of a tryout, to see if you like my take on it."

"Sounds like a plan," Mia said, still focused on the spot. "You can use my office."

"Use mine," Cammie jumped in. "I'll take you there."

Mia shot Cammie a look that said, *seriously*? "I thought you were leaving."

"Not anymore," Cammie said, fixated on Shane.

"Good-bye, Cammie." Mia picked up the bags Cammie dropped and placed them in the woman's hands. She took Cammie's arm, led her to the front door, and gently pushed her out. Mia's cell phone rang. On the chance it might be a customer, she took the call. "Belle View Catering Manor, hold on a minute, please." She covered the phone with her hand. "Dad, can you take Shane to my office?"

"You betcha. *Andiamo, il mio amico.* Come, my friend."

The men disappeared and Mia returned to the call. "Thank you for waiting. Can I help you?"

"Mia, hi, this is Alicia Cohen."

Alicia Medaglia Cohen. Grand niece of the late Gugliemo and high school arch nemesis. *This should be interesting.*

"Hi, Alicia. It's great to hear from you." Mia lied. She walked toward her office as she talked. "What's up?"

"I'm hoping you can help me. I don't know if you heard but Versailles on the Park went out of business."

"Yes, I know. The owner and his chef were arrested." *Thanks to me,* Mia thought but didn't say. "Talk about drama, huh?" She couldn't resist slinging Alicia's put-down of Belle View back at her.

"I'm throwing a surprise party for my husband Max a week from Saturday, but I need a new location now. I thought I'd see how much it might cost to move it Belle View. You know, seeing how we're friends and all."

Cheapskate was Mia's annoyed reaction to this ploy on Alicia's part to milk a deal out of Mia. She arrived at her office, where the preternaturally gorgeous Shane was bent over the computer keyboard, typing and mousing up a storm. He gestured to the screen. "I redid the Belle View gallery of photos," he said in a whisper.

Mia peered at the gallery's new design. There were less pictures and the ones he'd kept were framed and la-beled with a crisp new font. "Shane, that looks great."

She heard a small gasp from Alicia. "Did I just hear you say Shane?"

"Yeah."

This elicited a squeak from the woman. "You-you wouldn't be talking about Shane Gambrazzo, would you?"

"Yes, he happens to be in my office right now."

"OMG. He's back in town?"

I had no idea he ever left. "I guess so. So, back to your party. I'll price a couple of options for you and—"

"Whatever you say. It's booked. We are *so* there." Ali-cia spilled this out with the excitement of a tween at a meet-and-greet with her favorite boy band. She ended the call by squealing, "*OMG! Shane Gambrazzo!*"

Shane, absorbed in updating the Belle View website, embarked on another flurry of typing. "I fooled around with the homepage. What do you think?"

Mia didn't even bother to check out the changes he'd made. "I think," she said with a wide grin, "you're hired."

Recipes

Easiest Lasagna Ever

Ingredients:
1-2 tablespoons olive oil
2 cloves garlic
1 lb. ground turkey
A box of no-boil lasagna noodles (you won't use it up)
1-2 containers of 2% (part-skim) ricotta cheese
1-2 cups shredded part-skim mozzarella
1 cup grated parmesan
1 tablespoon Italian herbs
2 jars of your favorite tomato sauce (mine is any from
    Trader Joes!)

Directions:
Heat up the two cloves of garlic in some olive oil, and then add a pound of ground turkey.

Cook the turkey through, and then add a jar of TJ Organic Basil Marinara Sauce (or the sauce of your choice). Simmer for ten minutes on low heat.

In an 8-x-8-inch—or bigger, if you think you've got too much turkey—glass or metal pan, put down a layer of sauce, and then add a layer of the no-boil lasagna noodles.

Top the lasagna noodles with another layer of sauce, and then cover with some of the mozzarella, parmesan, and ricotta. Sprinkle some of the herbs over this.

Keep layering pasta, sauce, cheese, and herbs until you fill the pan. The final layer can be pasta covered with sauce. And cover the pasta thoroughly so that the sauce softens the pasta.

(NOTE: I try to make my lasagna the night or morning before I'm serving it so that the lasagna pasta gets thoroughly softened. I find if you don't do that, the pasta can get hard and not cook thoroughly.)

Bake at 350 degrees for about a half hour or an hour, depending on the lasagna size. Since the meat is cooked, what you're doing is cooking the noodles through and melting the cheese. Determine this by sticking a knife in the center and seeing if it comes out hot. If it pulls out some stringy cheese, you're in good shape.

Then, *mangia*!

Serves 4-6.

Potato and Beet Salad

Ingredients:

3 lbs. Yukon Gold (or red) potatoes, *cooked, chilled, and cut into chunks.* Whether you peel the potatoes or not is up to you. I generally don't, especially with the Golds. I also cut them up before I cook them because the smaller pieces cook quicker.

3 hardboiled eggs, diced

1 lb. cooked, chilled beets, cut into small chunks

¾ cup low-fat (or regular) mayonnaise

½ cup sweet relish

2 T. minced scallions

1 T. minced banana peppers

1 T. brown mustard

1 T. minced dill pickle

1 T. white wine vinegar

1 tsp. Worcestershire sauce

¼ tsp. black pepper

Paprika for garnish

Directions:

Combine all the ingredients *except for the potatoes and diced eggs.* When the other ingredients are all well blended, gently fold in the potatoes and diced eggs. "Gently" is the operative word here, in case the potatoes are a bit overcooked. You don't want your potato salad turning into mashed potato salad!

Serves 6-8.

Honey Phyllo Rollups

Ingredients:

The cookies:

2 cups ground nuts—walnuts, pecans, pistachio, or
   almonds work. Baker's choice
¼ cup sugar
2 tsps. cinnamon
1 tsp. allspice
24 sheets phyllo dough, thawed
½ cup butter, melted

The syrup:

½ cup honey
½ cup white sugar
½ cup water
1 T. lemon juice

Directions:

Preheat oven to 350 degrees.

Combine the ground nuts, sugar, cinnamon, and all-spice. Set aside.

Place two sheets of phyllo dough on a sheet of parchment paper larger than the dough. Brush the phyllo dough with melted butter. Sprinkle the dough with ¼ cup of the nut mixture. Roll the dough tightly but carefully from the long side upward, creating a slim log. Slice the log into four pieces and set each into a greased 13 x 9 baking dish. You can pack the rollups tightly—they won't expand. (Note: keep the unused phyllo dough covered with a wet cloth or paper towel so that it doesn't dry out.) When you've finished making the rollups, bake for 14-16 minutes until they're light brown. Let them cool.

While the rollups are in the oven, make the syrup. In a small saucepan, combine the honey, sugar, water, and lemon juice. Bring to a boil, then reduce heat and simmer for around five minutes. Remove from the heat and let cool for about ten minutes.

Spoon the syrup over the rollups. If you have any leftover nut mixture, sprinkle it over the rollups.

Serving: 24 rollups.

Cannoli Cake

NOTE: Step one is draining the ricotta so that your filling doesn't end up watery. I wrap mine in cheesecloth, then place it in a strainer that fits over a mixing bowl. I set a heavy can on top of the cheesecloth-wrapped ricotta and let it drain overnight in the refrigerator.

Ingredients:

Cake:
1 package white cake mix
¼ cup plain Greek yogurt
½ cup vegetable oil
1 cup water

Filling:
1 16 oz tub ricotta, drained (see above instructions)
1 8 oz container mascarpone cheese (doesn't have to be
    drained if it has the consistency of cream cheese)
1 8 oz container cream cheese (regular or light)
3 cups powdered sugar
1 tsp. vanilla
1 tsp. almond extract
1 tsp. orange juice
½ tsp. cinnamon
¼ tsp. salt
½ cup to 1 cup of mini chocolate chips

Instructions:

The cake:
Preheat oven to 350.

Beat the cake mix with the yogurt, oil, and water—slowly at first to combine the ingredients, then on medium speed for two minutes. Pour the batter into two 8" cake pans.

Bake for 25-35 minutes until a toothpick inserted in the center comes out clean.

Let the cake cool completely.

Filling and frosting:

Beat the ricotta, mascarpone, and cream cheese together until thoroughly blended. Add the vanilla, orange juice, almond extract, cinnamon, salt, and powdered sugar until all are well combined. (NOTE: add the sugar one cup at a time and mix slowly at first so that powdered sugar doesn't go flying out of the mixing bowl. Trust me, it happens!)

Gently fold the chocolate chips into the filling mix by hand. Start with half a cup of chips. Add more if desired.

Assembly:

Flip the first cake layer out of its pan onto a plate upside down, so that the flat bottom is on the top. Add a heaping amount of filling and spread it. Place the second layer on top and frost the top and sides with the filling. (NOTE: add the second layer right-side up, so the flat bottom sits on top of the first layer.)

Serves 8-16, depending on the size of the slices.

EVENT TIP

Looking for a fun party favor? Try personalized refrigerator magnets. We gave out pretty ones at our wedding, decorated with our names, our wedding date, and a tiny rose because we got married in a rose garden. My husband and I have been married over twenty-five years and friends tell us they still have the magnets on their fridges. They're great for birthdays, anniversaries, and even baby showers. If you know a baby's name and gender, they even make a sweet gender reveal. Order them in pink or blue, personalized with the baby's name.

A quick note about giving edible favors. In *Long Island Iced Tina,* stepmom Tina gives chocolate rattles as the party favor. Yes, they're delicious, but edible favors don't make lasting memories. They're gone as soon they're eaten!

ACKNOWLEDGMENTS

Heartfelt thank-you to my wonderful editor, John Scognamiglio, as well as everyone at Kensington for offering constant support and enthusiasm for this series. A shout-out to my agent, Doug Grad, whose unerring instincts found the perfect home for the Catering Hall Mysteries. Buckets of love to Jer and Eliza, for putting up with me and not becoming annoyed when I say, "I can't talk, I'm writing!" even though my head is in the fridge and I'm scrounging around for snacks. To my dear friends at Chicks on the Case and the Guppies, and all the bloggers who've reviewed and shared my posts (hi, Dru Ann Love!). Special thanks to Vickie Fee for fact-checking my Catholic memories. And a bazillion *grazies* to my fantastic Italian family . . . especially *mia mama*, Elisabetta DiVirgilio Seideman.

To the copy editor: Thanks for a great edit!

Connect with Us

Visit us online at
KensingtonBooks.com
to read more from your favorite authors, see books
by series, view reading group guides, and more.

Join us on social media

for sneak peeks, chances to win books and prize packs,
and to share your thoughts with other readers.

facebook.com/kensingtonpublishing
twitter.com/kensingtonbooks

Tell us what you think!

To share your thoughts, submit a review,
or sign up for our eNewsletters, please visit:
KensingtonBooks.com/TellUs.